Dark Encounters

OF THE UNEXPECTED KIND

THE CHILDREN OF THE GODS
BOOK SEVENTY-FIVE

I. T. LUCAS

Dark Encounters of the Unexpected Kind is a work of fiction!
Names, characters, places and incidents are products of the author's imagination or are used fictitiously and are not to be construed as real. Any similarity to actual persons, organizations and/or events is purely coincidental.

Published by Evening Star Press

EveningStarPress.com

ISBN-13: 978-1-962067-02-7

Also by I. T. Lucas

THE CHILDREN OF THE GODS ORIGINS

1: Goddess's Choice

2: Goddess's Hope

THE CHILDREN OF THE GODS

Dark Stranger

1: Dark Stranger The Dream

2: Dark Stranger Revealed

3: Dark Stranger Immortal

Dark Enemy

4: Dark Enemy Taken

5: Dark Enemy Captive

6: Dark Enemy Redeemed

Kri & Michael's Story

6.5: My Dark Amazon

Dark Warrior

7: Dark Warrior Mine

8: Dark Warrior's Promise

9: Dark Warrior's Destiny

10: Dark Warrior's Legacy

Dark Guardian

11: Dark Guardian Found

12: Dark Guardian Craved

13: Dark Guardian's Mate

Dark Angel

14: Dark Angel's Obsession

15: Dark Angel's Seduction

16: Dark Angel's Surrender

Dark Operative

Dark Choices

Dark Secrets

Dark Haven

Dark Power

Dark Memories

Dark Hunter

Dark God

Dark Whispers

PERFECT MATCH

The Children of the Gods Series Sets

Books 1-3: Dark Stranger trilogy—Includes a bonus short story: **The Fates take a Vacation**

Books 4-6: Dark Enemy Trilogy —Includes a bonus short story—**The Fates' Post-Wedding Celebration**

Books 7-10: Dark Warrior Tetralogy

Books 11-13: Dark Guardian Trilogy

Books 14-16: Dark Angel Trilogy

Books 17-19: Dark Operative Trilogy

Books 20-22: Dark Survivor Trilogy

Books 23-25: Dark Widow Trilogy

Books 26-28: Dark Dream Trilogy

Books 29-31: Dark Prince Trilogy

Books 32-34: Dark Queen Trilogy

Books 35-37: Dark Spy Trilogy

Books 38-40: Dark Overlord Trilogy

Books 41-43: Dark Choices Trilogy

Books 44-46: Dark Secrets Trilogy

Books 47-49: Dark Haven Trilogy

Books 50-52: Dark Power Trilogy

Books 53-55: Dark Memories Trilogy

Books 56-58: Dark Hunter Trilogy

Books 59-61: Dark God Trilogy

Books 62-64: Dark Whispers Trilogy

Books 65-67: Dark Gambit Trilogy

Books 68-70: Dark Alliance Trilogy

Books 71-73: Dark healing Trilogy

MEGA SETS

INCLUDE CHARACTER LISTS

The Children of the Gods: Books 1-6
The Children of the Gods: Books 6.5-10

Perfect Match Bundle 1

CHECK OUT THE SPECIALS ON

ITLUCAS.COM

(https://itlucas.com/specials)

FOR EXCLUSIVE PEEKS AT UPCOMING RELEASES & A FREE I. T. LUCAS COMPANION BOOK

JOIN MY *VIP CLUB* AND GAIN ACCESS TO THE VIP PORTAL AT ITLUCAS.COM

TO JOIN, GO TO:
http://eepurl.com/blMTpD

Find out more details about what's included with your free membership on the book's last page.

TRY THE CHILDREN OF THE GODS SERIES ON

AUDIBLE

2 FREE audiobooks with your new Audible subscription!

"This wasn't one of your smarter ideas." Dagor's voice was tinged with barely veiled annoyance.

"Really?" Aru arched a brow. "I thought it was quite clever."

Dagor swiveled his laptop toward him. "Instead of showing up in person, they sent a drone to scout the area, and now they know it was a ruse and that we are not there."

It had seemed like a great idea to plant the trackers in the remote canyon, put a couple of surveillance bugs in place, and watch who showed up.

Aru shrugged. "How was I supposed to know that they would do that?"

The mysterious abductors or perhaps rescuers of the Kra-ell had outsmarted him, but that didn't mean that the move had been a waste of time and effort. Getting a drone instead of people was disappointing, and he still didn't know who they were, but at least they had shown up in some form, which meant that the trackers had done their job.

"I told you they wouldn't fall for that." Dagor let out a breath. "If you were in their position, would you have rushed to investigate the sudden emergence of new signals without taking every precaution you could think of?"

"I wouldn't." Aru had to admit that he had wagered on the abductors or rescuers taking the bait, but he'd known it was a long shot. "It was a gamble, and it was worth a try. The good news is that we know much more about these people now than we did before the drone showed up."

"Like what?" Dagor asked.

"We know that they have the ability to decipher the location of the trackers, and we also know that humans don't have the technology to decrypt the signals they are emitting. Also, they came to investigate, just not in person."

Dagor didn't look satisfied. "All we really know is that they are too sophisticated to fall into our trap. We still don't know who they are, and we won't know how to proceed without determining whether they are Kra-ell or human. The two require very different approaches."

"I agree with Aru," Negal said in his usual monotone voice. "What's important is that they showed their hand. It was a smart gambit that prompted the opponent to make a counter move, which, in turn, will inform our next one. The fact that they can decipher the location of the signals means that they captured Gor and tortured the information out of him. He never would have volunteered it. We should assume that he's dead."

Surprised that the old trooper was backing him up, Aru nodded his thanks.

Usually, Negal grumbled about the rookie getting promoted because of damn politics or nepotism, and every time Aru made a wrong move, Negal smirked in satisfaction.

Still, despite the trooper's attitude and occasional snarky comments, Aru appreciated having the guy on his team and wouldn't swap him for someone more accommodating even if he could. Negal had the experience that Aru lacked, kept him on his toes, and would never sabotage the mission just to try to prove that their commander had been wrong to nominate Aru as their team leader.

Dagor leaned back in his chair. "The fact that Gor's tracker stopped broadcasting doesn't mean that he is dead. It only means they took the tracker out of him—like they did to the other settlers before him."

When nearly all the trackers embedded in the Kra-ell settlers had simultaneously stopped broadcasting, Aru had assumed the cause was interference. Not many things could disrupt signals produced by the sophisticated trackers, though, so he and his teammates had to assume that the interference hadn't been caused by a natural phenomenon or an accident.

Regrettably, they had been too far away to get to the compound in time to see what had gone wrong.

At the time, they had been investigating a possible pod landing in Tibet. The remote location was four days on foot from the nearest paved road and nowhere near any international or even local airport.

Getting to Karelia to investigate what had happened had taken a long time, and in the meantime, the signals had come back online from the Baltic Sea, not too far from the port of Helsinki.

When they had started winking out one after the other, Aru had feared for the lives of the Kra-ell.

Not that he would have been allowed to intervene even if he and his team could do anything about it. Their job was observing and reporting, which they had been doing since discovering the surviving Kra-ell in Gor's compound five years ago.

Nevertheless, they hadn't reported anything about the latest events in the compound yet, and if what Aru suspected was true, they wouldn't be submitting a report regarding the fate of the Kra-ell anytime soon.

Thankfully, they had one hundred and fifteen Earth years before anyone came to check on them. That left plenty of time to collect all the relevant information and come up with a compelling story to tell their commander about why they had failed to discover the others before they had taken over Gor's compound, or rather Igor's, which was the name he had chosen to be known by on Earth.

What they knew so far was that someone had blown huge holes in the wall surrounding the compound, taken out everyone who was still alive, and put them on a ship. Then, the invaders had either killed everyone or just taken out their trackers.

What gave Aru hope that the Kra-ell were still alive was that it didn't make sense for the invaders to storm the compound, kill only a small number of Kra-ell, capture the rest, put them on a ship, and then kill them all. The invaders had to be a formidable force to take the Kra-ell captive to begin with, and the prime suspects were other Kra-ell settlers who had also woken up from stasis. But unlike those in Gor's compound, the others must have figured out that they had tracking devices implanted in their bodies and had taken them out before Aru and his team arrived on Earth and started tracking all the settlers whose devices were active.

It was a perfectly reasonable hypothesis, but Aru knew it wouldn't be good enough to appease their commander, who would view it as a failure. Their team's next mission would undoubtedly be in an even more godforsaken sector of the universe.

Hopefully, the other person Aru was secretly reporting to would intervene on their behalf and prevent their exile.

After all, Negal's rumblings about nepotism weren't entirely unfounded. In fact, they were spot on. Aru had earned the promotion not because of anything he had done in the service but because of his unique talent and its usefulness to that person whose name should not be mentioned even in thought.

Still, their commander could find other ways to make their lives miserable. Just the loss of favor would devastate Dagor and Negal. An unfavorable evaluation from the commander would ruin any chances of promotion for them, and no one wanted to spend hundreds of years in some wretched corner of the universe doing work that was of little importance to anyone back home.

In all fairness, though, Aru and his team had been instructed to stay away from the Kra-ell and not let their presence be known, so if the Kra-ell had gotten themselves free somehow, even with outside help, the commander couldn't blame Aru's team for being ignorant of what had been brewing inside the compound. That being said, if the rescuers were other settlers who had woken up from stasis, the commander wouldn't forgive their ignorance of that.

At the time of the attack, Gor and two other purebloods had been away, which suggested that the invaders had been waiting for just such an opportunity and had been helped by rebels from the inside, either with just intel or with active participation.

When Gor and his two companions had subsequently been captured and taken to Los Angeles, it had been the lucky break Aru had needed. It had given him a clue as to the whereabouts of the other settlers. But then their signals had winked out as well, and his team had been left in the dark.

Desperate for any thread or clue, Aru had come up with the idea to go to China and locate the trackers of the first Kra-ell who had arrived on Earth—the scouting team that the Kra-ell queen had sent ahead of the settler ship.

The location where the bodies of the dead scouts had been cremated was known, and since the trackers were impervious to fire, it was only a matter of finding them. It hadn't been easy, but they had found five, of which only three were still operational. They could have kept digging, but Aru had decided that three was just the right number to lure the invaders out of hiding and show their hand.

His gamble had paid off, and they had gotten a response from the invaders. The question was what to do next.

Kian walked into the war room, pulled out a chair next to the conference table, and sat down. "Syssi had a vision earlier today," he said without bothering with a long preamble. "She saw three men in a canyon, which was sparsely covered in vegetation." He flicked his gaze to the screen mounted overhead, where footage from the canyon the signals were coming from was still playing on a loop.

Shifting his gaze to his war room team, Kian assessed their reactions. They all knew of Syssi's reputation, and he doubted any of them would be foolish enough to make light of her prophetic vision.

Turner nodded, but his expression remained impassive. It took a lot more than a foretelling to get the guy rattled.

William wasn't showing any reaction either. But since he was focused on scanning the footage from the drone and looking for anything he might have missed at the first pass-through, he might not have heard Kian.

Jade seemed nervous, which given the Kra-ell's esoteric beliefs was to be expected, and Kalugal looked curious and somewhat amused, which could've been perceived as him downplaying the importance of the vision or of Kian's regard for it, but Kian knew it wasn't so.

His cousin's mate also occasionally experienced visions, so he knew to give Syssi's foresight its due respect. Unlike Kian, though, Kalugal didn't mind Jacki having them, and he didn't fear their negative effect on her well-being.

Then again, Jacki probably wasn't as drained after having prophetic visions as Syssi. She was a resilient female and not nearly as sensitive as Syssi. Her visions were also mostly less intense in nature, but not always.

The one she'd had about Wonder's caravan had been quite shocking.

Jacki's gift worked by touch, and when she'd held an ancient figurine, she'd seen Wonder fighting to save the lives of her caravan companions. A powerful earthquake had opened a chasm in the desert floor, swallowing wagons, animals, and people alike, and eventually Wonder herself had fallen victim to it despite her heroic efforts.

The vision Jacki had been shown was of an event that had happened thousands of years in the past. If Syssi had seen something of such a catastrophic nature, she would have been shaken by it for weeks, or even months, but not Jacki.

Perhaps Kalugal's wife was tougher because her life had been less sheltered than Syssi's, or maybe she'd just been born different.

As a father, Kian often wondered whether nature or nurture had a more significant influence on his child's character, and he leaned toward nature. There was no doubt in his mind that Allegra had been born with a strong personality, which she'd most likely inherited from him. Hopefully, though, she'd also inherited her mother's empathy and emotional intelligence, which would make her a much better leader than he could ever be.

Onegus was the only one to actually respond to his proclamation. "I assume that the three men Syssi saw in her vision are the ones emitting the signals?"

The answer to that was complicated, and since there was no one in the canyon, Kian wasn't sure what exactly Syssi had seen, but he had a theory. "Since the drone footage from the canyon indicates that there is no one there, we have to assume that Syssi's vision was from the near future. On the next fly-by, we should switch to the high-altitude drone and hope they won't notice it."

"Why?" Jade asked. "They are not there, so they are not going to see it in either case. We can fly the smaller, low-altitude drone."

"They might have hidden cameras right next to the trackers," Kian said. "Since there is no one where the signals are coming from, we have to assume that they somehow managed to rig the trackers to transmit without the benefit of a live host. That means they could bury them in the ground or hide them in the bushes."

The alien trackers were the size of a grain of rice, so even if they weren't buried under the rocks, there was no way William could find them in the footage. Normally, the devices needed a live body to provide the energy for them to transmit the signal, so another possibility was that the men had implanted them in small animals. But to keep the critters from scurrying away, they would have needed to put them in cages, and that was probably what William was looking for as he scanned the zoomed-in footage in slow motion on his laptop.

"The vision could also be from the far future," Anandur said. "What were the men in the vision wearing?"

Kian lifted a hand. "Let me finish telling you about the vision first. When I'm done, you can ask your questions, and I'll answer them to the best of my ability."

Anandur nodded.

"When Syssi's consciousness flew over the men, they were arguing, and then something caught their attention, and they looked up. Naturally, Syssi's first thought was that they could see her floating overhead, but she quickly realized that it must have been something above or behind her. She couldn't see or hear what it was, but that's the dreamy nature of visions. Many of the details are missing, and others are unclear, and it's never obvious whether the vision is a window into the past or the future."

Kian took a sip from his bottle of water before continuing. "One of the men pointed a strange-looking weapon at what I assume was our drone, but then one of his companions stayed his hand, and their argument resumed." He put the bottle down. "Syssi didn't know that we were flying a drone or that the signals were coming from a canyon, so you can rest assured that her vision wasn't influenced by anything I told her."

"What exactly did you tell her?" Jade asked.

"All I told Syssi was that the signals were coming from a nearby location, and just like the rest of us, she assumed they were being emitted by the Kra-ell—either by members of the scouting team that had been sent ahead of the settler ship or some of the awakened settlers themselves. Most of the pods from the settler ship are still missing, so that's the most logical assumption, provided that they had learned of the trackers and how to manipulate them."

After more than seven thousand years, the Kra-ell scouts shouldn't be alive, but there was a small chance that they had gone back into their stasis pod to prolong their lives and stayed there for hundreds of years at a time.

It was the logical thing to do, and Kian still believed that at least some of the scouts had done that, but it no longer seemed like the signals were coming from them, and he had arrived at that conclusion even before Syssi had told him about what she'd seen in her vision.

His next suspicion had been that other settlers had come out of stasis before Igor had figured out how to track the signals, and since some of them were assassins who had been smuggled among the settlers to eliminate the Eternal King's direct descendants, they'd known about the trackers and had also known that they had to remove them from their bodies so they couldn't be found.

Those assassins must have been tracking Igor and had followed his signal to Los Angeles, which would explain the sudden appearance of the three signals in the clan's backyard.

But after Syssi's vision, he had to consider other options.

Perhaps the gods had left a sleeper cell on Earth?

Had members of that team been tracking Igor?

Had they been aware of what he had done to the members of each pod that had come online, and done nothing about it?

How could they have stood by while he'd murdered innocent males, adults and children alike, and subjugated the females?

Were they following a non-interference directive and were supposed to only observe?

If so, why were they interfering now?

Did they suspect the involvement of immortals? The hybrid descendants of the exiled gods they had been sent to eliminate?

Kian had so many questions and so few answers, and he hated relying on visions to form his strategy, but it seemed like he had no choice. Right now, Syssi's vision supplied the only clues they had.

Before meeting Jacki, Kalugal would have been dismissive of Syssi's vision, in a polite manner of course, but he'd been shown the power of clairvoyance by his mate and was no longer a skeptic.

Regrettably, Jacki was not in the same league as Syssi. He wouldn't have traded his Jacki for anyone, but there was no denying that Syssi's abilities far surpassed hers.

What his mate typically saw was small-scale, localized, and individual, while Syssi got to foresee or past-view epic events—like the Odus's decommissioning, or rather attempted eradication, and the Kra-ell who had been put in charge of it.

Kalugal didn't know all the details, but he imagined the vision had been cryptic, as all postcognition and precognition tended to be. Nevertheless, Jade had confirmed what Syssi had seen happening to the Odus.

In fact, he'd been told that Syssi had envisioned the Kra-ell years before the clan had learned of their existence. At the time, she hadn't realized that the fictional people she'd created for one of the Perfect Match Virtual Studios environments were not the product of her imagination but a glimpse into the future or maybe the past. She hadn't gotten all the details right, though, so despite her visions being legendary, they couldn't be taken verbatim.

There was another problem with the story Kalugal had been told about Syssi and her Krall version of the Kra-ell. The one detail everyone seemed to overlook was that the original Krall adventure had been created by the Perfect Match programmers before Syssi had come on board. She'd elaborated on and changed it, but someone had thought of it before her.

Was one of the humans working for Perfect Match a seer?

It wasn't such a great leap of logic. Humans had been known to have prophetic visions, and some weren't even aware of their abilities. They didn't realize that their minds had not created what they envisioned.

It was also possible that Syssi had played around with designs for the different Perfect Match environments even before Kian had bought a majority stake in the company for her and made her a board member.

Kian's team had been involved with Perfect Match almost from its inception, which probably included Syssi. He'd been a silent investor and stock owner in the company during the development stage, and when the original founders had gotten stuck and couldn't finalize the product, Kian had asked William to help them overcome their difficulties.

William had been instrumental in debugging the software and giving it the edge the founders had envisioned but couldn't quite achieve.

"What else did Syssi see?" Onegus asked.

Kian leaned back. "Syssi said that the weapon one of the men aimed at the drone looked like a monocular, which is odd on two accounts. One is that it had no visible trigger, so it couldn't have been a projectile weapon, and so we have to assume that it was a laser-based weapon or something that operated in a similar way. The other is that one of the males aimed it at our drone." He looked at Turner. "Correct me if I'm wrong, but as far as I know, no manmade handheld weapons can shoot down a drone at the height we were flying it."

Turner nodded. "That's correct."

"I wish the alien-looking weapon was the most troubling part, but it's not." Kian leaned forward and put his hands on the table. "When the three looked up at the drone, Syssi got a good look at their faces, and she was positive that none were Kra-ell. She thinks that they were gods."

Jade gasped. "I'll be damned. How the hell did they get here so fast?"

"My thoughts exactly. They couldn't have. They had to be here already," Kian said. "Syssi's impression was that they were friendly, but as much as I trust her visions, I wouldn't base our strategy on them."

"We all know not to take Syssi's visions lightly," Onegus said. "But gods? We've been searching for other immortals for centuries and haven't found any. Do you want to tell me that gods were hiding among humans this whole time, and we didn't know? Wouldn't they have recognized the technology we were drip-feeding to the humans? All they had to do was follow the breadcrumbs to us."

"It depends on when they arrived on Earth," Turner said. "We know that they are not part of the original group."

"Why not?" Jade asked. "Maybe more have survived. Until recently, you didn't know about Toven, and he didn't know about you."

The cogs in Kalugal's mind started spinning.

If the three males were indeed gods, they couldn't be contemporaries of the original group of rebels. Annani might not have known about another group who had settled somewhere else on Earth, but Mortdh would have, and he wouldn't have bombed the assembly while knowing that other gods could find out about his crime.

These gods must have arrived long after the original ones had perished. In fact, they had likely arrived after the Kraell ship had exploded and the pods had landed on Earth, which had been thousands of years later. That meant they possessed more advanced technology and know-how, which were priceless.

If Syssi was right and they were friendly, they might have sought out the clan to get its help or cooperation, and if contact was established, he should seize the opportunity and become instrumental in the negotiations.

That would not only grant him access to what those gods would offer up as part of the negotiations, but it would also increase his influence in the clan and get him the second council seat that right now was looking even less likely than it had originally.

With Toven joining the council and possibly Jade as well, Kalugal would have no grounds to request another seat. Jade represented nearly half of the village population, so if he got two seats, she could ask for six, and Kian would never allow the majority of the council to be comprised of non-clan members.

Leaning back in his chair, Kalugal crossed his arms over his chest. "Syssi's vision reinforces my earlier assessment that the three activated the signals as a way to make contact with us and not to lure us into a trap and harm us. In fact, I'm so sure of their intentions that I volunteer to head to the canyon with a team of no more than two warriors to meet them on equal terms. I think that would be received better than showing up in force, which would signal that we are afraid of them." He smiled at Kian. "Not to toot my own horn, but I'm a much better negotiator than you are, so if you were thinking about heading to the canyon yourself, I would advise against it."

"I wasn't planning to." Kian regarded him with thinly veiled amusement. "Thank you for the offer, but let's not get ahead of ourselves." He braced his elbows on the table. "We must not forget who created Igor and the other assassins and who programmed them to dispose of all legitimate heirs to the Eternal King's throne. These three might be the assassins' handlers, or alternatively, they could be genetically modified gods who were sent to Earth to complete the mission that the original assassins had been tasked with but failed to complete because their ship exploded and their stasis pods were damaged."

Turner nodded. "I agree with Kian. For some, assuming the best in people is natural and safe, but it is not so for us." He scanned the faces of everyone present. "We don't have the luxury of being naive and trusting. We need to assume the worst and hope to be surprised for the better."

As much as Kalugal wished he could argue with that, he couldn't.

Too much was at stake, including the lives of his mate and son. He'd rather succumb to Kian's paranoia than make a rushed decision that might endanger everyone he loved and cared about.

After all, he was a descendant of the Eternal King as well. Ekin, his great-grandfather, had not been the official heir to the throne because he'd been born to a concubine and not the official wife, and the same was true for his mother, who Ahn had fathered with a concubine. Still, Ekin had been the Eternal King's son, and Areana was the Eternal King's granddaughter.

Kian regarded him with his intense eyes. "Even if we decide to send a small welcoming party with a massive backup in case things go wrong, you can't be a part of it.

As a council member, you are privy to information we can't allow to fall into enemy hands."

Kalugal was immune to most compulsion, but not all, and if any of the three possessed Igor's ability, he wouldn't be able to resist the compulsion to reveal all of his secrets, and those included much more than the location of the village and how to get there.

"Unfortunately, you're right." Kalugal sighed. "As the saying goes, with great responsibility comes great sacrifice."

Kian chuckled. "Actually, the saying is 'With great power comes great responsibility, and with great responsibility comes great accountability,' but in your case, sacrifice and accountability are probably one and the same."

Kian

It was apparent to Kian that Kalugal's motive for volunteering was the same one that had prompted him to offer assistance with the Kra-ell rescue mission.

His cousin wanted to be in the know.

Kian didn't mind, but what Kalugal had forgotten was that as a council member, he was already privy to nearly everything that was going on in the clan and that the price for that knowledge was certain restrictions.

"I should be the one to go," Jade said. "And my team should be comprised of only Kra-ell. If these gods are recent arrivals, they don't know about the exiled gods producing half-breed descendants with humans. If they did, they would have tried to make contact with you or the Doomers, either in a friendly or unfriendly manner. But we should assume they know about the Kra-ell or they wouldn't be here. They must have been tracking us, and once we got rid of the implanted trackers, they lost us and needed to find out what happened to us. That's why they are making contact."

Jade's reasoning was solid, but Kian still had trouble treating her like he would any other warrior and not trying to shield her because of her gender. His instincts rebelled against letting her walk into danger without Guardians to protect her.

Given how strong and well-trained Jade was, it was a ridiculous sentiment, but he couldn't just ignore two thousand years of conditioning.

"That might be so." He shifted in his chair. "But we don't know if their intentions toward you and your people are friendly or hostile."

Jade shrugged. "If they meant us harm, they would have already disposed of us. Since they didn't do that and kept their presence a secret, we have to assume their goal is not to eliminate us. They were probably sent to complete the mission the assassin on our ship failed to complete." She shifted her gaze to Kian. "After discovering that the gods were gone, their mission was probably to locate the other descendants of the Eternal King, meaning the twins."

Kian tilted his head. "Why would they think we can lead them to the twins?"

Jade took a deep breath. "Perhaps they need Igor back because he can find the other pods and the Eternal King's grandchildren. Regardless of their intentions, it is better to keep them ignorant of your existence until we know what they are after. That's why I should take a couple of purebloods with me when I meet them."

Kian wasn't convinced that Jade was right about the gods wanting Igor, but he agreed with her assessment that it was better to keep them in the dark about the clan. "I'd rather keep our existence from them as well."

"I'm glad we see eye to eye." Jade squared her shoulders. "There are additional benefits to sending a Kra-ell team. We are faster and stronger and stand a better chance in the event of a confrontation." She looked at William. "Naturally, we will need to be equipped with compulsion-filtering earpieces."

Compulsion was a rare ability even for the gods, but that was according to Annani, and her information was seven thousand years old. The gods had had a long time to improve their genetic know-how and breed more compellers.

"Of course." William waved a hand without lifting his eyes from the screen.

"I see two possibilities," Turner said. "And each requires a very different approach."

It was about time the guy voiced his opinion on the situation. "I've been waiting for you to come up with a new angle no one has considered yet." Kian cast him a smile. "Let's hear it."

"I'm not sure it's a new angle," Turner said. "I'm just clarifying things. The first possibility is that these gods—provided that we are indeed dealing with gods—were sent by the Eternal King to make sure no threat to his throne remains on Earth. The second one is that they were sent by his wife to protect her children and grandchildren from the Kra-ell assassins. If it's the former, walking up to them would be foolhardy because we do not know what capabilities were engineered into them and their weapons. If it's the second option, and these gods were sent by the queen, they might assume that the Kra-ell approaching them are the assassins, shoot first, and ask questions later."

"They left Igor alive and didn't touch the rest of us," Jade scoffed. "If they were sent by the queen, they would have taken him out long ago to prevent him from going after her son."

"Maybe they couldn't," Kian said. "We're assuming that the queen operates secretly and pretends to be loyal to the king. If Igor had a way to communicate with someone on Anumati and the queen was aware of that, she couldn't tell her people to launch a direct attack on him without showing her hand."

Turner nodded. "That's possible. Also, don't forget that if they were sent to eliminate Ahn and the other exiled gods or to find the twins, they had no reason to bother with Igor. But as soon as a new player appeared on the stage, they followed the trail in hopes of potentially finding the exiled gods. Who else could have liberated the Kra-ell? Humans? Not likely. And they should know it couldn't have been a different Kra-ell faction, because if it was, they could have tracked the signals they emitted."

"Not necessarily." Onegus crossed his arms over his chest. "Those other Kra-ell could have removed their trackers before the gods arrived. I'm sure that's a scenario they took into consideration."

"Why would they?" Jade asked. "We didn't know that we were implanted with trackers. Igor knew, and yet he didn't remove his. Knowing how the gods operate, I wouldn't be surprised if the assassins were programmed to keep their trackers."

Kian was losing patience. They could engage in what-ifs for hours and get nowhere.

He lifted his hand. "The way to address both possibilities is to send a mixed group. Two pureblooded females and two immortals. Igor claimed there were no female assassins because of the gods' attitudes toward females and their reluctance to involve them in military missions. Therefore, this new team would know that the female Kra-ell couldn't be assassins, and they would have no reason to shoot at them. The two immortals could pass for humans, so even if these gods were sent by the king, they would have no reason to shoot them either. Naturally, we will provide the team with an aerial defense of armed drones and a backup force nearby."

Jade nodded. "I wish Kagra was here. She's my best fighter, and she's good under pressure."

Kagra was currently in China with Yamanu and the rest of the team that had been sent to find the origin of the signals. But then the broadcast location had changed while they had been en route, and instead of it coming from China, it was coming from Mount Baldy.

Onegus swiveled his chair to face Kian. "Speaking of the China team, what do you want them to do? Do you want them to continue to Lugu Lake to assist the crew working on Kalugal's archeological dig?"

Kalugal suspected that a pod was buried on the site, but since the place was rigged with booby-traps, digging had been progressing at a snail's pace, and the assistance of several super-strong Kra-ell would be greatly beneficial to speeding it up.

The team was awaiting instructions in Chengdu, the capital of China's Sichuan province, but Kian hadn't decided yet whether he wanted to send them to Lugu Lake to help with the archaeological excavation of the suspected pod crash or to instruct them to return home.

"Not yet. Keep them on standby."

Nodding, Onegus turned to Jade. "Do you have anyone else you trust for a mission like that?"

"Borga is a good fighter, but she's not a diplomat, and I don't trust her. I prefer Morgada, but she hasn't kept up with her training. I'll have to give it some thought." Jade looked at Onegus. "I leave the selection of the immortals to you."

"Do you have a preference for anyone specific?" Kian asked.

She shrugged. "It makes no difference to me."

Kalugal regarded her with an arched brow. "Don't you want Phinas to go with you?"

She shook her head. "Phinas is an excellent fighter, but he's even better as a father figure for Drova. One of us needs to stay alive for her, and it's not a good plan to have us both face danger together. I wouldn't mind taking Rufsur, though, and if Dalhu is a choice, I wouldn't mind having him by my side either." She leaned back in her chair. "He claims that he can smell evil, and if that's true, I would like him to sniff those supposed gods to ascertain their intentions."

"Dalhu is not a Guardian," Onegus said. "He's also happily pursuing his art and prefers to stay out of conflicts. I don't think he would want to take part in this."

Onegus didn't know Dalhu as well as Kian did. His sister's mate would have enjoyed some action, but the problem was that Dalhu was mated to Amanda, who was a council member and therefore privy to too much information.

Rufsur couldn't be part of the team for the same reason.

"Neither Dalhu nor Rufsur can go because they are both mated to council members and know too much. I suspect that mates don't keep secrets from each other even when they are supposed to." He looked at Kalugal. "Do you have anyone else?"

Kalugal shook his head. "Perhaps Boleck. He's an excellent sniper, in case you need one. Greggory is also a good fighter, and he's coolheaded."

Greggory had been Eleanor's inducer, and the two hadn't parted on the best of terms, but that didn't mean he was not a good choice. Still, he wasn't the right man for the mission.

"Frankly, I prefer Guardians to accompany the Kra-ell females." Kian raked his fingers through his hair. "It's not that I have anything against your men, but other than Phinas and Rufsur, none of them is qualified to handle a delicate mission like this."

Jade let out a sigh. "Fine, I'll take Phinas with me."

Phinas had proven himself during the Kra-ell rescue, both as a fighter and diplomat, and Kian had no problem with him meeting the gods, but Jade had a point about both of them going on a risky mission together.

"What about Drova?" He looked into her eyes. "You were right to point out that one of you should stay behind to be with her."

"You just have to ensure that both Phinas and I return to her."

"I'll do everything I can to ensure your safety, but I can't guarantee it." He turned to Kalugal. "Are you okay with Phinas joining the team?"

Kalugal nodded. "Naturally. Phinas is an excellent choice. "

"He's also charming," Jade said. "And he can pass for a human. His godly genes are not as apparent as in some clan immortals. He's not as perfect."

That was true. Navuh had never been concerned with the looks of the immortal warriors he bred. Until recently, the men selected to father them were chosen based mostly on brawn and aggressive tendencies, and lately on brains, but never on looks. In contrast, the clan females were much more discriminating about the humans they chose to father their children, and looks played an important part in their selection process.

Jade squared her shoulders and pinned Kian with a stern look. "Just to be clear, Phinas's imperfections make him more attractive to me, not less. No offense to all of you pretty boys, but I prefer my man rugged and masculine."

Kian chuckled. "No offense taken."

Turner's face lit up in a rare grin. "I'm just flattered to be bundled with the pretty boys."

Jade held on to her impassive expression, but she was stunned Kian wanted her to lead the team.

Could she have misinterpreted his intentions, though?

He'd said that he preferred a Guardian to accompany her and a female Kra-ell of her choosing, and he would probably nominate that Guardian as head of their team.

Kian would never leave such an important mission in her hands even though, strategically, she was the best choice.

Frankly, if she were in his shoes, she would also choose a trusted Guardian. He needed someone to represent the clan, and Jade hadn't been a member long enough to do such a role justice.

Was she even a member?

The clan had welcomed her and her people, but as members of their community and not full-fledged members of the clan itself. The only way to join that inner circle was to mate a clan member, and that didn't include Kalugal and his men, so her mating Phinas hadn't earned her a clan membership.

The clan was comprised solely of Annani's descendants and their mates.

Leaving issues unresolved was not Jade's style, though, and she wasn't about to wait until Kian informed her of his decision. She needed to know whether she was leading the team or not. "What about the fourth member of our team?" She looked at Onegus and then shifted her gaze to Kian.

"I suggest Magnus," the chief said. "He is the most senior Guardian on the force after the head Guardians. He's also coolheaded and eloquent."

As Kian nodded in agreement, Jade asked, "Who will head the team?"

"That depends." Kian crossed his arms over his chest. "If Magnus and Phinas have to pretend to be human throughout the meeting, then you will naturally be in charge. But if they don't, then Magnus will take over the lead as the clan's representative."

"Makes sense." Jade wasn't surprised or even disappointed.

Kian trusted her enough to lead the meeting in at least one of the scenarios, and he did not give his trust easily, so she considered that an accomplishment.

Saving his life had probably earned her a spot on the list of those he trusted, but letting her lead the team meant that he also valued the skills she brought to the table.

That being said, he knew that her loyalties were split.

She was oath-bound to protect the twins, but even though Kian had refused to accept her offer of a life vow in gratitude for saving her people from Igor's tyranny, she owed him an immeasurable debt, and he knew she would do anything in her power to protect him and the clan.

Hopefully, she would never be faced with a situation where she had to choose between Kian and the clan, and the royal twins.

The irony was that the twins had more right to membership in the clan than she had. They were Annani's half-siblings and Kian's aunt and uncle, but even though they were his own flesh and blood, knowing that Jade might side with them probably didn't sit well with him.

The truth was that if she was forced to choose, Jade would probably select the clan, and she could even get away with that without losing her place in the fields of the brave.

Her vow to protect the queen and her family could be deemed invalid because it had been extorted under false pretenses, and that was a loophole Jade could use to her advantage. She hadn't known that she was vowing to protect what everyone on Anumati regarded as abominations, which was what both societies deemed children born to a god and a Kra-ell.

Not that she still believed that they were indeed abominations. Now, she suspected that the combination produced offspring so formidable that both societies feared them, which was the real reason for the prohibition.

Had the queen's consorts known that the Eternal King's heir had been the twins' father?

All Kra-ell males knew right away when their seed took and fertilization occurred, so the consorts had to know that none of them had fathered the twins, but they still might not have known that they had been sired by a god.

As was true for any Kra-ell, the queen wasn't obligated to restrict herself to her official consorts, and she could have invited whomever she pleased to her bed—from the palace guards to one of the gardeners. But people talked, and although no male was allowed to officially make a claim on the queen's children, it was difficult to keep such a thing a secret.

Perhaps Turner was right, and the queen had commanded one of her consorts to claim them in order to silence the talk.

"We need a contingency plan," Kian said. "Any thoughts?"

Jade had a few suggestions in mind, but Kian's question was directed at Onegus and Turner, and she preferred to hear their ideas first before offering hers.

Onegus swiveled his chair to face Kian. "No matter how well we prepare, our away team will be at risk, but we can take steps to even out the odds. Naturally, everyone on the team will wear the compulsion-filtering earpieces. They should also wear our specialty protective vests, although those are only good at stopping bullets, and we don't know what the gods' weapons can do." He looked at Jade. "Did you ever see the gods carry weapons like the one Syssi saw in her vision?"

She shook her head. "It must be something that was invented at a later time. The weapons they used during my time were much larger and looked like javelins, but they were not meant for throwing or piercing armor. They released an energy blast that I doubt your protective vests can stop. The blast stopped the heart. It was instant death."

The weapons were developed to combat Kra-ell, not humans, and they had been designed accordingly.

Kian grimaced. "The more I learn about my ancestors, the less I like them." He shifted his eyes to Onegus. "The vests are better than nothing, so I suggest the team members wear them just in case they can do any good. Our other option is exoskeletons, but those are not practical for a mission that is supposed to be diplomatic in nature."

"Actually, I think that's a great idea." Onegus smiled. "First of all, the gods won't know who's inside the suits, and secondly, those things provide a powerful advantage."

Jade snorted. "I've seen those suits, and they look super intimidating. If we wear them, I can guarantee that the gods will shoot first and ask questions later."

"True." Kian nodded. "Besides, Syssi said that we shouldn't come as aggressors. The vests will have to do."

"Reluctantly, I have to agree," Onegus said. "We will have to provide the team with aerial defense and ground reinforcements that will be on standby and they should have exoskeleton suits with them in case they need to engage. Our missile-armed drones will be in the air just beyond the canyon, and a large force of Guardians will be stationed as near to the meeting place as we can get them without detection." He glanced at William. "Can we retrofit the sound cannon onto one of the drones? That might be the most effective weapon we have against the gods."

Scratching his neck, William seemed unsure. "That is an interesting idea, and I regret not investigating it before. It would require some re-engineering and components that I will have to manufacture in our lab because we don't have enough time to buy or order anything, and I doubt I can make those parts in time for the mission."

"That's regrettable," Kian said. "Any other options?"

"We can retrofit a helicopter to carry the system we already have," William offered. "We can mount the speakers at the bottom of the bird, with the sound wave pointed away from the cabin. With the crew wearing protective gear, they should be fine operating it. I probably can manage to do that with what I have."

"Good. Get on it as soon as possible." Kian turned to the chief. "You and Turner need to figure out the logistics of getting the backup force to the canyon while avoiding detection."

"What about the village lockdown?" Onegus asked. "Does it stay in effect?"

"Nothing has changed in that regard. For now, let's keep it buttoned down." Kian turned to Jade. "Choose the female you want to take with you and report back here in two hours." He looked at Kalugal. "Send Phinas over as well. We need to work on the right approach and what to tell these gods and, more importantly, what not to tell them."

"Hold on." Jade lifted a hand. "There is no one in the canyon. We are basing all of this on Syssi's vision, and it's not that I doubt it, but we are basically going in blind. What if we get there, and no one comes to meet us?"

"They will come," Kian said. "We have to assume that they are watching the canyon, and as soon as the team shows up, they will join."

Jade frowned. "But how? The drone scanned the entire area, and I saw no paved roads for miles around. They will have to either walk there, parachute down, or fly in on angel wings." She flapped her arms. "That doesn't fit the way gods work. It's too haphazard."

"Maybe they are there but using some alien cloaking technology." William let out a breath. "I'm also worried that there could be many more than three out there."

That was a valid point, and Jade wasn't too keen on trusting Syssi's assertion that the gods' intentions were friendly. But then there was nothing to be done about it, and the backup Onegus was arranging should suffice.

"When do you want the team to head out?" the chief asked.

"Midday tomorrow, provided that we can be ready by then. If not, the evening should be fine as well. The longer they wait, the more they sweat, right?"

Jade shrugged. "I don't know what sweating has to do with it, but they might get nervous. The question is whether their nervousness is good for us or not."

Leaning back, Turner regarded her with his penetrating gaze. "The more important question is whether they are indeed gods. If William's suspicion about a cloaking device is correct, they could be anyone."

Kian chuckled. "A cloaking device wouldn't affect Syssi's vision. That's not how visions work."

Jade wasn't sure that he was right about the nature of foretelling, but she trusted her logic more than she trusted visions, and right now, gods were the most likely candidates.

Onegus leaned back in his chair and crossed his arms over his chest. "I sincerely hope they don't have a cloaking device, or flying high-altitude drones over the area will be a waste of time."

Kian mirrored the chief's pose. "Nevertheless, I want that canyon monitored twenty-four-seven. We don't know that they have a device like that, although it would make sense for them to be able to keep themselves hidden."

"How far is the canyon from the nearest road?" Jade asked. "I need to know how long it will take us to jog there." She was a fast runner, and the immortals could probably keep up, but she needed more precise information.

"It's about an hour and a half on foot for a human," Onegus said. "I assume it will take you a fraction of that time."

"Assuming that an average human's pace is three miles per hour, that's four and a half miles. I can cover such a distance in ten to fifteen minutes." Jade smiled. "The question is how fast can your immortals run."

"They can keep up," Onegus assured her.

Gabi

With a sigh, Gabi put her book down and looked out the window of her hotel room. The romance novel was sweet, but it was predictable, and it didn't hold her interest. It was fine for reading in bed before falling asleep, but not as something to fill her day with.

Gabi was getting restless.

What was she going to do while waiting for the village situation to be resolved and for Uriel to let her know whether he could see her again?

He'd said that he would know by tonight whether he was staying in town or leaving because of the deal he was working on, but the whole story seemed iffy to her.

Flea-market flippers didn't negotiate huge deals that necessitated instant travel.

But then, what did she know about the flea-market flipping business?

Perhaps Uriel and his friends had found something truly amazing? Something even more valuable than the shoes of a Korean princess? And had several bidders they were negotiating with?

If the buyers in Los Angeles weren't offering them a price that was as good as or better than what the bidders from other places were willing to pay, then it would make sense for Uriel and his friends to fly over to where the better bidders were.

Another option was that the merchandise they were trying to find a buyer for was a contraband item that they were selling illegally.

Maybe Uriel suspected that the people they were negotiating with could sell them out?

That would necessitate a quick escape to avoid the authorities.

Nah, she was letting her imagination run wild again, and it was probably the fault of the book she was reading. It was about an international jewel thief trying to sell her loot to an undercover agent.

Uriel and his friends were probably actors, just as she'd suspected all along, and they were most likely working on a movie deal.

However, the problem with that assumption was that whether they got the movie deal or not, there was no reason for them to rush out of town—unless filming was about to start and the location was elsewhere.

Not a likely scenario.

Damn. It was so difficult to trust anyone. Life would be much simpler if everyone would just say what they meant.

It reminded Gabi of a movie that had had a profound effect on her. It was called *The Invention of Lying,* and it highlighted all the ways, big and small, that people used lies and platitudes to make life bearable.

It wasn't as if brutal truthfulness was desirable or practical, but she wished Uriel would be more straightforward with her.

When she'd asked him if it was a goodbye and his reply had been 'not if he could help it,' he'd sounded so sincere. But since he was probably an actor, it could have been a convincing act.

Well, it had been Uriel who had asked whether it was a goodbye, not her, and it was in response to her telling him that she'd enjoyed spending time with him and was glad that they'd gotten to spend two nights together, implying that she thought they wouldn't meet again.

Gabi had used Uriel's own tactics on him and thrown the question back at him, and that was when he'd said that it wasn't a goodbye if he could help it.

Ugh, it was pointless to guess what he would do, and staying cooped up in the hotel room was driving her nuts.

Reaching into her purse, she pulled out the phone Gilbert had given her and searched the contacts for Karen's number. Maybe she had an update about the lockdown and would be less cryptic than Gilbert.

The phone kept ringing for a long time before the call was finally answered.

"Hi, Gabi. What's up?" Karen sounded breathless, and the wailing babies in the background explained why it had taken her so long to answer.

"I just wanted to see if there was any news about the lockdown, but it seems like a bad time for a chat. You have your hands full."

"Yeah, Evan and Ryan are having a bad day, which is probably my fault because staying cooped up stresses me out, and they pick up on my moods. We are still in lockdown, and it doesn't look like they are going to lift it by tonight. I'm hoping for tomorrow morning." She sighed. "I need to get back to work so I can get a break from the little demons. I think they miss hanging out with Julia at the university, and that's why they are so cranky. They love their babysitter."

When another ear-piercing wail sounded in the background, Gabi winced. "I'd better let you get back to them. I'll call Darlene."

"Yeah, good idea. I'll call you later if I can."

As Karen ended the call, Gabi shook her head. "Poor Karen."

Gabi loved kids, and she loved her nephews, but she was very glad that she wasn't in Karen's shoes right now. Changing poopy diapers didn't faze her, but dual baby wailing was just intolerable.

Being a parent must be incredibly gratifying for people to be willing to suffer through that, not to mention the anxiety of raising little human beings while worrying about all the terrible things that could happen to them.

As Gabi scrolled through the list looking for Darlene's number, it occurred to her that Darlene worked in William's lab, so she probably knew more than Karen about the lockdown and when it might be lifted, but perhaps Kaia was even better informed. She was not only William's fiancée, but she was also privy to some secret project that the clan was working on, which meant that she had a high-security clearance and should know better than most what was going on.

Scrolling through the short contacts list on her clan phone, she quickly found Kaia's.

The phone rang a few times before her niece answered, "Hi, Gabi." She sounded rushed. "What's up?"

"I was wondering whether you knew anything about the lockdown and when it might end."

"Unfortunately, there is no news," she said breathlessly. "We are still in lockdown."

Kaia wasn't into sports, but she was young, not to mention immortal. She shouldn't sound so breathless unless—

Gabi sucked in a breath. "Am I interrupting something? I can call later."

Kaia chuckled. "Regrettably, you're not interrupting anything fun. I'm jogging home to get lunch for William and me. He's busy with the latest emergency project that Kian wants him to complete yesterday, and if I don't feed him something healthy, he's going to stuff himself with pastries from the café. When William is stressed, he's like a baby. Everything goes into his mouth. I'd rather he stuff it with healthy food that is good for him."

Gabi wanted to pat herself on the back. She'd been the one who had explained to Kaia about the importance of a balanced diet and how it affects the brain. Her niece had listened and adopted nearly all of it, but she'd refused to give up Coke, which was probably the worst offender.

Heck, even hamburgers and fries were better than that artificial junk. But hey, she was immortal now, and she could probably get away with a lot of unhealthy stuff before it negatively affected her.

"That's so nice of you, sweetie. I hope William appreciates how lucky he is to snag a rare gem like you."

Kaia chuckled. "Oh, he does, and I'm pretty lucky to have him, too. William is brilliant, kind, handsome, sweet, and caring, and it's an absolute joy to work with him every day in the lab, which is the best testament to how well we get along. We are together almost twenty-four-seven, and we love it."

Gabi could practically hear the love in Kaia's voice, and it made her so happy that she teared up a little.

"Indeed. Not many couples can spend so much time together without driving each other crazy. I can't imagine how wicked smart your kids are going to be, not to mention gorgeous and immortal."

"Well, our children won't be born immortal. They would have to be induced and go through transition like every other Dormant."

"About that. I'm still not clear on how it works."

Kaia laughed. "I thought that Cheryl had stated it bluntly enough. You have to have sex with an immortal male."

It had been so embarrassing to have her teenage niece explain how it was done. Well, technically, Kaia was still a teenager too, but at least she was legally an adult.

"I got that. But what about that mystical bond? I still don't know whether it's required for my transition."

She didn't remember who had said what, but she'd heard conflicting statements.

"Hold on. I just got home. I'll turn the speaker on so I can chop veggies while we talk." "Sounds like a plan."

"I can't hear myself think," Gilbert grumbled. "Can't you take the boys to the playground or for a walk? I need to go over these inventory lists."

Karen dipped the tea bag in the hot water for the twentieth time. "They've already been to the playground, and it's getting too hot to be outside."

The boys were watching one of their kids' shows while playing with toy cars and trucks on the floor, and as long as they weren't screaming and wailing, she was happy to leave them be. Karen was a pro at tuning the noise out while taking a breather from taking care of the kids, but Gilbert had no practice. Before moving to the village, he would spend his days in the office, and on weekends they had usually taken the kids out so they wouldn't be bored and cranky.

If they were, Gilbert would find an excuse to disappear from sight.

Now that he was forced to work from home, it still hadn't been a problem because the kids were usually gone most of the day, Idina in daycare and the boys at the university, but the lockdown was messing up everyone's schedule, and that included her plans for organizing a way for her to transition.

"Can you at least lower the volume?"

She shook her head. "They like it loud. It's either that or them wailing."

"Yeah, I know." Gilbert leaned back in the dining room chair. "I was thinking about taking my work to the backyard, but the bugs are a nuisance. I think they like my immortal blood." He rubbed his arm. "At least their bites don't cause a reaction, but I keep wondering if they get to live longer or multiply even more thanks to my potent blood."

"Dada!" Evan lifted his toy train and chucked it at Gilbert.

He caught it and smiled. "Good throw."

"No throwing toys at people," Karen scolded her son before turning to her mate. "Don't encourage him. If not for your new immortal reflexes, the toy would have hit you square in the face."

"Send him to his room," Idina said. "He's not playing nice."

"Who should I send to his room, sweetie?" Karen stifled a smile. "Your daddy or your brother?"

Idina gave Gilbert one of her semi-evil looks. "Both. Daddy wants quiet, and Evan needs to learn not to throw his toys at people."

"From the mouths of toddlers," Gilbert murmured as he closed his laptop and put it in his briefcase. "I really don't want to, but I'm going to work in our bedroom."

"We need to get a desk in there." Karen cradled the teacup.

"I hope the lockdown will be lifted soon, and you can take the kids to daycare so I can work right here."

"You're working on the dining room table while sitting on a dining room chair. That's far from ideal. You need an office, but since we don't have room for one, our bedroom will have to do."

He joined her at the kitchen counter and wrapped his arms around her. "I don't want to bring work to our bedroom on a permanent basis. That room is a sacred temple for worshiping my goddess."

Her lips twitched with a smile. "You say the nicest things."

"Only the truth." He nuzzled her neck. "And nothing but the truth, so help me Karen, my goddess, who I worship." He trailed kisses down her neck.

She laughed. "Stop it. We have an audience."

Gilbert turned his head to look over his shoulder at their three children. "They know that Daddy loves Mommy. Right, kids?"

Idina frowned at them. "Daddy loves me."

"I love you, your brothers and sisters, and your mommy. I also love Uncle Eric and Aunt Gabi and Aunt Darlene and the rest of our family."

Idina was still frowning. "You forgot William."

Karen stifled a giggle. "Daddy is still working on it. William is a new addition to the family, and it will take Daddy time to learn to love him."

"He said that he loves Darlene, and she is newer than William."

"True," Gilbert said. "But Darlene is a girl, and William is a boy."

Idina's face brightened with a broad smile. "So, you love me more than Evan and Ryan?"

"Dear Fates," Gilbert groaned. "Our daughter is going to be a lawyer."

Karen shrugged. "You always said that every family needs one."

"I did, didn't I?" He walked over to the couch and sat next to Idina. "I love all of my children with the same ferocity, but in different ways. Does that make sense to you, munchkin?"

She nodded at him sagely. "You love the girls because they are like Mommy, and you love her, and you love the boys because they are like Uncle Eric, and you love him too, but not like you love Mommy."

Gilbert opened his mouth to say something but then changed his mind and lifted Idina onto his lap. "Yep, more or less." He kissed her on each of her chubby cheeks, which were the only part of her that still retained some of her babyhood.

The living room glass door slid open, and Cheryl walked in, heading straight for the fridge. "What's there to eat?"

"There is leftover chicken from yesterday." Karen waved a hand. "We can cut it up and make a Chinese chicken salad with it. Want to help make it?"

"Sure." Cheryl took out the dish with the leftover chicken. "Do we have wonton strips?"

"We do." Karen opened the drawer and pulled out a bag.

"I have an idea." Gilbert put Idina back on the couch and joined them in the kitchen. "How do you feel about sharing your cabana with me during the day?"

Cheryl cast him a horrified look. "Why?"

"I need a quiet place to work, and I don't want to do it in the bedroom. It's bad juju. I only need a couple of hours, and I can do that while you're not there." He smiled. "I'll pay you. Twenty bucks for each hour of use."

Those were the magic words Cheryl couldn't resist.

"You've got yourself a deal." She offered him her hand. "On one condition. I don't want to hear a word about the mess."

He took her hand. "As long as I have a stretch of table to use, I don't care about the condition of the rest of the place."

Karen frowned. Cheryl wasn't the messy type. "What happened to your cabana?"

Cheryl scrunched her nose. "I'm redecorating. With all due respect to Ingrid, her interior design is outdated, and it doesn't look cool in my product videos."

Her Instatock account was gaining followers, and brands were paying her to promote their products.

"Can't you use screens, or filters, or whatever it was that you were telling me about?"

It seemed like a new feature was being added every day, and Karen had too much on her mind to pay attention to all the Instatock wonders Cheryl had been gushing about.

Cheryl shook her head. "It needs to look authentic and age-appropriate, but the house and the cabana both look like they were decorated by the same person who did the Venetian hotel in Las Vegas. It's old."

"You should talk to Ingrid," Gilbert said. "Maybe she's open to making some changes. I will pay for the new furniture and whatever else you need there."

Cheryl's eyes widened. "You will?"

"Sure thing. I'm investing in my dau—." He stopped himself. "In your business."

"It's okay." She put her hand on his arm. "You can call me your stepdaughter even though you and Mom are not married."

"I'd rather call you my daughter, but I know that you are not ready for that."

She patted his arm. "You can call me your daughter if you wish. But you will always be Gilbert to me."

Gabi

Gabi listened as Kaia opened and closed the fridge, ran water in the sink to wash the veggies, and then dropped the cutting board on the counter.

Those were such mundane sounds for such an extraordinary girl to make. But evidently even immortal geniuses needed to make food and eat it, clean up, and use the bathroom.

As the saying went, even a king puts his pants on one leg at a time.

In the grand scheme of things, people were slightly more evolved than their nearest relatives—the chimpanzees—and immortals were the next step in that evolution. It was a huge one, but at the end of the day, they were still just animals made of flesh, bones, and blood.

The question was whether people had something extra—an eternal soul that joined the universal consciousness once it was freed from the body.

In one of her deep dives down the YouTube rabbit hole, Gabi had stumbled upon a video of a near-death experience and had gone on to watch many more on the subject.

It had gotten her all philosophical.

Did consciousness emerge from the brain? Or did it exist prior to the brain's creation and continue after the brain's death?

Some claimed that it did, describing incredible encounters that, for some reason, tickled her memory.

Had she died in her sleep and revived without registering the event?

Could it be that her parents still existed in some form?

Were they following her life?

Did they approve of her and her life choices?

Why hadn't they contacted her?

A dream would have been nice, or a comforting whisper after she'd discovered that she'd been living a lie and that her husband had been cheating on her left and right while she'd been oblivious, believing that her life was going great.

Shaking the depressing thoughts off, Gabi forced a smile even though no one could see her. Sometimes, the act of smiling was enough to improve her mood, and lifting her head and squaring her shoulders could make her feel more confident when she was anything but.

It was a nifty trick of faking it until making it.

"So, what's that project that the boss wants William to complete yesterday?" she asked. "Does it have to do with the lockdown?"

"Of course," Kaia said. "How much did Gilbert tell you about it?"

"Only that another clan location was compromised and that Kian ordered lockdowns in both locations out of an abundance of caution."

"Yeah. That's more or less the reason, but there is much more that I don't want to get into at length because we would be on the phone for hours. The gist of it is that not too long ago, we welcomed into the village another group of long-lived people who are kind of related to us. They are a large group, and we took precautions when bringing them in, but we have reason to believe that another group of their kind followed them, and they are potentially hostile. We are not sure what their intentions are, and we are not taking any chances." She chuckled. "I'm saying 'we' and talking as if I'm in charge of the village security, but I'm just parroting what I've been told."

Kaia didn't sound concerned, but Gabi didn't think that a threat like that was trivial. "So those people who may or may not be hostile know where the other location is?"

"More or less. The place is located in downtown Los Angeles, but it's underneath an apartment building, and they wouldn't know how to get in even if it wasn't locked down. They can search the apartments, but all they will find are humans."

Gabi's hackles rose. "Would they harm the humans?"

"Not likely. They are searching for their people."

"I really hope you are right. Those innocent humans who live in that apartment building wouldn't know what hit them."

"We are watching the building, so it's not like they are being left without any defenses."

"Is that what William is working on? A way to defend that location?"

The truth was that Gabi had no idea what William's job description was.

Genius could describe many different things.

"He's working on outfitting a helicopter with a noise cannon. Immortals and other long-lived people have very sensitive ears, and a noise cannon can incapacitate them long enough for our people to slap handcuffs on them and bring them in for interrogation to find out what their intentions are."

Gabi had heard about noise cannons as an effective tool to disperse protestors and stop riots. It was a nonlethal weapon, and that made her feel better about the prospect of a possible confrontation.

She couldn't stand the thought of anyone getting hurt or dying.

"What about the humans in that building? Would they be hurt by the noise cannon?"

"We are not going to use the cannon there. These people seem to want to meet us in a remote location outside the city, and if they are friendly, we might not have to use it at all. It's just one more safety precaution to protect our team in case things go south."

"Good. I'm all for safety, and I'm worried about all the enemies the clan has. I assume that these people are not the Doomers that Onegus and Orion talked about in the restaurant?"

"No."

"So, two groups of immortals are enemies of the clan."

"Well, one that we know of. These new ones might be friendly."

Gabi sighed. "I have a feeling that the price of immortality will be more than just leaving everything I've worked for behind. I would be living in a constant state of anxiety. I don't like the idea of having known enemies who want me dead just because I belong to a group of people they disagree with. I hate it when humans do that, and I'm disappointed that immortals are just as bad."

"I don't live in fear," Kaia said as she closed a container with a loud pop. "And I don't regret it for a millisecond. I had to leave a career at Stanford behind and give up having articles written about me and by me in scientific journals, but I get to work on things I could have never even dreamt of, and I'm also less stressed than ever." She laughed. "That's probably thanks to all the great sex. Once you go immortal, you can never go mortal. The sex is just out of this world."

Gabi and Kaia had talked about intimate stuff in the past, and she loved being the cool aunt whom Kaia could ask for advice about boys. Except now the roles were reversed, she was the one doing the asking, and Kaia was the one supplying the information.

"In what way is it out of this world?" Gabi asked.

"Oh, boy. Where do I start? I need to put the containers in an insulated bag and then run to the bathroom. Can I call you back in a minute or two?"

"Sure. Take your time. It's not healthy to rush peeing. You need to relax and just let it flow."

Kaia chuckled. "Don't make me laugh, or I'll have an accident on the way to the bathroom."

"What's funny about keeping your bladder healthy? When you are stressed and rush things, the muscles in your pelvic floor tense up, which can lead to problems. Ask me how I know."

Whenever Gabi went through periods of stress, symptoms of bladder infection would send her running to the doctor, but most of the time the tests would come back negative. Eventually, she'd realized the connection between stress and the physical symptoms and had started making a conscious effort to relax her pelvic muscles.

The mind-body connection was more real than most people realized.

"I'm immortal," Kaia said. "I don't get infections, bacterial or viral, and everything heals fast. Got to go, Gabi. I'll call you in a bit."

"Time for lunch." Syssi closed her laptop and swiveled her chair to face Amanda. "Shall we adjourn to the kitchen and check on our daughters?"

Amanda lifted a pair of unfocused eyes to her. "Yeah. I was so absorbed in writing this paper that I didn't notice my stomach was growling." She stretched her arms over her head. "I have to admit that working from home has its advantages. I don't need to dress up. I have an excuse to wear my new Prada flats, and Okidu is in the kitchen making a tasty meal for us."

Syssi stifled an eye roll.

Amanda might be wearing flats, but that didn't mean she wasn't dressed in designer attire or that she looked any less than a million bucks. For someone so naturally stunning, it was odd that she felt the need to invest so much time and effort in perfecting her appearance, but perhaps it had something to do with her mother.

Annani's unearthly beauty was incomparable, so maybe the daughter felt as if she needed to work hard to measure up?

The mind was a strange and wondrous place, and each person had to navigate the landscape of their creation.

"Indeed." Syssi smiled at her sister-in-law. "But at home, you won't get the attention you're getting at the university."

Amanda waved a dismissive hand. "That used to be a factor, but it's not anymore. I'm happily mated."

"You are, but you still crave attention. Admit it."

Pursing her lips, Amanda shrugged. "It's much less important to me than it used to be. Still, as much as I'm enjoying this, working from home is not an option. We need test subjects, and we need the lab."

"How about a hybrid arrangement? We can work a couple of days a week at the university and the rest at home." Syssi pushed to her feet. "It would look less suspicious in cases like this when we both have to claim to be sick because we can't leave the village."

"It's the first time in the village's history that it's locked down. I don't expect it to happen often." Amanda leaned forward. "You should try to get another vision and clarify these gods' intentions."

Letting out a breath, Syssi plopped back down into her chair. "You have no idea how much I want to, but Kian doesn't want me to force them. He gets really upset when I do that."

Amanda arched one perfectly shaped dark brow. "It made sense to worry about the visions taking a toll on you while you were pregnant, but you're not pregnant anymore, and you need to set boundaries. My brother can be overbearing and intimidating, and I know that you don't like confrontation and love to appease him, but he shouldn't be the one deciding when you should or shouldn't use your Fates' given talent."

Syssi swallowed. "You're absolutely right, but you are also right about my aversion to conflict, and if I put my foot down on this, it will definitely lead to a major one. Besides, Kian is not entirely wrong. Sometimes, the visions take a lot out of me, and I faint or lose consciousness. I shouldn't attempt them alone, but the problem is that I can't concentrate and get in a receptive state when someone is with me in the room."

"It's not a difficult problem to solve." Amanda crossed her legs. "We can set up a camera in here, and I can watch you from another room. If something goes wrong, I will rush back in."

"That could be a solution, provided that I manage to forget that I'm being watched. Otherwise, I won't be able to reach the meditative state."

"Let's put it to the test." Amanda rose to her feet. "I'll go to the kitchen and call you from there on a video call. You'll put your phone on the coffee table facing you, sit down, and meditate."

"You'll need to be very quiet," Syssi said as Amanda opened the door.

Amanda made a gesture, zipping her lips. "I'll mute my side." She paused. "Do you want to eat lunch first?"

"No, I'd rather do it on an empty stomach. Sometimes, the visions make me nauseous."

"Don't try too hard." Amanda paused at the door. "If the vision doesn't come within minutes, let it go and come to eat lunch."

"Yes, ma'am." Syssi closed the door behind her.

Kian would be furious, especially since she was about to do it in his home office. Well, it didn't really matter where she did it. He would be mad regardless of where and how, but Amanda was right. She needed to put her foot down and stop being so accommodating.

Chuckling softly, Syssi sat on the couch and waited for the call.

She couldn't change who she was, and the truth was that Kian didn't need the additional worry when he was already dealing with so much, but it was also true that she might be able to find out valuable information that couldn't be obtained any other way.

Gabi

Kaia's comment about immunity to infections got Gabi thinking. Since sexually transmitted diseases would no longer be an issue, condoms wouldn't be needed to protect against that either, so maybe she should consider going back on the pill.

After kicking Dylan out, she'd stopped taking contraceptives and had never gone back on them. At first, because there had been no point consuming chemicals that had undesirable side effects when she wasn't having sex. Then, when she'd become sexually active again, condoms had become a must, and since they did double duty, preventing disease and pregnancy, there was no need to consume extra chemicals.

While she'd still been married to Dylan, they had decided to wait for kids, and she had dutifully taken the pill, thinking there was no need for a married couple to use condoms. After all, they were supposed to be exclusive.

Right. Talk about naïveté.

Not only had Dylan been unfaithful, but he also hadn't been very discriminating, screwing every willing woman in his path. She'd been so lucky that he hadn't infected her with syphilis or some other cursed affliction.

Letting out a sigh, Gabi let her head drop back on the couch pillows.

She wasn't immortal yet, and until she turned, she should continue being careful and using protection, but she hadn't been careful with Uriel.

What had possessed her to decide that it was safe with him?

Why had she decided that she wouldn't mind getting pregnant with his child?

She'd believed him about being clean and about having a low sperm count, the same way she'd believed Dylan had been faithful to her.

Evidently, she hadn't learned from her mistakes, and she hadn't developed a healthy skepticism like she'd thought she had.

Healthy, yeah—what a joke.

Good nutrition and exercise might keep her body healthy, but her negative self-talk definitely didn't, and it was undoing all her other good work. After all, the body and the mind were interconnected, and one affected the other.

What she should do instead of berating herself was put a positive spin on the situation.

She was finally over Dylan's betrayal and was once again willing to take a risk and trust a man.

Yay, Gabi! You go, girl!

When her phone rang, she answered Kaia with a cheerful voice that was only slightly forced. "I see that you took my advice after all and didn't rush."

Kaia chuckled. "Yeah, but for a different reason. So, where were we?"

"You said that sex with an immortal is out of this world, and I asked you in what way."

"Right. Where do I start? I love William, so I guess it's not just about the mechanics and the chemistry but about how he makes me feel and the mystical bond we share. That probably amplifies the pleasure and takes it to a whole new level, but you are probably more interested in the other stuff."

"I'm interested in all of it. Hopefully, I'll find an immortal who will make me feel like William makes you feel."

The problem was that she kept seeing Uriel's gorgeous face whenever she thought of forever and mystical bonds, and that wasn't smart. She was setting herself up for heartbreak because he was human, and she would have to leave him even if he wanted more with her. The problem was that while she was with him, she didn't remember what she knew about immortals, and all the other obstacles to their relationship didn't seem so insurmountable.

"That's a good way to think about it." Kaia took a long breath. "I'm going to talk in generalities because it would feel awkward otherwise. Immortals are amazing lovers for several reasons. They are usually a lot older than they look, and they have a lot of experience pleasing women. It's also important to them to please the ladies even though they have to thrall them to forget the encounter. They pride themselves on being exceptional lovers, and they are totally focused on their partner, which takes some getting used to because it's intense and can reveal things you never suspected you were into. Their recuperating time is practically nothing. They are ready to go again in minutes, and they don't get tired even after the fourth or the fifth time." She chuckled. "That sounds like too much, and you might be thinking, ouch—that would be a lot of wear and tear on a human woman's intimate parts, but their venom and their saliva contain healing compounds, so instead of waking up sore and achy, you wake up feeling rejuvenated."

Instinctively, Gabi's hand went to a spot on her neck where Uriel had bitten her, or rather where she'd thought he had. She must have dreamt it because there was no sign of a hickey. Even if he had never broken her skin, what she remembered feeling should have left a mark.

"Tell me more about the bite. Does it hurt?"

Kaia snorted. "Of course, it does. The fangs slice into your skin and flesh, and there is only so much they can do to minimize the pain with their saliva. But their venom contains aphrodisiac and euphoric compounds, so as soon as it's released, the pain disappears, and it's replaced with the best orgasms you've ever had. Once you're done coming, you will float away into the best psychedelic trip you could have ever imagined having, and with zero negative side effects. You wake up feeling calm, satiated, and rejuvenated."

A pit of dread formed in Gabi's stomach.

That sounded a lot like what she'd felt this morning and the morning before that. Maybe Onegus and Orion had been right after all, and Uriel was an immortal?

But Darlene's son, who was a super hacker, had checked on him and found out where and when Uriel had been born, who his parents were, and plenty of other information that confirmed he was just a human living in Portugal and visiting the US frequently.

So why was she suddenly scared?

Wouldn't it be perfect if Uriel turned out to be immortal?

But what if he was one of those awful Doomers who kidnapped girls and sold them into sexual slavery?

Flea-market flipping could be a great cover for trafficking, and if the deal Uriel and the other two were working on involved buying women and transporting them somewhere to be sold again, that would also explain the need to fly out of town on a moment's notice.

Could the man she was falling for be a monster?

Gabi wanted to believe that she was a better judge of character than that, but she'd been proven wrong before.

"Are you there?" Kaia asked.

"Yeah, I'm here. I was just thinking."

"I bet." Kaia laughed. "You probably can't wait to finally visit the village and check out all the single guys. There are many hotties to choose from. It will be like a visit to a magical candy store. You can have as many as you want without rotting your teeth or making you nauseous, and the candy can make you immortal."

"Yeah." Gabi forced a chuckle. "I can't wait."

"Let's try again," Amanda said once they were done with lunch. "Allegra and Evie are napping, Alena is chatting with Orion on the phone, and Okidu is cleaning. You won't be distracted."

Trying to bring up a vision hadn't worked before. Syssi didn't know whether it was because she'd been hungry and her hunger pangs had been distracting or if it had been thoughts of her daughter waiting to eat lunch with Mommy.

Perhaps Amanda was right, and now that everything had been taken care of and there was nothing to divert her attention, she could do it.

Madame Salinka had always said that the mind needed to be calm to enter a meditative state. She'd even suggested taking a mild herbal relaxant, but Syssi didn't want to use chemical aids, especially since she didn't know what would work on her immortal body and how much of it was needed.

"Let's do it." She rose to her feet. "Are you going to stay here?"

Amanda nodded. "Call me from Kian's office."

"I will." Syssi picked up her phone and made her way down the corridor to Kian's home office.

Once there she called Amanda, propped her phone against her coffee cup, and settled on the couch. "Give me ten minutes. If nothing happens, come in, and we'll get back to work."

"Roger that," Amanda said. "I'll mute myself now."

Closing her eyes, Syssi started deep breathing as per Madame Salinka's instructions, but instead of emptying her mind, she thought about the three males she'd seen earlier in the day. The trick was not to force anything and let the information flow through her, but at the same time, direct it toward the desired outcome.

Easier said than done.

Soon, her mind was wandering in all directions, her thoughts floating in disorganized clusters that were becoming less and less cohesive the longer she was at it.

It felt a lot like the moments before falling asleep. It was a state of calm, a relief from the day's stress, and a portal into the dream world.

For a seer, it was also the portal into viewing events in the past or the future.

A female of otherworldly beauty appeared first, a goddess of such brilliant glow that Syssi had difficulty discerning her features. It was more of an impression of beauty. The female was tall and had long white hair that shimmered like diamonds. Her glowing skin made it impossible to see her eye color or the shape of her lips, but Syssi could make out her body shape from the parts covered by her silver gown.

She was exquisite.

There was another female with her, also a stunning goddess, but since she bowed as she entered the room, it was clear that she was the other goddess's servant.

Syssi couldn't understand what the servant was telling her mistress, but the impression was that she was delivering exciting news.

Who were they?

Could that be the past, and she was seeing Annani's mother and one of her servants?

The details of the room were fuzzy, but Syssi got the impression that it was a receiving room—a lady's salon.

As the vision started to fade, Syssi tried to catch some last details, but all she caught was a gleam of gold. She didn't know whether it was a vase or a statue, but the shape intrigued her. It looked like a modern piece, and it didn't match the goddess's dress or the rest of the room, with its delicate silks and ornate patterns and the dim light that added to the antiquated atmosphere. Was that a hint?

It was almost as if two worlds had collided in that singular vision.

Pulled back to reality, Syssi tried to dissect the fleeting moments she'd experienced. Why had she seen this? And what significance did the golden artifact hold?

Could it be a connection, a bridge between the present and the past?

The goddess and her servant surely held some importance to their current situation with the three gods, or perhaps it was a glimpse into the future. And that modern piece of golden art, was it an anchor to her time, a clue to aid her in deciphering the message the vision was trying to convey?

As the last vestiges of the vision evaporated, Syssi opened her eyes and let out a breath. "You can come in," she told Amanda.

A moment later, the door opened, and her sister-in-law walked in. "Well? What did you see?" She sat next to her on the couch.

"Nothing that's connected to our current crisis. I saw two goddesses, a lady, and her servant. I didn't hear them talking, and I don't know if the vision happened in the past or the future. The only clue I got was a gold vase or statue that looked like a piece of modern art." She shook her head. "I'm not even going to tell Kian about it because it's not going to help him with what he's dealing with now, and it will only stress him out that I forced a vision."

Amanda chuckled. "As if there is anything you can keep from him for longer than five minutes. How are you feeling? Are you okay?"

Syssi nodded. "I'm drained, but it's nothing a few minutes of rest won't fix." She leaned her head against the couch cushions and closed her eyes. "There was another clue. The goddess I saw shone so bright that I couldn't see her clearly. Do you know if your grandmother had a particularly strong glow?"

"My mother never mentioned it. She was very beautiful, though. More so than the other goddesses." Amanda smiled. "Nai was an insignificant goddess and underage when she seduced Ahn. Given that he was such a stickler for the rules and that every goddess vied for his attention, Nai must have been extraordinary to succeed in tempting him to break the law for her."

Syssi laughed. "Your grandfather was much naughtier than he made himself out to be. He was a rebel, had an illicit affair with the Kra-ell heir to the throne, got her pregnant with twins, and then later allowed the underage Nai to seduce him. I wonder how many other naughty things he did."

On her way home, Jade debated between the two candidates she had in mind for the mission. Borga was better trained, and she was also coolheaded and functioned well under pressure, but Jade didn't like the female, and she didn't fully trust her either.

It would have to be Morgada, even though she wouldn't be much help if things got dicey. She wasn't a great diplomat either, but she was a pleasant, non-threatening female, which was uncommon for pureblooded Kra-ell.

Who knew? Maybe that was precisely what was needed for this odd situation.

The thing was, Jade didn't expect the meeting to turn violent. Whoever was broadcasting the signals wanted to find out who they were dealing with, and attacking the team sent out to meet them would be counterproductive to that goal.

Yeah, Morgada was probably the right choice.

Entering the house through the backyard, Jade found Drova in the area they had designated for training. For a long moment, she watched her daughter go through the stances, admiring the fluidity and accuracy of her movements. The girl was a born fighter.

Holding the staff horizontally behind her with both hands, Drova swung it overhead in a powerful arc, mimicking the dive of a hunting bird. The staff sliced through the air, creating a resonant hum. Transitioning smoothly, she twirled the staff deftly in front of her, the rotations tight and close to her body, making her a moving fortress.

It would be impossible for an adversary to get close without confronting the relentless rotations of her staff.

Next, using the staff as a vaulting pole, she kicked out both her feet in front of her, then landed and pivoted, sweeping the weapon around at ground level to target an imaginary opponent's legs. She fluidly shifted, twirling the staff above her head, creating a barrier and then striking diagonally.

With each movement, her feet danced in perfect synchronization, never missing a beat. She showcased not only power but also grace—each combat stance was a balance of strength and elegance.

To finish, she held the staff vertically in front of her, took a deep breath, and exhaled, pushing the staff in an upward motion. As it rose, she followed its trajectory with a leap, spinning in the air, and landing with the staff grounded beside her, standing tall and proud.

"Looking good," Jade complimented her daughter. "That was flawless."

Drova regarded her with a raised brow. "Thank you. Hearing praise from you is unexpected. Usually, you only bother to comment on my technique if it needs improvement."

"That's the traditional Kra-ell way. Excellence is expected, less than that is corrected. But even an old horse can learn a new trick, right?"

Drova chuckled. "I don't think that's how the saying goes, but I get what you're trying to say. You're learning many new things, and I guess giving out compliments is one of them?"

"More or less."

This was actually something Jade had picked up from Phinas. She'd seen him training with Drova and complimenting her left and right. The girl seemed to do much better with praise than with criticism, and Phinas had claimed that it was universally true and urged Jade to try it.

Drova leaned her staff against the fence. "So, what was the meeting about?"

"Come inside, and I'll tell you. Is Phinas home?"

"Yeah, he is." Drova followed her into the living room.

Jade found her mate sitting at the kitchen counter and eating a sandwich.

Poor guy didn't get to have dinners with his family. His mate and stepdaughter didn't eat the same things he did and never would.

He put the sandwich down and turned to her. "How did the meeting go?"

She pulled out a stool next to him and sat down. "It was surprising, to say the least. Kian wants me to lead the team, at least to start with. And if our immortal companions need to pretend to be human, I will lead the talk throughout the meeting."

Phinas grinned. "That's great. It means that he trusts you."

"It would seem so. He also let me choose who I want to take with me. The plan is to send two Kra-ell females and two immortals who can pass for humans. I didn't decide who the other female is going to be, but I chose one of the immortals." She smiled at him. "You."

"Me?" He put a hand on his chest. "And Kian is okay with that?"

"Kalugal suggested Rufsur, but since he's mated to Edna, who's a council member, that's not an option. Initially, I didn't want you to be part of the team in case things went wrong." She looked at her daughter. "I wanted at least one of us to be here for Drova, but I reconsidered. I'd rather have you by my side than a Guardian I don't know."

Frowning, Drova lifted her hand. "I assume that it has something to do with the village being locked down, but it seems like I'm missing crucial pieces of information. What's going on?"

When Jade was done explaining about Syssi's vision and who they suspected was sending the signals, Drova's eyes widened with excited determination.

"I want to be part of the mission, Mother."

It hadn't even occurred to Jade that Drova could be a candidate. Her daughter was a damn good fighter, but she was just a kid.

"You're too young."

Squaring her shoulders, Drova cast her a hard look. "I'm almost seventeen, and according to Kra-ell tradition, I am old enough to take part in defending our tribe. Besides, after you, I'm the best female fighter you have, and you know that."

Jade looked at her daughter with pride. "I appreciate your confidence and desire to help, but this mission requires diplomatic skills that you haven't mastered yet."

The stubborn expression on Drova's face wavered for a split second. "Who do you have in mind for the mission?"

"Borga or Morgada. Each has things going for and against her."

"Let me guess. You are considering Borga for her fighting ability and Morgada for her amiable nature."

"That's right."

"Neither of them has diplomatic skills, and you're not planning on letting them talk. You will do all the talking."

Jade had to smile. Her daughter knew her well. "That's right."

"Then you can take me." Drova cast Phinas a sugary smile. "It can be a family mission."

Phinas looked appalled. "You're too young, and this mission is full of uncertainties. I can't risk your safety, and even if I was okay with that, Kian would never let an underage girl join the mission. Don't waste his time even suggesting it."

Drova shifted her gaze to him. "Kian is not in charge of me or my mother. If Jade deems me ready, he can't say no."

Phinas snorted. "That's what you think. But go ahead and give it a try."

Drova returned her gaze to Jade. "It's up to you, and I hope you choose me. I won't be reckless. I promise to follow your guidance to the letter, and I'm a better choice than Borga or Morgada. Please, let me prove myself."

There was a very good chance that Kian would put his foot down and forbid Drova's participation, but even if he didn't, Jade couldn't deny that Drova was right. According to Kra-ell traditions, she was old enough, and she had the skills, and Jade had no right to keep her away from danger because she was her daughter.

"Fine. But if Kian refuses to let you go, I don't want you to argue with him. I need you to act professionally and accept whatever he says. We are forging an alliance with the clan, and this mission is a test. I don't want anything to screw it up."

Drova didn't look happy with that, but she nodded. "I'll be the picture of the obedient underling. Professional all the way. I won't let you down."

"Chocolate or vanilla?" Gilbert tugged on Idina's foot.

She was sitting on his shoulders, her sandal-clad feet dangling over his chest and her small hands clasping his forehead.

He loved every freaking moment of it and dreaded the day she would no longer want to ride on top of her daddy's shoulders.

"Vanilla with sprinkles." She leaned her pointy chin on his head.

"They don't have sprinkles in the café."

"So tell them to bring some. Vanilla with no sprinkles is boring."

"The boys want chocolate," Karen said.

"I don't want ice cream." Cheryl turned the double stroller toward the playground.

"Wait." Karen caught her hand. "Look over there." She pointed with her chin. "Isn't that Ingrid?"

"It is," Gilbert said. "Go talk to her about decorating your cabana."

"She's busy." Cheryl chewed on her lower lip. "I don't want to bother her."

The designer was sitting at a table with a muscular guy who reminded Gilbert of the actor who played the military dude in *Avatar*. Cropped blond hair, a square jaw, and the aura of a drill sergeant.

"That's Atzil," Karen said. "He's Kalugal's cook."

Gilbert took another look. "That guy is a cook? Are you sure?"

She chuckled. "He looks like a bodybuilder, but he's the cook, and he's a very nice guy."

"How do you know that he's nice?" Gilbert narrowed his eyes at her.

"That's what I heard." She lightly slapped his bottom. "Go get the ice cream for the kids. I'll introduce Cheryl to Ingrid."

Half an hour later, Cheryl had an appointment at Ingrid's design studio for the next day, and she happily took her younger siblings to the playground, leaving the adults to talk in peace.

"So, Atzil," Gilbert started. "Karen tells me that you are Kalugal's chef."

"Cook," Atzil corrected. "I never studied in a fancy culinary school, but I can cook a hearty meal, and I hear no complaints from the men." He sighed. "I wish there was someone who could do my job, but there are no takers, and someone needs to cook for the men, or they will live off frozen pizzas and sandwiches from the café."

Ingrid put her hand on Atzil's massive shoulder. "Atzil has his eyes set on running the new bar, but there's more involved than just finding a replacement cook for Kalugal. Kian wouldn't allow a former Doomer in his secure section of the village, and that's where the bar is located. It's such an awesome place, and I put so much effort into decorating it authentically, but it stands empty, collecting dust because no one other than Atzil is interested in running it."

"The bar was built to look like a hobbit's home," Atzil said. "Ingrid decorated it with rustic furniture and earthy colors, and all it needs now is someone to pour the drinks and serve some food. It could be the new social gathering place for everyone in the village, but since it's located in Kian's secure enclave, that's a problem."

The wheels in Gilbert's head started spinning. "When you say that it's built to look like a hobbit's home, do you mean that it's hewed out of the earth?"

Ingrid nodded. "From a distance, it appears as a gentle hill with a circular door. It's made from dark wood and adorned with ornate iron hinges and a big rustic knob right in the center. Two round windows flank the door to let in some natural light to the entrance, which leads to a tunnel-like hallway with walls that are lined with earth and reclaimed timber beams. The floor is paved in rounded stones, made to look as if they were worn smooth by the footsteps of countless patrons." She smiled. "Not too comfortable for high heels, I'm afraid, so I covered them with hand-woven rugs in rich, earthy tones."

"The bar area has an arched ceiling that's supported by timber beams," Atzil said. "It gives the entire space a cave-like feeling. It's chilly even on a hot day."

Karen grimaced. "That sounds dark and dreary."

"Not at all," Atzil said. "Ingrid placed lanterns on the walls that fill the space with a soft glow, and the round windows at the front let some light in as well. The tables and chairs are crafted from polished wood, and each is uniquely shaped because they were handmade by a local craftsman."

"I added cushions and throws in deep reds and golds to make the place nice and cozy," Ingrid said. "But the real masterpiece is the bar counter. It's a single elongated slab of wood, polished to a gleam, showcasing its natural grain and knots. Behind it, I had shelves carved into the walls to display bottles." She cast Atzil a fond glance. "When I was coming up with the design, I had you in mind. Perhaps that's why you fell in love with the place at first glance."

The poor guy looked speechless, his Adam's apple bobbing in his throat. "You never told me that before."

Ingrid shrugged. "I didn't want it to go to your head."

Gilbert wasn't interested in all the decorating details or Ingrid and Atzil's sappy romance. He was concerned with more practical issues, like opening the bar doors to the public. "Since the bar is hewn from the hill, perhaps it's possible to dig a tunnel leading to it from another section of the village and block off the entrance from Kian's side. That way, everyone can use it. Once this latest mess is over, I can stop by the architect's office and review the plans with him to see what can be done." He leaned back in his chair. "Or I can have a word with Kian about the segregation of the village. I understand his concern with security, but everyone living in the village should be a trusted community member. If they are not, they shouldn't be here."

Ingrid snorted. "Good luck with that. The village might look like a democracy to you, but it's not. Kian has the final word, and the only one who can overrule him is Annani, but she never does because she doesn't want to undermine his authority. Besides, as much as I would like Atzil to have his bar, I don't think it's worth creating social unrest."

The interior designer was feistier than she looked, and Gilbert liked her. "So let me get this straight. Are you willing to accept every rule that Kian makes? How is that different from living in a dictatorship?"

"Kian doesn't make rules to benefit himself. He makes them to keep all of us safe."

"Really?" Gilbert cocked a brow. "So, the rest of us plebs are okay to intermingle with everyone else and live with the Kra-ell and the former Doomers, no offense meant, but Kian and the rest of the aristocracy are not?"

Ingrid opened her mouth, closed it, and then opened it again. "I guess there is something to that, but on the other hand, the rest of us are not important enough to merit threats. It's like the president. He or she needs to be protected twenty-four-seven because they are public figures, and some might wish them ill. The average Joe and Jane don't need to worry about safety because they are of no interest to anyone other than their family and friends."

Smiling, Gilbert lifted his soda bottle. "To the average Jane and Joe. We have it so much better than the aristocracy in many ways."

Karen clinked her bottle with his. "To being nobodies."

"To nobodies." Atzil and Ingrid joined the toast.

"I have an idea," Karen said. "How about the two of you come to our house for drinks? We can have a cheese and cocktails night."

Atzil grinned. "That's a wonderful idea, but I have a better one. Since you have a house full of kids, you should come to Ingrid's house, and I'll treat you to cocktails and appetizers Atzil style." He smiled apologetically. "I would have invited you to mine, but I live with a roommate."

Leaning forward, Ingrid whispered, "Atzil hasn't slept in his house for months. He's living with me, but we didn't make any official arrangements, so no one knows."

"Why not?" Gilbert asked.

Ingrid shrugged. "That's what works for us."

Under the table, Karen lightly kicked his shin. "It's like us," she said. "Everyone keeps asking why we are not married even though we have three kids together, and my answer is very similar to yours. That's what works for us."

Gilbert couldn't disagree more, but he was wise enough to keep his mouth shut.

Atzil and Ingrid weren't fated mates. That was the reason they were not making any official announcement. Both of them were still waiting for that special someone to show up.

He and Karen were a completely different story. There was no doubt in Gilbert's mind that they were truelove mates, and hopefully, there weren't any doubts in Karen's mind either.

After a short break for lunch the team reassembled in the war room, and as everyone took their seats, Turner was the first to speak up. "I've thought about the situation, and I realized that we shouldn't just show up at that canyon and hope they will meet us there. We need to send a message to let them know that we are sending a team to talk to them and when we want to meet them."

"How do you propose to do that?" Onegus said. "Leave a big sign in the canyon saying meet us here tomorrow at two o'clock in the afternoon?"

Turner didn't even crack a smile. "Something along those lines. We know they are monitoring the canyon, either with cameras on the ground or a drone from above that our own drone can't detect. We can attach a banner to our drone with that information or drop a sign."

"Why not do a fly-by and announce it with a megaphone?" Kian asked.

"They might be using only video," Turner said. "Not that I think it's likely given the technology they possess, but just in case they are collecting visuals only, we should put down something in writing."

As a knock sounded on the door, Kian swiveled his chair to look at the monitor, and when he saw who was standing at the door, he shook his head. "Jade must have lost her mind," he murmured. "Let them in."

Onegus released the lock remotely, and the door swung open.

"Good afternoon." Jade walked in with Phinas and her daughter. "Meet my team members. Drova is the other Kra-ell female I chose to accompany me." She sat on the chair Phinas pulled out for her and motioned for her daughter to sit beside her.

Kian shook his head. "Not happening. How old are you?" he asked Drova.

The girl squared her shoulders and jutted her chin out. "I'm almost seventeen."

"Which means you are sixteen." He looked at Jade. "Whose idea was this?"

"Drova volunteered, but I approved. According to Kra-ell traditions, she's old enough to fight, and she's the best female fighter I have. If things go wrong, Drova will be more valuable to me than Borga or Morgada."

The Kra-ell were different, Kian was well aware of that, but only a couple of hours ago, Jade had been reluctant to take Phinas with her because she was worried about leaving her daughter with no parental figure. What had happened between now and then for her to do a one-eighty like this?

"Are you willing to risk your daughter's life?"

Jade winced. "I can't play favorites. I realized that if Drova was someone else's daughter, I would have considered her for the team based on her fighting skills and my level of trust in her. The only reason I didn't was that she was mine, and that's not fair. If I'm willing to risk other people's children, I have to be willing to risk mine."

Kian understood that all too well.

One day, Allegra would have to take up the mantle of leadership, and he wasn't looking forward to that day. He was torn between wishing that she would never develop the necessary traits to lead or the desire to become a leader and hoping that she would.

In the end, it wasn't up to him.

It was up to fate.

However, in Jade's case, he could play the role of fate and relieve her from the burden of having to either refuse her daughter or put her at risk when it was evident that she didn't want to.

"I'm sorry, but you represent the clan in this mission, and according to our traditions, Drova is too young. Choose someone else."

He could see the tension leave Jade's shoulders. "I understand." She turned to her daughter. "You'll have to be patient and wait until you are seventeen."

"Eighteen," Kian corrected. "Seventeen is the age of consent, but eighteen is the age of enlisting in the Guardian force." He smiled at Drova. "If you wish, you can join the training program as soon as you catch up on your general studies. I'm willing to bend the rules for you and allow you to join right now. If you are as skilled as your mother claims, then you might be ready for Guardian duty at eighteen, which would be unprecedented. It usually takes decades of training until a cadet is ready to be sworn in."

Drova glanced at her mother. "Can I join the training?"

"If you so wish. But you heard Kian. You have to pass your high school equivalency test first."

"I can do both. I can study and train at the same time." She turned a pair of defiant eyes at Kian. "It's not like I have anything better to do with my time, and I can't spend sixteen hours a day sitting in front of the computer and studying. I'll go insane."

He could understand that.

The Kra-ell were not made for stuffy classrooms. They needed fresh air and plenty of physical activity, but the problem was that most of the Guardian training happened underground.

"This is a discussion for a different time." Jade pulled out her phone. "I'm going to ask Morgada to join us. You can go back home, Drova."

Reluctantly, the girl rose to her feet and dipped her head in deference to Kian. "Thank you for the offer to join the Guardian training."

"You're welcome."

Onegus lifted his hand. "Come to my office after this crisis is over."

"Yes, sir." She turned on her heel and left the room.

"I'm sorry about that," Jade said after the door closed behind her daughter. "She is a good fighter, but I'm glad you didn't allow her to join the team."

"You're welcome." Kian smiled. "I just hope someday you will return the favor when my daughter demands to participate in a dangerous mission."

She cracked a smile. "I hope to still be here when Allegra is Drova's age, and I also hope to have a say in her decisions. I promise to do my best."

"Can we go back to the message issue?" Turner asked. "If we want to fly a banner, we should get to it before it gets too dark."

Kian looked at Jade. "Will you be ready to be at the canyon at noon?"

She nodded. "You still need to coach me on what you want me to say to those gods or whoever they are. But that shouldn't take too long, right?"

He nodded. "The list of things you can't tell them is much longer than the list of what you can."

"That's what I thought. We should be able to make it by noontime."

Aru

Negal stood next to the hotel room window with his hands tucked in the back pockets of his jeans. "It's getting dark. No one is going to show up at that canyon today."

"They flew the drone over the area again," Dagor said. "This time, it was a high-altitude military drone they thought we couldn't detect." He snorted. "Who do they think they are dealing with?"

Aru frowned. "Are you sure the military drone was theirs? Maybe there is an Air Force base nearby."

Dagor shook his head. "There isn't, and civilians don't have drones like that. It's another clue as to the military ability of our adversaries. In my humble opinion, we should take the drone down to show them that we are not to be messed with."

Dagor was young and hotheaded, but thankfully, Negal wasn't.

"We can't take their drone down," the old trooper said. "It would be considered a hostile act, and rightfully so. Our objective is to find out who took the Kra-ell and what they did with them. Not to start a war." He pinned Dagor with a hard look. "Above all, we need to keep our presence on the planet a secret. Humans can't be allowed to find out about us."

"We also don't want to get shot at by that drone." Dagor turned to Aru. "We are hard to destroy, but if they blow us up, even we can die. I don't intend to end my life on this godforsaken planet."

"Clever." Aru snorted. "You couldn't have said it better if you tried."

Earth had indeed been forsaken by the gods. It had been erased from all historical records and all the astronomical maps. No gods were ever supposed to visit the cursed planet, and except for a select few, no one on Anumati knew that this sector was still being patrolled.

The remark didn't pull a smile out of Dagor like Aru had expected.

"We need to take that bird down. Whoever they are, they are not familiar with our technology and will not know that we were responsible for the drone's demise. They will think it malfunctioned."

Negal sat on one of the beds and leaned his elbows on his knees. "How many times do I need to tell you that we can't? Even if the cause of the drone's demise could be blamed on a malfunction, once the drone is disabled, it will crash, and it's a big bird that can cause a lot of damage. I don't want innocent human lives on my conscience."

"There is nothing to destroy on Mount Baldy," Dagor insisted.

Negal cast him an exasperated look. "It could start a brush fire, and given how dry everything is, it would spread so fast the humans wouldn't be able to contain it. Do you want to explain that to the commander?"

That got Dagor to finally nod in agreement. "Fine. I just hope that these people are other Kra-ell and not humans. I don't want to think what the commander would do to us if we reported that the Kra-ell from Gor's compound were taken by humans. The cleanup job would be massive."

"Yeah, and we would have to do it," Negal said. "But that's neither here nor there. I'm tired of sitting around and waiting, and since it's getting dark and no one is going to show up, I say we get out of here and get something to eat."

"Not yet." Aru pushed to his feet and opened the balcony door. "I need to make a phone call."

"To your human?" Negal asked.

Shrugging, Aru ignored the question and stepped outside.

Negal followed him. "You've been seeing her every night since we got here. You know that's irresponsible."

"It's not your place to lecture me about responsibility, Negal. I know what I'm doing."

"Do you? Are you thralling her to forget what you do to her every time you are with her? You know what repeated thralling can do to a human. If you care for the girl, you should stay away from her."

"We don't know that's true. It might have been part of the propaganda." Aru didn't sound convinced even to himself.

He could already see the damage his thralling was doing, even though it shouldn't have after only a couple of times. The female was getting headaches and often looked confused as if she couldn't remember the most basic things.

Perhaps she was already mentally compromised, and his thralling was exacerbating the problem?

"It's not propaganda, Aru. It's science. Human brains were designed to be susceptible to our manipulation, but we were warned that too much of it can fry them and to use our powers with caution."

"Not only humans," Aru murmured. "Every species our scientists created was designed to allow us to control it."

"All except for the Kra-ell." Negal smiled sadly. "They were the first, and the scientists didn't think to modify their genetics with a safety feature that would give us control over their minds. With that one simple modification, a lot of the bloody mess on Anumati would have been avoided. The Kra-ell wouldn't have sought equal rights, and there would have been no rebellion."

Aru waved a dismissive hand. "You know better than to believe everything they say, or anything for that matter. The propaganda machine is so massive that it's nearly impossible for commoners like us to know the truth."

Negal huffed. "Don't tell me that you believe the Kra-ell legends that claim they were the first people and that we are a modified version of them and not the other way around?"

"Why not? It's just as plausible as us creating them as our first modified species. What's recorded in history is what our rulers want us to believe, not the absolute truth."

Gabi

After three hours of getting pampered in the hotel's spa, Gabi felt refreshed and much less irritable than she had been going in, and she had Karen to thank for the idea.

In fact, she should call her.

Once she exited the elevator on her floor, she pulled the phone out of her robe pocket and dialed her sister-in-law.

"Hi, Gabi," Karen answered right away. "Regrettably, I have no news. We are still in lockdown."

That wasn't a big surprise. If the lockdown had been lifted, Gilbert would have called her already to schedule a time to pick her up. Then again, she'd been around people, so everything pertaining to immortals, the village, and the lockdown had retracted to the recesses of her mind, and all she'd remembered was that her brothers were working on some big business deal and that was why they couldn't see her.

It was all very confusing, and it was a miracle she was still clinging to her sanity.

Uriel had a lot to do with that, no doubt. Without him to distract her, she would have gone nuts. But on the other hand, if it wasn't for him, she would have gone to the village when she'd arrived and would have been locked down together with her family, and her mind wouldn't be in danger of getting fried.

He was worth it, though.

Being with him was a once-in-a-lifetime experience, and she would cherish it for many years to come.

As sadness threatened to obliterate her good mood, Gabi took a deep breath and forced a smile. "I guessed as much. I'm just calling to tell you that I listened to your advice and splurged on a spa treatment. I got a massage, a pedicure, and a manicure and had my hair done. I feel like a new woman."

"Awesome. I'm glad you are not wasting your vacation by sitting around in your room and waiting for your brothers to call."

What Karen had probably meant by that was that Gabi wasn't waiting for Uriel to call her, not Gilbert or Eric, but the truth was that she'd held the phone in her hand throughout the spa treatments in case Uriel called.

She chuckled. "Hopefully, tomorrow I can finally come visit you in the village. I can't afford another spa treatment."

"Didn't they give you a discount?"

Karen had told her to say that she was Mr. MacBain's guest so she could get a discount, but when Gabi had gotten to the salon, she couldn't remember the name. It was part of the thralling or compulsion or whatever it was that Orion had done to her. She was only free to remember what she'd been told during the meeting with her family and their new friends when she was alone, and apparently, it included the names of those friends.

"I couldn't remember the name, so I didn't say anything. They charged it to my room."

"I'll take care of it," Karen said. "Don't worry about the bill."

"I don't want you to pay for it." Gabi pulled the room key out of her pocket and opened the door.

"I won't. I'll speak to Onegus and ask him to tell the front desk to give you a discount on the spa treatments."

"Don't bother him with that." Gabi sat down on the couch and lifted her feet onto the coffee table. "He needs to concentrate on solving the security issue and lifting the lockdown."

"That's okay. I won't mention it until the crisis is over."

"Good. Are the boys sleeping? I don't hear any ruckus in the background."

Karen chuckled. "That's because we are not home, and Cheryl took them to play in the sandbox. Gilbert and I are in the village café, sitting with a lovely couple and enjoying an adult conversation. You have no idea how great that feels after dealing with the little ones all day long."

Should she be offended that her brother was there and hadn't asked to speak with her? Evidently, Gilbert was enjoying the adult company as much as Karen and didn't want to be bothered by his sister.

"I'll let you go so you can enjoy your evening. Say hi to Gilbert for me, will you?"

"Of course. He sends his love."

Gabi rolled her eyes. Gilbert would never say something like that. Karen was just being nice. "Right back at him. Call me as soon as anything changes with the lockdown situation."

After ending the call, Gabi let out a sigh and wiggled her toes, admiring the bright red nail polish. She'd wanted dark green, but the beautician had convinced her to go with a traditional red, saying that it went better with her skin tone.

She was right, of course.

Her toes looked amazing, and it was a shame she didn't have open-toe sandals to show off the pedicure.

It would also be a shame if Uriel didn't call up and they didn't go out, and all that pampering went to waste.

Gabi wasn't the type who went out alone and picked up guys in bars, and she had no friends in Los Angeles whom she could call up and invite to a girls' night out.

The only people she knew were her family, and they were stuck in the village.

When her phone rang a few minutes later, she knew it was Uriel, and not because she had any supernatural senses. The call came on her regular phone, not the one she had gotten from Onegus, and her clients and friends from Cleveland would text her first.

Onegus had offered to forward her calls to the new phone, but Gabi had declined, preferring to keep her old life separate from the one she was about to embark on.

Letting it ring several times before answering required a deliberate effort, but she didn't want Uriel to think that she was just sitting around and waiting for his call.

"Hi," she said as nonchalantly as she could. "Are you done with your meetings?"

"For today, I am. Did you hear anything from your brothers?"

"They are still not back. Their deal must be as complicated as yours."

"Their loss is my gain. I get to invite you to another dinner. We could go to the same restaurant or find something else in the city. What's your pleasure?"

"I'm in a mood for something more exciting. How about a nightclub? I can ask the concierge to recommend a classy place."

Looking at her painted toes, Gabi regretted again not having sandals. Perhaps she could go on a quick shopping run and get a pair. But that would be wasteful. She'd already bought a pair of new shoes on this trip.

"I don't like nightclubs," Uriel said. "They are too noisy."

She was so used to men agreeing to do everything she wanted that her first response to his answer was surprise.

The second was suspicion.

Uriel was too young and too hip to be bothered by the noise level in nightclubs—unless he had very sensitive ears—like the immortals.

Still, Onegus, or rather Roni, had checked Uriel's background, and everything had looked legit. Uriel was human.

Was he, though?

What if they were wrong?

It didn't make much sense that she could uncover something that the mighty clan hacker couldn't, but perhaps there were subtle hints she could pick up on?

What else gave immortals away?

Fangs, of course, and glowing eyes, which they got when they were aroused, but they could thrall their partners to forget seeing those things.

They were also super strong, but it wasn't as if she could tell Uriel to bench-press a car.

"We could go to a comedy club," Gabi suggested. "They are much less noisy."

"I'd rather go to dinner. I'm hungry, and not just for food."

Well, if he put it that way. "I'm hungry too. When can you get here?"

"Are you sure you want to eat in your hotel restaurant again?"

"Yeah, the food is okay, and the cocktails are great. But the best thing it has going for it is the convenient location. It's only two and a half minutes away from my room."

"I'll be damned." Dagor leaned closer to the screen. "They are sending us a message."

Aru put a hand on Dagor's shoulder and leaned over his head to look at the screen. A low-flying drone, the kind anyone could buy on the internet, was making passes over the canyon with a banner flying behind it.

On one end, there was a circle with a vertical line down the middle and an upside-down Y shape inside the circle. It was what the humans considered a universally accepted peace sign. On the other side, it had a dove holding an olive branch in its beak, which was another human peace sign. Between the two signs, written in bold letters and numbers, was 12:00 noon Wednesday.

"They want to meet us tomorrow at noon, and they come in peace," Negal translated the sign, as if it needed translation. "Or, more accurately, they want us to believe that they come in peace." He looked at Aru. "Should we send them a message back?"

"Not yet." He looked at the nearly dark sky. "They are not expecting an answer today anyway."

"They know we are watching the canyon." Dagor turned to look at Aru over his shoulder. "They expect some type of response."

"And they will get it. Just not today." He smiled. "Do they really expect us to accept that their intentions are peaceful and walk into a trap?"

"Maybe." Negal shrugged. "We expected them to rush in to check who was emitting the signals. They outsmarted us and sent a drone instead, and evidently, they also figured out that we must be monitoring the canyon."

Aru headed toward the door connecting Negal and Dagor's room to his. "They are not stupid, and once they realized that there was no one there, it was logical for them to assume that we were watching." He opened the door.

"Where are you going?" Negal asked. "We need to plan what to do tomorrow."

Aru smiled. "You know what to do. We talked about it. We will implement plan B, but we will wait until the last moment to do so."

"Smart but risky," Dagor said. "They might bolt."

"They won't." Aru stepped into his room and closed the door behind him.

They had rented a two-bedroom suite in the hotel, and although he usually didn't like pulling rank on his teammates, having a room to himself was the one exception.

Since the walls were thin and the doors provided no soundproofing at all, there was no real privacy to be had, but for this communication, he didn't need to say a word out loud.

Taking his boots off, he lay on the bed, closed his eyes, and opened a channel.

Can you talk?

Yes, Aria's voice sounded in his head. *Are you well, Aru?*

I am very well, thank you for asking. The plan worked, and the other party responded. They flew a banner that specified the day and time of the meeting. They also added two peace signs to reassure us that they meant no harm.

There was a long moment of silence on their mental connection. *What did they use to symbolize peace?*

She was always so literal. Even when they were children, Aria needed to know every detail. It was a wonder that she had not become a scientist, but then the Fates had decreed a different path for them, one that might be more pivotal to the future of Anumati than any new scientific or engineering marvel.

They used human symbolism. Luckily, we have been here long enough to be acquainted with them, so we knew what they meant.

It might be a trap, she said.

Aru smiled even though she could not see him. Hopefully, she could hear it in the tone of his mental voice. *It might be, but I am not going to walk into a trap. I have a plan.*

You always do. Aria sighed. *I miss you, and I miss your hugs. They are the only thing capable of bringing me peace. The years you've spent in stasis were the most difficult of my life. The silence in my head was depressing.*

Leaving Aria behind was the hardest part of joining the crew of the ship patrolling this sector, but it wasn't as if either of them had a choice. They had literally been born for this mission.

I miss you too, but now we get to talk whenever we please, and we can do it in complete privacy.

That was not something that Negal or Dagor could do. If they wanted to communicate with loved ones on Anumati, they had to route the call through the patrol ship, and even though the entire enormous interstellar vessel was staffed with people who supported their cause, everything they said on those calls had to be recorded and reported. It was protocol.

Semi-complete privacy, Aria chuckled. *The Supreme knows every word we exchange.*

Of course. Neither of us can keep secrets from the Supreme.

The Supreme could have several meanings in their language, and that was why they were using the term to describe their leader, even though it was probably an unnecessary precaution. No one had ever heard of anyone capable of eavesdropping on a telepathic communication, but he and Aria were not taking any chances.

No one knew that they possessed the ability to talk to each other telepathically, so no one had reason to penetrate their private channel. But if anyone was listening to their conversations, they could only accuse Aru of disclosing classified information to a loved one.

The one they called Supreme had to remain shielded at all costs, even if the cost was their lives.

Gabi

Gabi put on lipstick, smacked her lips even though all the makeup tutorials said not to do that, and brushed her hair with her fingers.

"How am I going to trick Uriel into revealing whether he's immortal?"

Maybe she could whisper something scandalous from far away and watch his reaction?

She could go to the bathroom and, once she was out of his hearing range, say something about fondling his balls or licking him up and down like a popsicle. That would get a response out of him for sure. No guy, whether human or immortal, could keep a stoic expression when hearing a woman make a promise like that.

Not that she knew much about immortals, but since they looked like humans and had the same anatomy, it was safe to assume that what worked on regular men would work just as well on them.

Smiling, she took her purse, checked that her room key was in her wallet, and walked out. Uriel had offered to pick her up at her room, but Gabi knew that if they met there, they would never leave, which would have been fine with her if she wasn't hungry and didn't need to also talk to him and test whether he was immortal.

The problem was that she would forget her plans as soon as she entered a room full of people. Heck, she would forget it as soon as she saw him.

But maybe if she held the thought firmly in her mind, it wouldn't disappear, and she would remember to execute her plan. But then, if Uriel was indeed immortal, he could pluck those thoughts from her head, which was why Orion had messed with it to start with.

But what if she framed the test in her mind as a sexy game?

She could whisper naughty things to him and try to determine if he was actually hearing her or if he was guessing what she was saying just from her body language. She should be able to hold on to that thought.

The bullet elevator no longer made her nauseous, and as she exited on the restaurant level, she wasn't dizzy as she walked up to the hostess. "I'm meeting Uriel Delgado for dinner tonight. Is he here already?"

The hostess smiled. "He is. I'll take you to your table."

As Gabi followed the woman, something bothered her, but she couldn't put her finger on what it was. When had Uriel told her his last name?

She couldn't remember him actually saying it, but she knew it somehow. She also knew that there was something she needed to do later in the evening, but she couldn't remember what that was either.

When the hostess turned into the alcove and Uriel came into view, the bothersome thoughts flew out the window, and all Gabi could think about was how sexy he looked in the pale pink dress shirt and charcoal gray slacks.

The guy was magnificent no matter what he was wearing, and even more so when he had nothing on at all, but she liked seeing him in dress clothes that she would later peel off him one item at a time.

Standing with the chair pulled out for her, he leaned to kiss her cheek. "You look beautiful tonight."

"Thank you. So do you."

He grinned, flashing two rows of perfect white teeth. His canines were slightly longer than average, and in the back of her mind, Gabi knew that it was significant for some reason, but when she tried to remember why, a pulse of pain blasted through her head.

Wincing, she sat down and let Uriel push her chair in. "So, how did it go today? Did you close the deal?"

"Not yet." He sat across from her. "But we made significant progress. Tomorrow is going to be the pivotal day. How about you? Did you hear from your brothers?"

"No, not yet. I spoke with my sister-in-law earlier, but she had no news for me." Gabi could only remember telling

Karen about the spa visit but not about when Gilbert and Eric were coming back.

"What about your nieces and nephews?"

To her shame, Gabi couldn't recall having asked Karen about them.

She shook her head. "I don't know what's wrong with me. I guess I forgot to ask her about them. But since she didn't mention anything, I assume that they are alright."

Uriel's eyes filled with worry. "Does forgetting things like that happen to you often?"

"Not normally, no, but since I got here, it happens a lot. At first, I thought that I was suffering from PTSD because I was so scared of flying across the continent, but thanks to you, the flight wasn't that traumatic. Besides, it has been days, and I shouldn't still be experiencing side effects." She rubbed her temples. "Maybe it's all the changes, and I will be okay once I return to my routine, and if not, I'll get my doctor to run some tests. I heard that thyroid imbalance can cause memory issues."

He seemed even more unsettled as he reached for her hand. "Regrettably, I'm ignorant about everything that has to do with medicine and what it takes to keep the body in balance. That being said, the main thing that has changed since you got here is me. I feel guilty because I keep you awake at night, and you might not be getting enough sleep."

This time, her smile wasn't forced. "If not for you, this trip would have been a complete disaster. With my family unable to meet me, I would have nothing to look forward to."

His worried expression turned into a guilty one. "Every night, I think it's going to be the last, and I prepare myself mentally not to see you again, but then you call me, or I call you, and I'm overjoyed that I will be seeing you again, even though I know that it will make parting from you so much harder."

It was nice of Uriel to say that, and he might have even meant it, but Gabi knew as well as he did that there was no future for them. She had a life in Cleveland, and he had a life wherever it was he lived.

"I feel the same," she admitted. "You still didn't tell me where you are based or what you do when you are not hunting for treasures and making deals to sell them. For all I know, you might have a wife and six kids waiting for you to finalize your deal and bring home the bacon."

"Bacon?" He arched a brow. "Why would I be bringing home bacon?"

That was what had bothered him about what she'd said? Not the wife and six kids?

She narrowed her eyes at him. "When someone says they are bringing home the bacon, it's a reference to their role as a provider for their family, implying that they are earning a living and supporting their loved ones. Usually, their wife and kids."

Gabriella Emerson was breaking his stupid heart.

He should have never allowed her to get under his skin like that, but there was something about her he just couldn't resist. She wasn't like any of the other women he had been with, not because she was more beautiful, or had softer skin, or a smile that was more alluring, and it wasn't that she was smarter, more charming, or a better lover, although to him she was all those things.

It was that she had that something extra he had never expected to find here or back at home.

"I'm not married, and I don't have children. You are the only woman in my life right now."

She arched a brow. "That's convenient. How about last week? Was there someone special back then?"

Answering truthfully wasn't the smartest move on his part, but he had never claimed to be particularly clever. Sometimes, he just had to follow his gut. "I never stay anywhere long enough to have someone special, but for some reason, you have become special to me in the short time we've had together, and that's why I know that saying goodbye to you will hurt like hell."

For a long moment, she just looked at him, seemingly debating what to say. "We are both single adults, and we get to decide what our future will look like. We could decide that giving this relationship a chance is more important than you chasing the next treasure or my nutrition practice. We could forge a future in which we can be together."

Her words were like a javelin to his heart. It was so gutsy of her to say them, but regrettably, nothing could be further from the truth.

She was human, and she could never find out that he was not, but to keep thralling her was irresponsible. The right thing to do would be to part ways with her tonight without taking her to bed, but he wasn't strong enough to just walk away.

He could refrain from biting her, but that wouldn't be helpful because he would have to thrall her to forget seeing his fangs and his glowing eyes.

Maybe he could blindfold her?

Would she trust him enough to allow him to tie her up?

He would never do that without her full consent.

Gabi let out a sigh. "Your silence is answer enough, and you're probably right. I don't know enough about you to fantasize about a shared future. For all I know, you might be a terrible person."

"I would like to think that I'm a good guy, but then no one thinks of themselves as evil, not even the most evil ones. They think that they are justified in their evil-doing."

She tilted her head. "Have you ever deliberately hurt someone?"

He was a soldier, but he was young, and he hadn't taken part in a violent conflict yet, so he was lucky enough to have never used force to hurt anyone, but there was no guarantee that he wouldn't in the future. In fact, it was almost a certainty.

But for now, he could answer her question truthfully. "I have not."

Her smile was radiant. "Then you are a good person. It's as simple as that."

"I wish it was." He sighed. "The truth is that I'm not free to do as I please, Gabi. In a perfect world, I would have been overjoyed by the chance of a relationship with you, but my world is far from perfect, and I can't really tell you much about it. My partners and I are involved in something pretty big, and I'm not in a position to walk away and do my own thing."

She nodded. "I understand. Is there anything at all that you can tell me about yourself?"

He could tell her his fake identity, but he didn't want to lie to her. Lies of omission were bad enough.

"I can't. I'm sorry." He leaned over the table and took her hand. "All I can tell you are anecdotes from my travels and the various finds my friends and I have discovered, if those are of any interest to you."

Looking defeated, Gabi nodded. "Maybe I'll get to know you a little better from those stories. I just wish I knew why you need to be so secretive. Are you a spy?"

In a way, he was, so he could admit it. "I am."

Her eyes widened. "For who?"

"No one you know, and I'm not spying on anyone you care about. I'm looking for a group of people that might be hiding somewhere around here."

That should be vague enough.

Her brows pulled down in a frown. "What are you going to do to them once you find them?"

"Nothing. My job is to observe and report. Nothing more."

Gabi was still frowning. "Okay. Let me ask it in another way. What are those you report to going to do to these people?"

"Nothing. They just want to know what they are up to."

"So, your treasure hunting is just a cover?"

"It is more than a cover. We actually make good money from it, and we enjoy doing it. It's like being part anthropologist and part archeologist."

Gabi was a smart woman, but there was no way she could guess from what he was telling her what he was up to or who he was, and yet he felt like he was saying too much.

Keeping his identity and that of his teammates a secret was of paramount importance to their security, and he should reach into Gabi's mind and erase the last few moments of conversation. The thralling would be minimal, and it wouldn't harm her, provided that he didn't thrall her again later.

As Uriel excused himself to use the restroom, Gabi smiled until he could no longer see her and then slumped in her chair.

Throughout the evening, she'd felt torn between the urge to get up and leave in a huff or drag Uriel back to her room to have her way with him. It was a miracle she had survived all the way through dessert.

He infuriated her with his refusal to tell her anything personal about himself, including his age, where he'd attended college, or even if he had attended. His answer to every question was that he couldn't tell her without lying to her, and he didn't want to lie. But why would he need to lie about the college he'd attended? Or where he'd been born? Or about his family?

He'd said that he was working on a project that required complete confidentiality, and he wasn't allowed to disclose any details, personal or otherwise. The only things he was willing to share with her were that he was single, childless, and didn't have anyone special in his life.

Did she believe him?

Given her experience with men, she shouldn't, but she did.

Why?

Maybe it was because he refused to lie to appease her curiosity, or perhaps it was the sincerity in his eyes and his tone of voice, but she didn't think he was lying about that.

Still, it didn't diminish her aggravation with him or the constrictive ache in her chest.

Tonight might be their last, and Gabi very much doubted Uriel would seek her out in Cleveland once his project was over.

He hadn't asked her any questions about her family except to inquire when her brothers would return from their emergency business trip, and those questions had been related to information she had volunteered.

He hadn't even asked her if she was married or had children, which was the clearest indication that he was only interested in the here and now.

On her part, Gabi hadn't volunteered the information either, and not just because he hadn't asked or because she was angry with him for insisting on remaining a mystery.

She didn't like talking about her parents dying when she was still a kid, or about the marriage that had failed so miserably, or about her turbulent relationship with food and why she'd become a nutritionist.

Who wanted to hear her depressing stories about loss and failure?

People were much more interested in success, which Gabi could now front with confidence. She was fully in charge of her life, and she was doing well—fear of flying and many other things notwithstanding.

"Ready to go?" Uriel startled her from her reveries.

"Yes." As Gabi's mind took a leap in a different direction, imagining Uriel's gloriously naked body moving against hers, she felt her cheeks warming, which was ridiculous given that she had no reason to feel embarrassed about her attraction to him.

Maybe the reason for the flash was the surge of desire and not shame for her lustful thoughts. Yeah, that was it.

Hiding a smile, Gabi lifted the small cappuccino cup, finished the last few drops, collected her purse, and pushed to her feet.

As he wrapped his arm around her middle, his large hand encircling nearly her entire waist, the heat in her body rose by several degrees, and as his hand traveled down her hip and then back again, it was all she could do to stifle a moan.

"What are you doing to me?" she murmured as they stood in front of the elevator doors, waiting for them to open.

"What do you mean?" he asked with mock innocence.

"I can't get enough of you. It's like you are an addiction that I never want to be weaned off."

"Same here." His hand on her waist tightened, and the moment the doors opened, he moved so fast Gabi didn't know how she found herself with her back pressed against the wall and the entire cabin shaking from the force of the impact as it lurched down.

"Uriel," she whispered against his lips.

"Gabriella." His hips pressed into her, and his mouth hovered a fraction of an inch away from hers.

Was he waiting for her to kiss him first?

She could do that.

Tilting her head, she drew his bottom lip between hers and gently nipped it with her teeth.

The growl that erupted from his chest sounded more like something coming out of an animal's throat than a man's. It belonged to a ferocious beast that was about to devour her, but instead of fear, all she could feel was a blast of lust.

As he took her mouth in a hard kiss, his hands landed on her ass and hauled her up, so she had no choice but to lift her legs and wrap them around his waist.

The friction was delicious even though his hard length and her moist center were separated by layers of fabric.

If she could just reach his zipper and free him, he could move her panties aside and be inside of her in a split second.

The annoying beep of the elevator reaching the lobby put an end to that fantasy.

"Gabi," Uriel whispered into her mouth as if her name was a prayer. "You need to let go."

The doors started opening as she finally dropped her feet to the floor, and it wasn't a moment too soon.

Two couples stared at them as they got out, and one of the women cleared her throat before getting into the elevator.

"She's just jealous," Gabi said before the doors closed.

Uriel chuckled. "I'd rather think that she's inspired. If there wasn't another couple with them, her husband would have been in for a treat." He led her to the other bank of elevators going to the hotel rooms on the top floors.

Holding on to his arm, Gabi smoothed a hand over her dress. "How do you know he was her husband? Maybe he was a boyfriend or a lover?"

"They both had wedding rings."

Gabi winced. "To some, that's meaningless. Some people have no problem cheating while wearing their wedding rings."

Some even thought it was sexy, which was really depraved, in her opinion. But then, who was she to judge? Actually, as a woman who had been cheated on, she had every right to pass judgment.

Had her husband worn his wedding ring while cheating on her? Had the women he'd picked up been turned on by it?

The acrid scent of betrayal hung around Gabi like a fog, making him think that she hadn't been talking in generalities. It had been something she'd experienced. But it wasn't his place to ask. Since he couldn't tell her anything about himself, he had no right to inquire.

If she wanted to, she would tell him, and when she did, he would find the guy and avenge her.

Right now, all he could do was take her into his arms and comfort her, but as he reached for her hand to pull her to him, an older couple joined them, so handholding was all he could offer.

"Good evening," the older lady said. "Are you staying in the hotel?"

"Yes, we are," Gabi answered while squeezing his hand.

The lady smiled. "You make such a beautiful couple. Are you on your honeymoon?"

Gabi shook her head. "We are visiting my family." She leaned on his arm. "I'm going to introduce Uriel to my brothers." She lifted her head and smiled sweetly at him. "I hope they like him."

"What about your parents?" the lady asked as the four of them entered the elevator.

The smile slid off Gabi's face. "Regrettably, they are gone, so it's just my brothers and their families."

His heart clenched with sympathy, and he squeezed her hand.

"I'm so sorry to hear that," the lady said.

"Thank you. They passed a long time ago." Gabi pressed the button for her floor. "Which floor are you on?"

"The sixty-ninth," the man said. "Same as yours."

Thankfully, the lady refrained from asking any more questions, and they said their goodbyes as each couple headed to their room.

"I'm sorry," he said as he closed the door behind them.

Gabi put her purse on the entry table. "It's not your fault, and as I said, it happened a long time ago."

"How old were you?" He shouldn't have asked, but if Gabi's parents had passed away a long time ago, she must have been a kid when it happened.

"I don't want to talk about it now." She sauntered toward him. "We were in the middle of something, and we were interrupted." She pressed her body to his, pushing him against the door and lifting her head to trail moist kisses along his neck.

Smiling, he put his hands on her waist. "I can't remember where exactly we were interrupted. Can you remind me?"

"With pleasure." She covered his hands with hers and guided them to her ass. "You lifted me as you kissed me, and I wrapped my legs around your torso."

"Oh, yes." He hoisted her up so her center was at the exact spot where it could rub against his erection. "Now I remember. But you were kissing my mouth, not my neck." He tilted his head to allow her better access.

As she kissed and nibbled the column of his neck, he struggled to maintain the shroud that would mask his glowing eyes and elongating fangs. Under normal circumstances, it wasn't difficult to do, but Gabi evoked something so primal in him that he had trouble multi-tasking while being with her.

"God, how do you smell so good?" she murmured against his skin and then totally unexpectedly licked him. "Hmmm. You taste good, too." She lifted her head and looked at him with glazed-over eyes. "The question is whether you are good or poisonous to eat."

He laughed. "I'm probably both." His venom had healing properties, and his thrall was dangerous to her, but he wasn't going to do either tonight.

Her smile was brilliant. "I had a feeling you would say that," she teased.

"Do you feel brave tonight?" He carried her to the dresser, put her on top of it, and leaned over her. "Do you feel like the meaning of your name? A strong hero of God?" He pushed her hair over her shoulder and cupped the back of her neck.

"I do," she breathed with a challenge dancing in her blue-gray eyes. "You are intoxicating." She started humming a tune he didn't recognize. "You and I are in a twisted romance."

He covered her mouth before she had a chance to sing another verse, and when she tried to kiss him back, he tightened his hand on her nape to keep her from going in and nicking her tongue on his rapidly elongating fangs.

"Close your eyes," he commanded.

A crooked smile twisted her lips as she obeyed. "Are we playing that game again?"

"We are playing a new game." He opened the top drawer and pulled out a pair of skin-tone stockings. "These are perfect." He pulled out another pair that was black and silky to the touch.

"What is perfect?" Gabi opened her eyes.

Thankfully, his shroud was still holding, or she would have run out of the room screaming.

"These." He held the two pairs of stockings up. "One to blindfold you and the other one to tie your wrists together. Are you game?"

Was she?

If Uriel wanted to hurt her, he didn't need to blindfold her or tie her up. He was so much stronger that he could incapacitate her in a split second. This was just a sexy game, and she was curious to see where he took it.

Well, she wouldn't see anything because she would be blindfolded, but that was beside the point.

"I'm game," she whispered. "I've never done anything like this before."

"Neither have I." He wrapped the black stockings around her head, tying them in the back. "If it gets uncomfortable at any moment, tell me, and I'll take it off."

"Okay." Gabi opened her eyes to test whether she could see anything through the nylon.

She could see the general outline of Uriel's body as a dark silhouette, but that was only because the lights were on. If he turned them off, she wouldn't be able to see anything.

"Let's get you out of this dress first."

Excitement thrumming through her, Gabi lifted her arms as he pulled the dress off over her head.

The air conditioning vent was right across from her, and as her nipples pebbled, Uriel dipped his head and took one in his mouth through her flimsy lace bra.

"Yes." Moaning, she threaded her fingers in his hair and held him to her.

He kissed her other nipple, first through the fabric and then once more after releasing her breasts from the lace.

When he lifted her into his arms, she had only her panties on, but apparently, he planned on removing them once he got her where he wanted her, which was spread out on the bed.

"Hands up." He didn't wait for her to obey and lifted them over her head. "I'm going to secure them to the headboard. Is that okay?"

"Yes," she breathed.

This game was incredibly arousing.

Not being able to see and having to rely on hearing and touch alone added to the acuity of the sensations, and being at Uriel's mercy, even though it was only perceptibly more so than at other times, was exciting as well.

Were all women strange that way? Or was it just her messed-up mind that found this arousing rather than scary?

It was like the classic beauty and the beast scenario, not that Uriel resembled a beast in any way, but in that he could do anything he wanted to her, and yet she trusted him not to harm her. More than that, she trusted him to protect her.

If anyone chose that moment to burst into the room and attack her, she knew that Uriel would defend her, not because he loved her, but because that was who he was.

Her ex, the captain of the football team, would have run away and left her to die. That was who he was, only she hadn't seen it throughout the years they had been together. She'd only realized it when things had started to unravel.

"Are you okay?" Uriel asked. "You seem tense."

With her head going places it shouldn't, Gabi hadn't even noticed that he was done tying the pantyhose to the headboard.

After giving them a gentle tug, she knew that her hands could easily slide out from the loose knot he'd made, and that was reassuring.

"I'm perfect." She gave him a smile.

"I'm glad." He leaned over, the long strands of his hair brushing over her chest as he took her lips in a sweet kiss. "Now I'm going to remove the last barrier." He hooked his thumbs in the elastic of her panties and dragged them down her thighs.

When he kissed her belly button, she expected him to keep kissing down, but he surprised her by taking her mouth. Arching into him, she rubbed her aching nipples against his chest, melting into him.

Sliding his tongue into her mouth, he feathered his fingertips over her heated center, the touch too slight to give her what she needed.

"Touch me," she said as soon as he let go of her lips. "Don't tease me."

"Why?" There was a smile in his voice. "It's so much fun to tease you, to bring you to the edge and have you beg for more."

"You're cruel."

"Cruel to be kind," he sang before taking her lips again.

The sound of his singing had an unexpected effect on her. His speaking voice was beautiful, deep, and resonant, but when he sang, it was hypnotic, and even though he'd only sung those four words, the rest of the tune kept playing in her head over and over again.

Gabi had no idea how she remembered the lyrics of a song from the seventies that she hadn't heard more than once or twice throughout her lifetime. It was as if Uriel's voice had unlocked a hidden treasure inside her head.

Cruel to be kind in the right measure— Cruel to be kind in the right measure—

How appropriate for the game they were playing.

Uriel

Gabi was so damn beautiful, but it wasn't the sum of her features that made her so appealing to him. It was the personality that animated her, her expressions, her intelligence, the spark of mischief, and even her irrational fears. The sum of who she was, was unique, and for some inexplicable reason, a perfect fit for the sum of who he was.

The blindfold hid her eyes from him, which was regrettable, but it accentuated her delicate heart-shaped face and her lips, which were still covered in that hot red lipstick that didn't come off no matter how hard he kissed her.

And the rest of her body, Fates, it was perfection.

She was delicately built, not petite but close, with slender shoulders, a slim waist, and long, slim limbs. He could spend hours kissing every inch of smooth skin and map every freckle on her chest, her arms, her nose, and her cheeks. Even her imperfections were perfect to him, and he wanted to tell her not to cover them with makeup, but he knew better than to make such suggestions.

Beauty was indeed in the eyes of the beholder, and the more he got to know Gabriella Emerson, the more beautiful she appeared to him.

"Please," she whispered. "Pretty please with a cherry on top."

He chuckled. "Is that your version of begging?"

"That's the best I can come up with."

"Well, if you are asking so nicely."

Sliding down, he flicked his tongue over one nipple and then sucked it into his mouth while parting her moist folds with his fingers. As he slid one in, she moaned and arched her back, and as he slid in another, she tugged on the pantyhose restraint but didn't pull her hands out, even though she could have done so with minimal effort.

Gabi liked the game they were playing, which was fortunate for both of them. He could stop worrying about losing the shroud and about thralling her afterward to forget all the things that gave him away. He might even be able to bite her if he did that during a climax.

Sliding further down, he was transfixed for a moment by the sight of his fingers pumping in and out of her, but when she arched again, he treated the seat of her pleasure to a gentle lick that had her moaning his name.

As she lifted her legs and rested them on his shoulders, he cupped her round bottom and brushed kisses against the swollen nubbin. When he sucked it into his mouth, she undulated her hips against him with lewd abandon, and as she cried out, he shuddered with pleasure, his erection kicking up and demanding his attention.

Ignoring it, he kept licking and pumping until she came again.

"I love seeing you fall apart for me," he whispered against her pink, swollen petals and blew air over her heated flesh.

"I haven't even begun." Her lips lifted in a satisfied smile.

He was out of his clothes in a split second, and as he climbed on top of her, her smile widened.

"Can you release my hands? I want to touch you."

"Not yet, beautiful." He gripped her hips, angling her for his penetration and rubbing the head of his erection against her engorged clitoris.

"Uriel, please. No more teasing."

As he surged inside of her, they both groaned. It was a struggle to keep still until she stretched around him, and he took her mouth in a ravenous kiss to distract himself from the need to start moving. Only when he felt she was ready for more did he start to pound into her, but never while unleashing his full power.

No human female could survive that without major damage, and he would rather die than cause her harm, but it was damn hard when she was arching up to meet him thrust for thrust.

Needing to slow himself down, he reached between their bodies and stroked her, but when she exploded into another orgasm, he could no longer hold back both the intensity and the venom bite. One had to give, and it was better to bite her than to pound into her with the force he was capable of.

"Uriel," she groaned.

Clamping a hand over the back of her head, he tilted it to the side and sealed his mouth over the soft spot where her neck met her shoulder. A couple of seconds of sucking and licking was all the preparation he could afford to give her before his need overwhelmed him. He sank his fangs into her soft flesh, pumping his essence into her at the same time.

Gabi gasped, and her body tensed under him, but a moment later, she went lax.

As pain turned into pleasure, and pleasure turned into a climax, and then another, he retracted his fangs and licked the puncture wounds closed.

Long moments after her body had stopped shuddering, he braced his forearms and gazed at the blissful expression on her beautiful face.

Was he falling in love with his human?

He couldn't love Gabi. As wonderful as she was, there could never be anything more between them than these few moments of lust—these few moments of closeness that were more precious to him than all the other moments he'd collected so far.

Gabi

The velvety cushion beneath Gabi's cheek lacked plushness, yet it radiated a comforting warmth and pulsed with a rhythmic heartbeat.

Now, that was a pleasant surprise.

She hadn't expected Uriel to be there in the morning, and for a moment she thought that it was still night, but a swift glance towards the window revealed a gleaming sliver of golden sunlight peeking through the gap where the heavy curtains met, hinting that the morning was well underway.

Being cocooned against the gentle rise and fall of Uriel's chest, reveling in the security of his arms encircling her and the warmth of his bare skin against her cheek, was a morning greeting more intimate and sweet than any words could offer.

If not for the insistent nudge of her bladder, Gabi would have relished this tranquil moment a little while longer.

She was reluctant to break the embrace, but nature's call was not to be denied.

Perhaps she could make a dash for the bathroom, take care of business, and return to bed without waking Uriel?

However, the moment she shifted in his arms, his eyes popped open, and a smile bloomed on his gorgeous face. "Good morning." He leaned in and kissed her on the lips. "Did you sleep well?"

"Good morning. I slept splendidly, and finding you here in the morning was a nice surprise, but I really need to go to the bathroom. Wait for me?"

"Of course." He released her. "Hurry back."

"I will."

As she padded naked to the bathroom, the weight of his gaze was palpable, a gentle pressure against her skin. She wanted to treat him to a sultry saunter, but given how pressing her need had become, she probably looked like an ungainly duck, awkwardly hustling forward with her thighs clamped tight.

Having attended to her most immediate need, Gabi walked over to the vanity, and as she washed her hands, she lifted her gaze to the mirror and surveyed her reflection. Even with tousled hair cascading wildly over her shoulders and makeup slightly smudged from the night's escapades, a radiant glow emanated from her. It was the unmistakable sheen of satisfaction, the postcoital luminescence of a woman after a thoroughly satiating encounter between the sheets. A renewed energy coursed through her, a sense of well-being as though she had been revitalized by a deep, uninterrupted ten-hour sleep.

Had she slept that long?

Uriel had removed her wristwatch last night before tying her up, and her phone was in her purse, which was still on the entry table where she'd left it when they had entered the room, so she had no way to check what time it was, and the only clue Gabi had was how refreshed she felt.

As more memories of the evening surfaced, she brushed her hair aside and examined her neck. He'd bitten her just as he was climaxing, and it hadn't been a gentle nip, but somehow, there was no sign of it on her skin—not even a hickey.

Maybe she remembered it wrong, and he'd bitten her on the other side?

Tilting her head the other way, she moved her hair and examined her left side, but the skin there was just as unmarred as on her right side.

"What the heck? Did I dream it?"

It wouldn't be the first time she'd had an erotic dream, but none had ever felt so real. Well, she'd had that one dream a long time ago about a certain actor she'd been crushing on as a teenager, and that one had felt quite real, but it couldn't compare to the phantom bite. She could still feel the momentary slashing pain of his teeth breaking her skin and the panic she'd felt for a split second before it had been replaced by an indescribable pleasure.

Oh, goodness. The pleasure.

"If it could feel that good in dreams, I would never get anything done. I would just try to dream as much as I could."

"Gabi?" Uriel called out. "Were you saying something?"

Damn. She didn't even have the phone with her so she could pretend to have been talking with someone or listening to a podcast, and Uriel would think that she was a crazy woman talking to herself.

Oh, heck, whatever. Let him think whatever he wanted. It wasn't as if it would change his mind about wanting to stay with her.

He was leaving no matter what.

"Sorry about that. I was talking to myself." She reached for her toothbrush. "By the way, there is a hotel-provided spare toothbrush and a razor, so if you want to come in and freshen up, you are welcome."

The door opened a moment later and Uriel walked in, wearing his birthday suit, which included a very prominent erection.

Gabi's mouth watered. "Is that just a good morning greeting, or is he happy to see me?"

For a moment, Uriel looked confused, but as he followed her gaze, a laugh burst out of him.

What was it about the sound of his laughter that was like a switch on her libido?

"He's definitely happy to see you." He turned around, giving her a great view of his ass as he entered the toilet compartment.

As the door closed behind him, Gabi let out a sigh. It wasn't fair that he was so perfect in every way, yet she couldn't keep him. Hey, maybe that was why he could allow himself to be so great. He didn't need to push her away with jerky behavior because he'd just stated flat out that he couldn't share anything with her.

Then again, Gabi had dated plenty of men whom she'd informed right from the start that she only wanted to have fun and wasn't looking for a relationship, and that hadn't prevented some of them from exhibiting jerky behaviors.

When she was done brushing her teeth and applying her moisturizer, Uriel sauntered over to the vanity and turned on the faucet. "What are your plans for today?"

"I don't have any. Why?"

He grinned at her through the mirror. "It's only a few minutes after seven in the morning, and I don't need to leave until eleven, which gives us enough time for play-time and breakfast at the hotel restaurant."

Uriel

Gabi's cheeks pinked with what he knew was desire, not embarrassment. She was comfortable in her nudity, more than most of the human females he'd been with, and rightfully so.

He wouldn't have changed a single thing about her. She was perfect the way she was.

Lowering her lashes, she husked, "What do you have in mind?"

He glanced at the shower. "A way for us both to get ready for the day without wasting time."

She chuckled. "So, you are all about efficiency?"

"Today, I am." He lifted her by her waist and transferred her from the vanity into the shower.

"Hold on." She put her hand on his forearm when he reached for the faucet. "I don't want my hair to get wet. I had it done yesterday. We can use the handheld, so I don't get splashed from above."

"As you wish." He moved aside, transferring the command of the shower to her. "It's all yours."

Gabi cracked a smile. "Thank you." She twisted her hair in a bun and tucked the ends inside, securing it on the top of her head.

Pivoting on her bare heel, Gabi turned on the water in the handheld shower head, checked the temperature, and secured it on the long pole at the height of her breasts so her hair was safe from the water spray.

Perhaps the joint shower wasn't one of his brightest ideas. Already, he was being forced to shroud his glowing eyes and elongating fangs, but when things got heated, he would have to thrall Gabi not to see them.

After all, he couldn't blindfold her in the shower. As trusting as she was with him, that would surely make her suspicious.

Thankfully, she seemed mesmerized by the view of his straining erection, and he hoped it would provide enough distraction so only a minimal thrall would be needed to keep things under control.

"If you keep looking at me like that, it will be a very short shower." He gently pushed her against the shower wall and knelt before her.

The height difference between them meant that in this position, his mouth was aligned with those perky breasts that had him salivating from the moment he had woken up with them pressed against his skin.

Twirling his tongue over one nipple, he licked it into a stiff point, closed his lips around it, and sucked in hard.

"Yes," she groaned.

Smiling, he leaned over to her other nipple and nipped it lightly with his blunt front teeth.

Gabi jerked in surprise, but the scent of her desire intensified tenfold.

As he laved it with his tongue, soothing the small hurt away, she uttered an impatient sound that he could only interpret as frustration with the gentle treatment.

Interesting.

Evidently, the feisty human was into more than just bondage. She liked a little pain served with her pleasure.

Given his incredible strength, it would be tricky to control the precise level that would provide a little spice to her pleasure but no more.

Pushing to his feet, he spun her around. "Hands on the wall."

He could pull it off. For her, he would hold himself in check and delay his own gratification so he could give her precisely what she craved.

Doing as he'd ordered, she turned her head to look at him over her shoulder. "What are you going to do to me?"

"Cruel to be kind in the right measure," he sang before landing a light smack on her left cheek.

"Ow! What was that for?" She tried to sound indignant, but her voice was husky, and the scent of her arousal grew so overwhelming that he got lightheaded, probably because all his blood had traveled to his erection.

"Your pleasure." He massaged her bottom, spreading the heat, before delivering another smack to her other cheek.

She didn't contradict him. Instead, she pushed her butt out and spread her legs a little farther apart.

If that wasn't an invitation to continue the play, he didn't know what was.

Leaning down, he kissed the side of her neck and slid two fingers between her slick folds and then rubbed them around her entrance without penetrating her.

"What about you?" Her whisper would have been barely audible if he were human. "Do you enjoy this?"

"Very much so." He slid his fingers into her moist heat and pumped in and out slowly while his thumb circled the bundle of nerves at the apex of her thighs.

He could have told her that anything that heightened her pleasure was an aphrodisiac to him, but that might have diminished her enjoyment. She had to believe he was as much into the game as she was.

Two more light smacks had her sheath tightening around his fingers, and he had a feeling that she could have climaxed just from that play, but he needed to taste her again.

"Turn around." He went down to his knees and picked her leg up, resting her dainty foot on his shoulder and opening her glistening center to his ravenous gaze.

"Close your eyes," he commanded, afraid his shroud wouldn't hold.

"I want to watch." She threaded her fingers into his hair.

"Close your eyes," he reiterated with a featherlight slap to her wet folds.

"Ouch," she mewled. "You're not supposed to do that."

The outpouring of moisture said otherwise, but since she had closed her eyes, he didn't correct her. Instead, he licked the small hurt away and moved higher to suck her clit.

"Oh, yes." She thrust her hips forward and rocked them on his tongue while holding on to his head.

He breathed in her intoxicating scent and added his fingers to the play, penetrating her with two while still sucking on her clit.

"Please," Gabi pleaded. "I want you inside of me."

His plan had been to make her climax on his tongue and fingers, but he couldn't deny her anything.

"Well, since you asked so nicely." He planted one last kiss on her moist petals, lowered her leg down to the shower floor, and pushed up to his feet. "Turn around."

"So bossy," she whispered but did as he'd asked, planting her hands on the wall, pushing out her heart-shaped ass, and stretching up on her tiptoes to compensate for their height difference.

Bending at the knees, he wrapped an arm around her waist to brace her and positioned his erection at her entrance. With one swift surge, he was inside of her, pounding away, hard and fast, his thighs slapping against Gabi's upturned behind with each forward thrust.

He braced his other arm on the tile wall to cushion her head and let himself go a little faster, a little harder, but nowhere near the ferocity coursing through him. His fragile human couldn't take that force, meaning he couldn't bring it out even if he wanted to.

When her orgasm hit, and her muscles clamped around his arousal, his seed erupted, and he bit into his arm to refrain from biting her again, but he didn't release his venom.

He'd bitten her last night, so holding back wasn't as excruciatingly difficult as it would have been otherwise.

When the urge to bite subsided and his seed was spent, he kissed the spot where he'd bitten her the day before and inhaled the unique scent of her skin.

He needed to memorize every touch, every smell and every taste, and lock those memories in a treasure chest in his mind to revisit for moments when the world seemed too dark to bear, and he needed a ray of light to remind him that there were things worth fighting for.

As the server refilled Gabi's coffee cup, she lifted it to her lips and smiled behind the rim. "You know, I never liked bossy guys." She leaned closer to Uriel and whispered, "But I liked it very much when you got bossy in the shower."

She would have never admitted enjoying it to anyone other than Uriel, which was odd because he was the kind of guy that she wouldn't want to have such potent ammo to use against her.

Besides being too good-looking to be for real, he was the most evasive, relationship-averse guy she'd ever met, and she'd met her share of men with commitment issues, learning that there was a collection of various phobias under that umbrella. There were gamophobes—those who fear marriage, philophobes—those who fear love, and pistanthrophobes—those who fear trusting others, especially loved ones. She hadn't encountered any genophobes—those afraid of sex and intimacy—but that was a fear that was more prevalent among those born female and, therefore, physically weaker.

Thankfully, she no longer suffered from those particular fears.

Well, suffering less was a more accurate description of her mental state. Right after the divorce, she had carried all those phobias along with many others.

Reaching for her hand, Uriel lifted it to his lips and brushed them over her knuckles. "I aim to please."

She twisted their conjoined hands and kissed the back of his hand. "You please me very much." She didn't add the second half of her thought, that it was a shame he wouldn't be pleasing her for much longer, but then what was the point?

They both knew that they didn't like it and despite being single adults living in a free country, they couldn't do anything about it. Or maybe couldn't wasn't the right word. As her mother used to say, there was nothing a person couldn't accomplish once they put their mind to it. She was willing to move mountains to give their relationship a chance, but he either couldn't or simply didn't want to.

As her phone rang in her purse, Gabi frowned. It wasn't her regular phone, it was the other one Gilbert had given her, and she couldn't remember why he had done that. Something about a family plan?

Shaking her head, she pulled it out of her purse and looked at the caller's picture.

"It's my sister-in-law." She looked at Uriel. "Do you mind if I take it?"

"Not at all. Please, maybe she has news about your brothers."

Nodding, Gabi accepted the call.

"Hi, Karen. What's up? Any news from Gilbert and Eric?"

"Good morning, Gabi. No news. I just wanted to check how you are doing. I feel so bad about you being stuck in that hotel. Are you in the restaurant right now?"

"Yeah. How did you know?"

"The background noise of people talking and of clanking utensils."

"Oh, yeah. I'm having breakfast with Uriel, the guy I told you about. The one I met on the plane."

"Oh, right." Gabi could hear the smile in Karen's voice. "Did he come to meet you for breakfast, or did he spend the night?"

She smiled up at him. "A lady doesn't kiss and tell."

Karen chuckled. "Then it's the second one. I'm glad that you are at least having fun with your guy. Otherwise, I would have felt really bad about Eric and Gilbert being away."

"I know, right? But we should meet up like we did the other day. I can come to see you at the university, or we can go to that Italian restaurant, or I could visit your new house without the guys being there. It's Wednesday already, and I'm flying back on Monday. I can't extend my visit any longer."

Karen sighed. "I wish I could, but Evan came down with a bad case of the flu, and I think that Ryan is coming down with it, too. I'm staying home with them so they won't pass the germs on to anyone else, and I would hate for you to come over, catch what they have, and ruin the rest of your trip."

That was a bummer, and it also sounded off. It wasn't unusual for the twins to get sick occasionally, but Gabi couldn't shake the feeling that things were not as they seemed.

"What about Kaia and Cheryl? Were they exposed to the twins?"

"Kaia wasn't, but Cheryl was. It's good that it's summer vacation still, and she doesn't have school."

Well, perhaps she could at least meet Kaia and her fiancé. For some reason, she didn't remember much about him except for his intelligent blue eyes. Had he been silent through the dinner they had shared in the hotel restaurant?

No, it wasn't that. She'd drunk so much that day that she could remember almost nothing from that dinner. Kaia's fiancé might have talked up a storm, and she wouldn't have remembered it, just as she couldn't remember why she'd been given another phone. On the other hand, she remembered shopping with Darlene quite well.

The mind was indeed a mysterious place, with some pathways clear as day and others obscured by fog.

"I'll call Kaia later. Maybe she can meet me for coffee somewhere. If not for Uriel, this trip would have really sucked."

"I know." Karen affected an apologetic tone. "I'm so sorry about that, but you know how it is when running a business. Emergencies arise, and someone has to address them, and that's usually the owner."

"Yeah, I get it, but at this rate, you will all have to come visit me in Cleveland because I'm not flying in again to see you only to be stuck in a hotel waiting for my brothers to make themselves available. You know how much I hate flying. The only reason I survived this flight was that Uriel was holding my hand the entire time."

"It's so strange that you can tolerate short flights but not long ones. Any idea why that is?"

"I convince myself that a short flight is like a bus ride, but I can't keep up the illusion for long, and after an hour in the air, I start panicking."

Karen chuckled. "You're a strange lady, Gabi."

"Yeah, tell me something I don't know."

It sounded like Gabi's family wasn't eager to meet with her. Maybe she'd been right all along, and there was something wrong with one of her brothers or nieces or nephews, which was why they didn't want her to come to their home.

He didn't know much about human medicine, but some treatments left people looking haggard, and maybe that was what they didn't want her to see.

When she ended the call, Gabi dropped the phone back in her purse. "I have a feeling that I won't see my family during this trip. Something is going on, and they are trying to hide it from me."

"My thoughts precisely. When you met your brothers the day you arrived, did they look okay?"

Gabi frowned. "They both looked great. Although Gilbert is still missing half of his hair, so my suspicion about him getting a hair transplant was a miss. His skin, though, looks amazing. He must have started seeing a dermatologist and getting some Botox and fillers or maybe laser treatments. Eric has had work done as well, which is strange. He's too young to do stuff like that." She leaned closer. "Tell me the truth, Uriel. Did you and your buddies have work done in Korea? You said that you didn't have plastic surgery, but they have fabulous creams and microneedling and laser treatments and a host of other things."

They hadn't even been to Korea, but the less she knew, the better.

"No, we didn't. So, what did Eric have done? Was it new hair?"

"Yeah. Eric definitely had a hair transplant." Gabi frowned. "Come to think of it, he didn't confirm that." She laughed nervously. "I had way too much to drink that day. I can't even remember what we talked about."

That didn't seem right. She'd been a little tipsy on the plane, but she'd been lucid and remembered everything they had talked about.

The story with her family was starting to creep him out. Humans got into some strange shit, and from what Gabi had told him about her brothers, their move to Los Angeles had been unexpected, and even more so was her niece's engagement to an older guy, who had recruited her for a secret project in bioinformatics.

Perhaps the entire family was involved in something illegal, and that was why they were keeping her away?

"What about the lunch you had with your sister-in-law? Was there something off about her or the fiancée of your other brother?"

Gabi frowned. "That's strange. I don't remember much from that lunch either. I remember playing with my nephews and gossiping about guys with the ladies, but that couldn't have accounted for the entire lunch." She smiled. "Although an hour can pass quite quickly when having fun. Later, I went shopping with Darlene."

That sounded innocent enough, and he was very interested in the gossip about men part.

"Did you talk about me?"

"Yeah." Gabi smirked. "They wanted to know about the hunk I met on my flight over. They all want to meet you. Maybe when Gilbert and Eric are finally back from their business trip, we could all go out to dinner. I want you to meet them."

He wanted to meet them and make sure they weren't doing something stupid that could get Gabi in trouble, but he wouldn't be around long enough to do that. After the mission, he and his partners were going to pull a disappearing act.

"I wish I could meet your family, but I don't think it will be possible this time. The deal my partners and I are working on might still require us to fly out on a moment's notice." He glanced at his watch. "I will probably know where things are heading after the meeting I'm supposed to attend in a couple of hours."

Nodding, Gabi lifted the coffee cup to her lips and took a sip. "I will keep my fingers crossed for you. I hope everything goes well and you won't have to leave town just yet. I hope to keep seeing you until I go back home." She put the cup down, leaned back in her chair, and closed her eyes.

She'd had a good night's sleep, he'd made sure of it, but she didn't look rested even though his venom bite from the night before should have given her a health boost.

"Are you tired?"

"A little." She opened her eyes and put a hand on her forehead. "I'm feeling a little under the weather. Maybe I caught the bug from my nephew when I played with him on Monday."

He'd heard her sister-in-law telling Gabi about her nephew coming down with the flu.

"Do you know a doctor in town you could see?"

Gabi waved a dismissive hand. "It's nothing, and I don't need to see a doctor for something as trivial as this. I'm very resistant to bugs, and even when I get the flu or a cold, I get over them quickly."

That was reassuring, but he felt terrible about leaving Gabi without anyone to care for her. "Can I get you something from the pharmacy?" He glanced at his watch. "I still have some time before I need to go."

"I don't need anything. I have my vitamins in my room. I always load up on vitamin C and zinc while going on trips, especially conventions when I'm around hundreds of people who bring in bugs from all over the country. Getting sick while traveling is the worst thing ever." She shook her head. "I shouldn't have said that. Getting sick on a trip is annoying. Losing a loved one is the worst thing that could happen."

As a wave of sadness followed her words, he remembered what she'd said to the lady in the elevator. Her parents had died a long time ago, which meant she must have been very young when that had happened.

He shouldn't ask her about it and get even closer to the woman he was about to leave, but he couldn't help himself. "I assume you are referring to your parents. I wouldn't have asked, but you told that lady in the elevator about them passing a long time ago."

"I don't like to talk about it." Avoiding Uriel's eyes, Gabi glanced around, looking for their server. "I need a coffee refill." Forcing a smile, she turned to him. "If I'm still craving coffee, I'm not sick. It's probably just an allergy, or it might even be the dry air in Los Angeles. I'm used to a more humid climate."

There was nothing like the weather to change the topic of conversation from personal to general.

"It's okay if you don't want to talk about your parents. I don't want to pry."

Of course, he didn't. If she revealed things about herself, he would have to reveal things about himself, and that was a big no-no for him.

As the server materialized with the coffee carafe in hand, Gabi lifted her cup for him to refill it. "Thank you." She smiled at the guy and waited until he refilled Uriel's as well.

"I'll make you a deal," she said after the server had left. "I'll tell you one thing about myself in exchange for you telling me one thing about yourself. It can be as small as your favorite book or as big as who was the most significant influence on your life growing up."

He hesitated for a split second. "Remember that you said it can be anything."

"Anything." She took a sip of the fresh coffee. "My father died when I was twelve. His heart just gave out with no warning. He wasn't sick, he didn't complain about chest pains or being tired, and he seemed perfectly healthy, only he wasn't." It still took effort to talk about it without getting teary-eyed or choked up, but she'd managed to deliver the information in a nearly flat tone. "Your turn."

"I'm not much of a reader," he admitted. "I like watching movies, and sometimes I can binge-watch an entire season in a couple of days."

She hadn't expected that—not from Uriel. Most of the men she'd dated hadn't been big on reading, but he seemed different, and it was a little disappointing to hear him say that.

"What attracts you to movies?" Gabi asked.

"The stories of human lives. I know it's fiction, but it provides me with a window to look through that I wouldn't have gotten otherwise. There is only so much that a person can experience himself."

Books were even better at that because they provided a window into the minds and souls of the protagonists and the antagonists, but some people were more visual than cerebral, and evidently, Uriel belonged to the visual group.

Except, he just didn't fit the profile.

"Fair enough." She took a sip from her coffee. "Why not books, though? You get so much more with books. You get into the characters' minds, their hearts. You don't get that with movies."

He shrugged. "We all have our preferences, and I prefer to guess what they are thinking from their facial expression and their body language. Also, I find that it's a great way to learn languages. I watch foreign films with subtitles."

"I've never heard of that method, but I can see how it can work for someone with a great ear and an even better memory."

"I have both."

"It's also great spy training," she said with a straight face.

He laughed. "Yeah, I guess it is. Your turn."

What he had told her wasn't earth-shattering, but she'd learned something about him that she hadn't known before, so it was well worth it.

"After our father died, our mother fell apart, and Gilbert basically took over running the household. Two years later, she died from an aneurysm, or what I call a broken heart. She just couldn't go on without our father. With time, I've forgiven her for giving up on life and abandoning us, but for a long while I was angry at her and feeling guilty for being angry. It was a very dark time in my life."

The choking sensation she'd expected arrived, but it wasn't as bad as it usually was, and a couple of deep breaths unclogged her throat.

"I bet." Uriel took her hand and gave it a light squeeze. "How old was Gilbert when your mother died?"

"Twenty-four. Eric was eighteen, and I was fourteen. Gilbert was already managing our household, including earning an income and supporting us, but after our mother died, he also had to deal with an emotionally broken kid sister and a young brother who was putting on a brave face but was as grief-stricken as I was." She forced a smile. "Your turn."

"I have a sister who I'm very close to but don't get to see."

That was another surprise. He hadn't mentioned any siblings.

A buzz started in the back of her mind, alerting her to some discrepancy she couldn't put her finger on. It was as if she had reason to believe that Uriel was an only child, but he hadn't told her that, so how could she know whether he had siblings or not?

"What about your parents? Are you close to them?"

He shook his head. "Not as close as I would like. They live far away."

For someone who was globe-trotting, visiting faraway places shouldn't be a problem, but there was probably more to his relationship with his parents than physical distance.

"Any other siblings?" she asked.

He shook his head. "Just one. Your turn. Have you ever been in love?"

"Yes."

She could swear that his eyes blazed with inner light for a moment, the dark brown turning a beautiful shade of amber. "What happened to him?"

"I divorced his cheating ass."

Uriel looked stunned, as if she'd slapped him across the face, and the sound he emitted was what she would have expected from a lion warning his prey.

"What kind of idiot could have cheated on an incredible woman like you?"

That was such a sweet thing to say. "A self-absorbed prick with an enormous ego that needed constant stroking. According to him, I didn't stroke it often enough." Gabi smiled sadly. "That was his opinion. I think that I stroked it too often, but I'm beyond the point of questioning myself about the failure of my marriage. It wasn't my fault. It was his. I'm just glad we didn't have children, or the divorce would have been much more difficult than it was."

Uriel

As Uriel's fangs punched out over his lip, he threw a quick shroud over himself, but that didn't do much to mask the growl that reverberated through his chest.

"How could you have fallen in love with someone like that?"

Gabi sighed. "I was young, and he was the guy every girl in the school wanted. When he became mine, I thought myself the luckiest girl on earth." She lifted the cup to her lips to hide the wave of embarrassment that washed through her.

Was she blaming herself for the mistake she'd made?

Humans had to rely on intuition and healthy skepticism to detect deceit, and Gabi had been a young girl who hadn't developed the skills yet.

"It wasn't your fault." He reached for her other hand.

"I was naive."

"Naïveté is a blessing, not a curse."

She arched a brow. "You're probably the only person I've ever heard say that. Normally, calling someone naive is a polite way of saying that they are stupid."

"Being naive is to judge others based on your own character. You were good and loyal, and you didn't expect him to be a lying scumbag. If you just tell me his name, I'll find him and avenge your honor."

To his surprise, Gabi laughed. "You are such a talented actor. You sounded so sincere, like a knight vowing to avenge the princess's broken heart."

"It wasn't acting. I meant every word."

"Sure you did." She patted his hand. "I appreciate the sentiment, but I divorced Dylan eleven years ago. It took me almost two years to mourn the end of the marriage, and during that time, I lost everything I had, but eventually I pulled myself up by the bootstraps, as they say. My brothers helped, of course."

He frowned. "What do you mean you lost everything? Was his betrayal financial as well as personal?"

Gabi briefly closed her eyes and let out a breath.

"I gained nearly as much weight after our divorce as I did after my parents died. Can you imagine what that did to my practice? I lost clients, couldn't get new ones, and couldn't support myself. I moved in with Gilbert and spent two years moping on his couch."

He'd seen enough movies to know that the cheating husband should have supported her. There was something called alimony that the former spouse was supposed to provide, but if her ex was a worthless loser in more ways than one, perhaps he hadn't earned enough to pay her alimony.

"What about the support he was supposed to pay you?"

"He wasn't. I was making more money than him when I started suspecting him. Gilbert hired a private investigator who provided proof of his cheating, but that had no bearing on the financial aspects of the divorce. I didn't need money from him, and I didn't want it. I just wanted to be rid of him." She closed her eyes again. "That's not true. I didn't want to be rid of him. I wanted the cheating to have never happened, and I wanted our fairytale life to continue. But wishing that was just as pointless as wishing my parents hadn't died, and the only solace I found in both cases was food.

"After my parents died, I gained nearly 100 lbs. A nutritionist helped me get that under control, and once I dropped the excess weight, I joined the cheerleading squad and boys started noticing me, including the captain of the football team. I fell in love with Dylan, and we were the prom king and queen. I felt on top of the world. I was finally over my grief and ready to start my enchanted life. We went to the same college, got married, and I started my own business. The nutritionist who had helped me get back in shape as a teenager inspired me to become a nutritionist myself. Life couldn't get better than that." She smiled sadly. "But, it was only downhill from there. "

"Not really. Look at you now. You have a successful practice, and you can have any man you want. You're gorgeous."

Her face brightened. "Thank you. I like to believe that fate had a different plan for me, and that Dylan was never meant to be the one for me. But I'm thirty-eight years old, and my clock is ticking. Soon, children will no longer be an option. Not that I'm convinced I want any, but having the possibility taken away is scary." She lifted her hand and wiped the back of it over her forehead. "I think I'm starting to develop a fever."

Uriel pushed to his feet. "Let me escort you back to your room so you can take those vitamins you mentioned."

"That's a good idea." She took his offered hand.

Dipping his head, he pressed his lips to her forehead. "You are only slightly warmer than normal. If you have a fever, it is very low."

She also didn't smell sick, which made it easier for him to leave her and head out to the meeting.

Still, it was a shame that he needed to go.

Gabi was finally opening up to him, and he wanted to keep talking to her and learn everything he could about her, but he'd run out of time.

"The teams are in place," Onegus said. "But our guests are nowhere in sight. We are monitoring the nearest paved road, and there are no cars parked along the stretch that is closest to the canyon. There are also no hikers in a five-mile radius."

Kian glanced at his watch. It was twenty minutes to twelve, and if their so-called guests intended to show up on time, they should be entering the canyon. Then again, if they were Kra-ell or immortals, they could cover the distance from the road to the meeting in much less time, and if they intended to parachute from a helicopter, they wouldn't need any time at all.

They could also use dirt bikes.

They could be hiding in a cave and planning to emerge a few minutes before the meeting, but Kian couldn't see any advantage to that. Given how noisy those vehicles were, it wouldn't give their riders the element of surprise.

What worried him more was the possibility of them arriving in an aircraft.

"I don't like that our meeting team is exposed down there. They can't even take cover in case of an aerial attack."

Onegus cast him a look that had just a tinge of exasperation in it. "Stop being such a pessimist. They would not have gone to all this effort to lure our people into a trap just so they could kill them. They want information, and to get it, they need to show up."

"Fuck!" William exclaimed in a very uncharacteristic manner. "One signal winked out, and the other two are moving. How the hell are they doing that?" He looked at Onegus. "Do you see any movement on the feed from the drone?"

The chief shook his head. "If they are physically moving the trackers, they are using devices that are too small for us to see. But I suspect that they can manipulate where the signals are coming from. They are probably stationary and are only simulating movement."

"Not possible," William said. "Not with those trackers. The device is a solid piece that disintegrates if you try to crack it open. They can't do anything to them. I still think that they have some sort of cloaking device."

Kian arched a brow. "We know that they can activate and deactivate the signals, which is more than we have managed to do, so obviously they have superior technology, and if Syssi's vision is correct, which I believe it is, we are dealing with gods, not Kra-ell. They are very likely to have technology that we can't even imagine."

"Where are the signals moving to?" Turner asked. "That's more important than how. They obviously want us to follow them."

It made perfect sense. The gods didn't want to walk into a trap either, so changing the meeting place at the last moment was a brilliant move. In fact, Kian should have thought of that and done the same.

He turned to William. "They are being cautious, and that's a smart move. How fast are the signals traveling, and in what direction?"

William took a long moment to answer. "They are traveling at about sixty miles an hour, give or take a few, and they are heading west. It looks like they are flying."

Turner chuckled. "We were wrong about them implanting the trackers in gerbils. They must have implanted them inside carrier pigeons." He swiveled his chair toward Onegus. "Can you rewind the footage and check if a pigeon took flight in the canyon when the signals started moving?"

"What for? As you've said, it doesn't matter how they are doing it, only where they are going. I'm redirecting the drones to follow, and I pray to the merciful Fates that they don't run out of fuel before they reach their final destination."

Turner flipped his laptop open. "We need a new refueling station for the war bird. You also need to send the van with the replacement batteries for the smaller drones in the same direction."

"I'm already on it," the chief said.

Kian pulled out his phone. "I'm calling the Odus in here. We need to verify the direction and the exact location of the signal when the trackers become stationary."

Onegus nodded. "Do we tell the backup team and the meet-and-greet team to head west, or do we wait until the clock strikes noon?"

That was a good question. The gods might have moved the signals precisely for that reason—a bait-and-switch tactic—so he would show his hand by moving the backup forces out of their hiding spot across from the canyon.

Once the Odus arrived at the war room, the signals kept moving for another twenty minutes or so and then stopped.

After Okidu and Onidu had gone into their trance-like stance, Okidu pulled a folded piece of paper and a pencil out of his jacket pocket, wrote down a list of numbers, and handed them to William.

"It's in Simi Valley," William said while zooming in on the location. "It's another canyon, but it's not as isolated. There are residential neighborhoods a few miles away, but there is a new development going up right on top of the adjacent hill overlooking that canyon, and it's also easily accessible from the road."

The new location was only semi-secluded, which meant that they would have privacy for the meeting, but moving a large force into the area was problematic because they couldn't effectively shroud it without Yamanu, who was in China. Not even Toven possessed the ability to shroud a force that size.

"That's brilliant," Turner said. "They can pretend to be construction workers and hop down to the canyon when they feel it's safe to do so."

Kian turned to Onegus. "Is the drone on location?"

"The big war bird just got there, but it's keeping a high altitude. The small drones will be deployed when the van arrives."

"Have the camera zoom in on the canyon. I wonder if they left a message for us."

"On it." Onegus leaned over his screen. "I'll be damned. How did you know?"

Kian smiled. "I had a gut feeling. What did they leave for us?"

"There is a cardboard sign on the ground with 1:30 pm handwritten on it."

It was just enough time to get the people from Mount Baldy to the new location, provided that they headed there now, but since they had started as soon as the signals moved, they had about fifteen minutes to spare. Not that it was enough time to find a place for the backup force to hide, but at least they would be nearby.

"Simi Valley?" Phinas arched a brow. "Where is that?"

"It's due west," Magnus said. "Almost in a straight line."

Jade pulled out her phone and searched the map for the location. It was a long drive.

As soon as they had been told that the signals had started moving, they had jogged out of the canyon and gotten back into Magnus's car. It had taken them only fifteen minutes at a pace that allowed the immortals to keep up, which was about half the speed Jade was capable of, and yet Morgada had huffed and puffed as if she'd run a marathon. The female had become seriously out of shape, which she would have never been allowed to do if she'd remained on the home planet.

Jade had always believed that the Kra-ell were inherently physically active, but like many of the other beliefs she'd held, it was a misconception. Evidently, people acted in accordance with what was expected of them, and since Igor had thrown the tentpoles of their society out the window, Morgada had decided to forgo physical training, become soft, and concentrate on other pursuits, whatever they were.

"How long is it going to take us to get there?" Jade asked.

They had been driving in the direction the signals had been going, but as long as the trackers had kept moving, their team hadn't known where they were heading and how long it would take them. Hopefully, Simi Valley was their final destination, and they weren't going on a wild chase.

"Another hour or so," Magnus said.

She didn't know the guy well, and she hadn't spoken more than a few words with him before the mission or during the ride to the canyon, but she trusted Onegus to choose the right person for the mission. Magnus could easily pass for a human, and he seemed levelheaded.

"I have more information about the location," the chief's computer-altered voice sounded in her earpiece.

William's team had redesigned the translation software to match an artificial narration with the tone and inflection of the speaker, so not everyone sounded the same, and in most cases, she could guess who the speaker was. It was a huge improvement, and it made the experience of listening to people through the specially-designed earpieces less disturbing.

"The good news is that there is a large construction site overlooking the location," Onegus said. "And that's also the bad news. There are multiple crews working on the subdivision, so there will be plenty of witnesses, which will limit what shenanigans either party can pull off. But that also means that our guests could be hiding among the construction workers and decide whether to show up based on who they see arriving at the meeting place. I'm glad that we decided to send two Kra-ell females and two immortal males who can pass for humans. Our guests will not perceive a small team of that composition as a threat."

"What about the backup?" Magnus asked.

"They are on their way, and I'm looking for the best place for them to hide. Our guests left us a cardboard sign invitation for one-thirty, so that doesn't leave us much time. Naturally, they did that on purpose."

"Smart," Phinas said. "I would have done the same."

Jade agreed. In fact, she was relieved. The new location was near humans, which meant that the gods didn't intend an armed confrontation. Even if one or more of them was a strong compeller, that couldn't protect them from an aerial assault, which was probably what they were worried about the most.

It was also what had worried her.

They had a military-grade drone providing aerial defense, but if the gods had more advanced weaponry, they might be able to take the drone out.

"I'm sending the location straight to your car navigation system," Onegus said. "You are about an hour away, which means you don't have time to make any stops on the way."

"Ugh." Morgada shifted in the seat. "I was hoping we could stop for a restroom break."

Jade cast her an incredulous look. "Are you unwell?"

The Kra-ell metabolism was such an efficient machine that using the restroom once a day was more than enough.

Morgada winced. "It happens when I get nervous. Other than Tom, I've never met a god face to face."

Magnus cast her a smile. "We don't know for sure that we are about to meet gods."

"Any more questions?" Onegus asked.

"Not for now," Jade said. "But I might think of something during the ride."

"I'm here. Onegus out."

Next to her, Phinas chuckled. "You know how in the old *Star Trek* show, the rookie crewman was always the one to die on away missions?" He shifted his eyes to Magnus. "Everyone knew that the one wearing a red uniform was not going to make it."

Magnus looked at his red Kevlar vest and grimaced. "I'm not a rookie, and you are not Captain Kirk." He looked at Jade through the rearview mirror. "But you remind me of Captain Kathryn Janeway."

The captain must have been a war hero, but Jade had never heard of her. "Who is Captain Janeway, and in what way do I resemble her?"

"Oh, lass." Magnus shook his head. "I've got to introduce you to *Voyager*."

Gabi

"I'll call you as soon as I can." Uriel leaned to kiss Gabi's forehead, probably to check again how warm she was.

"I'm okay." She lifted on her toes and kissed him on his cheek. "Don't worry about me. Just finish this business deal already and come back to me."

The guilty look in his eyes was like a spear to her heart. "I'll do my best."

He didn't think he was coming back.

Then again, she'd felt the same way every time they had parted, so she wasn't going to agonize over it now only to have him call her later, saying that he was coming over.

As he walked away, Gabi's gaze followed Uriel, each step echoing louder in the hallway until he reached the elevator. She offered a lingering wave, catching his gaze for a fraction of a second as the metal doors were closing.

But even as her heart contracted with a familiar unease, somewhere deep within her, Gabi felt a grounding assurance. Despite the doubts, a gut feeling whispered that she would be seeing him again.

This isn't goodbye...

But then the lock on her memories sprang open, and she closed her eyes and groaned.

Oh, damn, maybe it is.

This split personality thing couldn't continue. She would lose her mind if it did.

Wait a minute, was Evan really sick? Or had Karen just provided a plausible excuse for why she couldn't meet Gabi?

Sitting on the couch, she pulled the clan phone out of her purse and dialed her sister-in-law.

"Gabi? Are you still with Uriel?"

"No, I'm back in my room. Is Evan really sick?"

"No, thank goodness, he's not. I hate pretending that one of my kids is sick, you know, bad luck and all that, but it was the first thing that popped into my head."

"I'm glad that he's okay." Gabi put a hand on her forehead. "I'm not feeling so great, and I thought that I might have gotten what Evan had, but if he's not sick, I must have gotten it from someone else."

"Maybe you caught something during the convention or on the plane. Bugs sometimes take a few days to multiply before you start showing symptoms."

Gabi winced. "Gross. Now I'm imagining an infestation growing in my body."

"In a way, it is. But you can't see it, so there is that. What are your symptoms? Do you have a fever? Runny nose? Sore throat?"

At the mention of her throat, Gabi lifted her hand to her neck where a bite mark should have been but wasn't. "I don't have a thermometer, but I'm a little warm, and I feel lethargic."

Karen snorted. "Since you spent the night and the morning with Uriel, you probably have a very legitimate reason for feeling tired."

Thinking of what had happened in the shower, warmth spread into Gabi's cheeks. "Yeah, you might be right. I think I'll crawl back into bed and take a nap."

"Good plan. Call me if you need anything."

Gabi rolled her eyes. "As if you could help me. Any news about the lockdown?"

"Nothing yet, but I don't think they can keep it up for much longer. People are starting to get antsy. But I was serious before. Call me, and I'll get you help. Our babysitter at the university has nothing to do as long as we are stuck here. I can ask her to babysit you instead. I can also order delivery of whatever you need."

"I'm fine, Karen. I've lived alone for the past nine years, and I survived with no help. I can manage this small inconvenience."

"I know, sweetie. But I can't help worrying about you. Promise me that you will call me if things take a turn for the worse."

"I promise."

After ending the call, Gabi opened her pill organizer, popped a packet of vitamin C and zinc into a tall glass, filled it with water, and drank the whole thing in one go.

Feeling a little nauseated, she pulled out a mint and popped it into her mouth, but instead of helping with the nausea, it irritated her throat and made her cough.

Some tea could help, but all the hotel supplied was coffee, and she was all caffeinated out after consuming three cups during breakfast. She could call the front desk and ask them to send up some teabags, or she could take a short walk to the drugstore around the corner and stock up on other remedies. She was out of Motrin, and in case her throat started to act up, she could use some lozenges.

Besides, the fresh air might do her good.

The midday sun bore down on the building site, the shimmering heat waves radiating from the rooftops.

Aru pulled a handkerchief from his back pocket and wiped the sweat from the back of his neck. "I hope they get here soon so we can get out of here."

Not that it was any cooler at the bottom of the ravine where the meeting was about to take place. The spot they had chosen was under the gnarled limbs of a tree that provided almost no shade, but that was the best they had found.

"This is kind of fun." Negal slapped a blob of cement over the previous layer of tile shingles and pressed another clay tile on top of it. "There is something to be said about building things with your own two hands."

"I'd rather be doing anything but that." Dagor adjusted his protective glasses with a gloved hand. "The sun is glaring, my hair is saturated with sweat under this hardhat, and my shirt is sticking to me."

Aru patted his back. "Stop complaining and be glad that this is not how I chose for us to make a living while we are stationed here."

Dagor executed an irreverent bow. "I'm forever grateful, oh great leader."

The roofers who had donated their hardhats, protective eye gear, and gloves were currently enjoying an afternoon at a local bar, drinking beers in an air-conditioned space.

Persuading them to make the switch had taken a minimal thrall and a couple of hundred dollars each. It was more than Aru had expected to pay for the privilege of laying roof shingles, but everything had gotten more expensive these days, including bribes.

"Here comes the drone," Negal said. "That was faster than I expected."

The humans working on the other roofs were oblivious to the warbird flying above their heads. They couldn't see it or hear it, and even if they did, they wouldn't think it posed them any danger.

"They are decisive." Dagor wiped the sweat off his brow with the back of his gloved hand. "I'll give them that."

"It's a pretty big bird, and it's armed," Negal said. "They say that they come in peace, and yet they are flying a military drone above our heads."

"They are being cautious." Aru collected cement on his trowel and smeared it over the first shingle layers.

The real roofers would have a lot of work just undoing the mess the three of them were making while pretending to be working. From above, those looking through the drone camera eye wouldn't be able to differentiate between them and the real roofers, so in a way, he was glad that their adversaries were flying the drone and getting reassurance that no one was waiting for them in the ravine below.

However, if he were in their shoes, he would suspect that their intended hosts were hiding among the construction workers. The beauty of his plan was that this was a large development with hundreds of workers milling around. It would be impossible for their adversaries to sift through all the humans to find the three who didn't belong.

"Damn," Dagor pulled out his disruptor. "How did they get the smaller drone here so quickly? There is no way they could have flown it here on one charge."

"Obviously, they drove it here." Aru put his tool down. "And they are flying the damn thing low enough to see our faces."

"I should disrupt both drones' navigation systems and bring them down." Dagor aimed the disruptor at the device.

"Don't." Aru put his hand on Dagor's arm, bringing it down. "It could crash on the site, and people could get hurt. It could also start a fire, which might cause untold damage."

Dagor groaned. "Let me at least disturb the armed one. I can aim a weak blast and cause a malfunction that will only affect its navigation ability, so it won't crash here. If I do nothing, the moment we ditch our disguises, it could shoot us down."

Aru maintained his hold on Dagor's arm. "If we damage its navigation capabilities, it will eventually crash somewhere, and we can't risk innocent lives on the remote chance that our adversaries decide to fire upon us before hearing us out. They are no doubt just as curious about who we are as we are about them. They want to talk, not shoot. At least not at first. Besides, I hope that they are as concerned about staying under the humans' radar as we are."

Reluctantly, Dagor lowered the device. "You are the commander. If we die, it's on you."

Aru snorted out a laugh. "You've been watching too much television. We are not that easy to kill."

"Not true. If they blast us to smithereens, we can't be put together again. We are not Odu."

Aru couldn't help the shiver that ran through him at the mention of the disastrous creations. It didn't help that he knew now that what had been said about them had been a lie, just one more thread in the Eternal King's propaganda tapestry.

He'd grown up on horror stories about the Odus, a cautionary tale about creating soulless machines and the terrible unforeseen consequences.

"A car just pulled up to the curb," Negal announced.

That got Aru's attention. He watched as the four doors opened almost simultaneously, and the passengers got out. Two of them were tall, dark-haired females with sunglasses on their pert noses and tight-fitting clothes that didn't conceal their alien physiques.

"Kra-ell," Dagor stated the obvious. "Is the tall one Jade?"

"Given the swagger, it would seem so." Aru let out a breath. "I'm glad she's not dead. I think that the other one is Morgada. Both are original settlers."

"That's not good," Negal said. "They will immediately recognize who we are. And what the hell are they doing with two human males?"

Aru was wondering the same thing. "It would seem that humans helped liberate the Kra-ell from Gor's rule, which makes things much more complicated for us. If they are from the government, which they must be to possess such military might, we will have to abort the mission. We can't expose who we are, and the Kra-ell females will recognize us right away."

"Let's keep the hardhats and protective glasses on," Negal suggested. "They might suspect that we are not human, but they won't know for sure."

Dagor chuckled. "Does anyone want to bet how long it will take them to figure out who we are?" He looked from Aru to Negal and back to Aru. "My bet is ten minutes tops."

"I think we can do better than that." Aru adjusted his hardhat on his head. "Keep your heads down and try to walk with less fluidity."

A crease formed between Negal's eyebrows. "Do you want us to pretend to be human?"

Aru shrugged. "We can't pretend to be Kra-ell, so pretending to be humans is our only option."

Gabi

The city seemed to be suffocating under a relentless summer sun, and as Gabi walked the streets of downtown, she felt the weight of that heat pressing down on her. The very air seemed thick, making every breath feel like a conscious effort.

The sidewalk stretched out ahead, appearing to emanate its own misty aura. She could see the heatwaves rising in delicate spirals like ghostly fingers. They distorted the air, making the world waver and dance in a dizzying mirage. The buildings, cars, and people seemed to ebb and flow in this heat-induced haze, their edges softening, blending, and occasionally disappearing altogether.

There weren't many people on the sidewalk, and the few who passed her hurried by with faces that glistened with sweat. Everyone was in silent agreement that the quicker they moved, the sooner they could find respite.

Gabi pulled out a tissue from her purse and dabbed it at her forehead. The paper came away damp. She knew she should quicken her pace, find shade, or enter one of the air-conditioned stores lining the street, but she couldn't.

She hadn't expected it to get so hot, and although she'd been walking for less than ten minutes, the exhaustion from being sick, combined with the oppressive heat, was slowing her steps to a near crawl.

If only there was a bench she could rest on for a couple of minutes and catch her breath.

But there were none in sight, and the drugstore was just around the corner. A few more minutes and she could rest in the air-conditioned space while shopping for her items, and if she still felt so bad after she was done, she would call a taxi back to the hotel.

Fifty feet never seemed so far away.

Forty feet.

Twenty.

She could make it.

Only a few more steps—

Her knees gave out, and then she was falling, but the impact never came. Sometime between being upright and hitting the sidewalk, everything went dark.

The next time Gabi opened her eyes, she was no longer outside in the hot sun. In fact, she was freezing cold despite having a blanket tucked around her.

It took her a moment to take in her surroundings and realize that she was on a hospital bed. A curtain separated her from the rest of the room, but given the sounds, she was in an emergency room. She felt a dull ache at the back of her head, her fingers instinctively reaching to touch the tender spot.

A moment later, the curtain was pushed aside, and a nurse came in. Or was she the doctor?

"I'd advise against that," the woman said.

"What happened?" Gabi asked. "Where am I?"

"You fainted, fell, and knocked your head," the nurse or the doctor said while typing on the keyboard. "Someone called the paramedics, and you were brought here."

The woman didn't bother to introduce herself, and since she was facing the computer screen, Gabi couldn't see the name tag.

"Where is here?"

"City Medical Center," the woman said.

Gabi's eyes widened in realization, and a rush of memories flooded back. The intense heat, the shimmering sidewalk, the weight of the sun pressing down on her. "I... I remember walking. It was so hot," she whispered, her voice shaky.

"Heatstroke, likely. It's been a scorching week. We've run some scans to make sure there's no internal bleeding. You have a mild concussion, and we'd like to observe you for a little while."

Gabi tried to sit up, a wave of dizziness making her wince. "I need to call... I have to let someone know."

Ignoring her, the nurse asked, "Do you have medical insurance?"

"Yes, of course. I hope the paramedics brought my purse. The card is in my wallet."

As the woman turned toward her, her name tag became visible. Cortney Duke was an R.N.

"They did." Cortney pulled a bag from under the hospital bed. "Everything you had on you when you were brought in is in here." She handed it to Gabi.

Gabi opened the bag, pulled out her purse, and took out her insurance card. "Here you go." She handed it to the nurse.

"Thank you." She took it and turned to her screen.

"When will I see the doctor?" Gabi asked.

"The doctor is making the rounds. You're not an urgent case."

She'd heard that hospitals were understaffed all over the country, but she hadn't known it had gotten so bad that emergency room patients did not get to see physicians and were taken care of by nurses.

"I fainted in the middle of the street. There is obviously something wrong with me, and I need to find out what it is."

Cortney looked at her over her shoulder. "The most likely causes are heatstroke, dehydration, or a stomach flu. We are running tests to rule out a bacterial infection, and the results should arrive shortly."

"I don't have an upset stomach, and I don't think I was dehydrated either." She'd drunk mostly coffee, which wasn't great for hydration, but it wasn't the first time she had done it, so she doubted that was the culprit. "I wasn't feeling well, and I was on my way to the drugstore to get some Motrin and other supplies. The heat must have exacerbated my symptoms, and that was why I fainted."

"It's possible, but we need to rule out other more critical possibilities. Bacterial infections can be very dangerous." The nurse finished typing. "The doctor will be with you shortly." She ducked behind the curtain.

Gabi was stunned. Was that how people were being treated in hospitals these days?

Pulling the white phone out of her purse, she called her brother.

"Hi, Gabi," Gilbert answered right away. "Can I call you back in a few minutes? I'm on another call."

"No, you can't. I'm in the hospital, and they are treating me like some vagabond that was found on the street." Which wasn't far from the truth, but she had insurance and could pay for the non-treatment she was getting. "I need you or Eric to come get me."

"What happened?" Gilbert sounded alarmed, as he should be.

"I was feeling a little under the weather and went to get some stuff from the drugstore. I fainted, and someone called the paramedics. They brought me to City Medical Center. I just woke up, and the nurse said that they were running some tests. I haven't even seen a doctor yet. Can you or Eric cut your business trip short and come get me?"

"I need to make a few phone calls to see what can be done, and I'll call you right back. Can you hang in there for a little bit longer?"

That wasn't the answer she'd expected, but what choice did she have? "Please hurry. I don't feel safe here."

"I will." He ended the call.

In case Gilbert and Eric couldn't get back to Los Angeles as quickly as she needed them, perhaps she should call Uriel as well. If she was lucky, he was done with his business deal and could come to her rescue.

Pulling out her old phone, she dialed his number, but the call went straight to voicemail.

Damn. It wasn't her day.

With a sigh, Gabi typed up a message to Uriel and hit send.

Jade

Jade lifted her dark sunglasses and looked at the construction site. At least thirty houses were being built, and many crews were doing different tasks. Some were still in the framing stage, while others were getting their roofs installed.

If she were in the gods' shoes, she would have chosen the roof for obvious reasons, preferably on one of the houses overlooking the canyon. There were six of them perched near the edge, and each had a roofing crew of three to four people, but since all of them were wearing hardhats and protective eye gear, it was difficult to discern differences between the humans and the non-humans.

Gods could suppress their glow which, other than their unnaturally perfect appearance, was the only other thing that could give them away. So, hiding their faces behind safety glasses was a smart move.

Shifting her gaze from one crew to the next, Jade smiled. "Got you." She nudged Phinas's arm. "Look at the footwear of the crew on the roof of the fourth house from the street, and then compare it to what the other roofers are wearing."

"They are all wearing boots," Magnus said. "But the others are wearing work boots, while those three are wearing regular walking boots."

Phinas shrugged. "It could be a different brand of work boots, but we should keep an eye on them." He tapped his earpiece to let Onegus know he was talking to him. "Did you get that?"

"Yes. We are zooming in. We've got you covered."

The knowledge that the drone could shoot them down if needed was reassuring. It wouldn't kill the gods, and it would scare the shit out of the real construction workers, but it might give them a chance to get away if necessary.

She still couldn't shake the feeling that they were walking into a trap, and Syssi's vision had made it worse instead of better. Jade could handle other Kra-ell as long as they weren't compellers like Igor, and even if they were, she had the protective earpieces to shield her from that. Gods, however, were a different breed, and it was impossible to know what capabilities they possessed. With how they manipulated nature, they could have discovered a way to create compellers that didn't need to use sound to carry their commands. They might be able to reach directly into the minds of their victims.

"So, are we going down there or not?" Morgada asked.

"Start the descent," Onegus sounded in their earpieces. "Double-check your gear and make sure that it fits properly. If the earpieces allow any untranslated speech through, they are useless against compulsion."

Jade checked to make sure hers were sucre in her ears. Since the earpieces didn't alter the ambient noise and it was passing through unfiltered, it was sometimes hard to determine whether they were working correctly.

"What's the status of the backup force?" Magnus asked.

"Getting in position. The ETA of the helicopter with the sound cannon is less than five minutes. By the time you get down to the canyon, it will be there."

The problem with the cannon was that the earpieces weren't designed to filter out the noise it was producing. If the need arose to use it, their team would be as affected as the gods, and the backup force would have to collect them all. The immortals would heal the injury to their inner ear quite fast, but she and Morgada would take much longer.

"Can I give you a hand?" Magnus offered his arm to Morgada.

She cast him an offended look. "I might be out of shape, but I'm still Kra-ell. I can jog down this canyon."

Jade doubted that, but Magnus nodded and retracted his hand. "No offense, eh? I was just trying to be a gentleman."

"No offense taken." Morgada took the first step down the steep slope.

"Careful," Magnus said. "If you break something, it's going to ruin the meeting. We will have to evacuate you."

Morgada was wearing dark sunglasses, so Magnus couldn't see the red glow that his words had no doubt produced, but given the tight line of Morgada's lips, she was glaring at the Guardian. "I'm not going to break anything."

As Jade shook her head, Phinas leaned closer to her and whispered in her ear, "Do you think they are flirting?"

"How should I know? Kra-ell don't flirt."

He chuckled. "I beg to differ. They might not have flirted in the past, but they are learning new ways."

"Look at that." Magnus pointed to the bottom of the canyon. "Our hosts have graciously prepared a meeting place."

Hidden under the scraggy limbs of a tree, a brown blanket was spread over the ground and secured with a large jug, presumably filled with water.

Jade looked at the metallic container with suspicion. "Like I'm going to drink anything they offer me." She glanced up to see whether the roofing crew had made a move.

They hadn't, and by the looks of things, they were still laying shingles.

Maybe Phinas was right, and that crew just happened to be wearing different work footwear. But if those roofers weren't their hosts, who were?

As Jade led the group down the steep slope towards the makeshift meeting place, the canyon walls loomed high above them, and the echoes of the construction work above them made it difficult to hear movement in time to react. Not that she expected any dangerous animals to leap at them, but there could be snakes and spiders, and some of them might be venomous.

The ravine was a labyrinth of rugged terrain strewn with loose gravel and rocky outcrops. Hardy plants dotted its walls, which rose like ancient fortresses, imposing and weathered, their colors ranging from deep russet to burnt sienna, and their gnarled forms providing only a modicum of shade.

Jade's hand searched for the pommel of her sword, but it wasn't there. They were unarmed save for the daggers they had hidden under their clothing and in their boots. The banner Kian had flown over the other canyon promised their hosts that they were coming in peace, so they had to maintain a peaceful appearance.

As they reached the tree with the brown blanket, Jade's eyes darted around, scanning for signs of traps or threats.

"They expect us to sit down." She motioned for the others to sit while keeping an eye on the roofing crew above, and then joined the others on the blanket.

The tension in the air was palpable, and everyone was on edge.

Morgada's eyes fixed on the jug of water. "I don't like this," she murmured.

Magnus nodded. "If they pass it around, just pretend to drink."

Phinas kept watch on the roofing crew. "Maybe they're just construction workers after all, and our hosts will approach from a different direction."

"That's why I'm watching the other slope," Magnus said.

Jade's gaze remained fixed on the crew above. "Gods are the masters of subterfuge. But sometimes, things are just the way they seem."

Aru

Aru watched as the two Kra-ell females and two human males carefully climbed down the rocky terrain.

The rock formations towered on either side, their jagged edges casting sharp shadows that seemed to deepen the canyon's barrenness, and the four people climbing down found temporary respite in those shadows as they made their way to the bottom, where Dagor had left a little surprise for them.

It was an exceptionally hot day, and the arid canyon was baking in the unyielding sun. The canyon floor was dry and cracked, marked by the imprints of long-gone streams, but now only the occasional scattered tumbleweeds and patches of dry grass clung to survival, their pale colors offering little relief from the desert's harshness.

Above, the cloudless sky stretched like an infinite blue canvas, offering no respite from the unrelenting sun, with only their adversaries' large drone hovering high above like a bird of prey.

"It's showtime." Dagor put his trowel down. "They got the hint and are sitting down."

It had been Dagor's idea to lay down a blanket with a jug of water as a symbolic gesture of hospitality. He believed it would promote a relaxed conversation. "People like to sit around while talking," he had said with a grin.

"Don't mistake that for complacence." Negal walked over to the edge of the roof and used the ladder to climb down, even though he could have just as easily jumped down.

They didn't want to attract attention, which was why they shrouded themselves as they started their descent down the canyon wall. It wouldn't fool the Kra-ell females, who wouldn't be affected by the shroud, but the humans with them would be taken by surprise when they got there because they wouldn't see them approaching. If they wanted to maintain the illusion of being human for a little longer, they would have to drop the shroud midway to the ravine floor.

As Aru followed Negal down the ladder, his phone rang, but by the time he reached the ground, the call went to voicemail.

"You were supposed to put your phone on airplane mode," Negal admonished. "Who is calling you?"

It could have been a number of people he had done business with, a random wrong number, or Gabi, but it wasn't as if he could respond right now, so he didn't even bother pulling the device from his pocket.

Except, a moment later, he heard a message come in and instinctively knew that it was from her. "Start down the ravine. I'll catch up with you in a moment." He lifted the phone and read the message.

The blood chilled in his veins.

> *Hi Uriel. I don't want to bother you during your important meeting, but I wanted to let you know that I'm in a hospital. I fainted on the way to the drugstore, and they brought me here. They suspect dehydration from sunstroke, but they are running some tests to be sure. I don't like it here, so I called Gilbert, and he promised to try to get me out. But in case you can make it here sooner, I would really appreciate it if you could help me get back to the hotel. They are probably not going to let me go without someone to take care of me, so I need someone to show up, but after that, I will be fine on my own. It was just too hot outside, and combined with my cold, it got to be too much. Let me know when you think your meeting will be over.*

"She's in the hospital. I need to get to her."

"Have you lost your mind over that human?" Negal put a hand on his shoulder. "You can't go anywhere right now. Besides, what do you know about human medicine? If there is something wrong with her, she's at the right place and in the right hands. They will take care of her in the hospital."

Negal was right. Aru couldn't abandon the mission at this critical point to rush to the hospital.

"I need to text her back. Start on without me. I'll catch up."

"I'm not going anywhere without you," Negal said. "Dagor needs to stay back in case we are walking into a trap. You are our leader, and this was your idea. Just text her back quickly."

"This obsession with the human needs to stop," Dagor murmured.

Ignoring him, Aru typed. *I'm in the middle of something I can't get out of. I'll come as soon as I can. Which hospital are you in*?

Her answer came back immediately: *City Medical Center*.

That sounded like a generic term for a medical facility. There were probably several of them in every town.

Aru texted back, *which city*?

This time, there was no answer.

Had she gotten annoyed with him? Or perhaps the doctor walked in just then?

"Come on." Negal started walking. "We don't want to keep our guests waiting."

Aru pushed his worries aside and pocketed his phone. His heart was heavy, but he couldn't let his feelings jeopardize a critical mission. He had to believe that Gabi would be okay until he could reach her.

As Kian's phone buzzed with an incoming message, he tore his eyes from the view of the canyon and his team at the bottom of it.

Seeing that it was from Gilbert he was tempted to ignore it, but since nothing was happening yet, he could allow himself a moment to read what the guy wanted.

> *Gabi called me from the hospital. She fainted in the middle of the street, and paramedics were called. I have to get out of the village and go see her. Is there any way you can lift the lockdown to allow me out? I'd like to bring her to the village, but if that's not an option at the moment, I will stay with her until she's discharged.*

That was such bad timing, but Kian could empathize. If any of his sisters were in trouble, he would have moved mountains to get to them.

Instead of texting back, he called the guy. "Come to the war room. Do you know where it is?"

"Yes. I'm on my way."

Kian ended the call.

"What's going on?" Onegus asked.

"Gilbert's sister is in the hospital, and he wants me to let him out of the village."

The chief's brows furrowed. "What's wrong with her?"

"All I know is that she fainted on the street."

Onegus drummed his fingers on the table. "She's been seeing that Uriel Delgado guy. Maybe our initial suspicion was correct, and he is an immortal. He could have induced her transition, and that was what put her in the hospital. If that's the case, we need to get her out of there as soon as possible and do a thorough cleanup job to erase all records of her being there."

"You said that Roni had checked his background and that he seemed legit."

"Seemed is the operative word. I didn't think that Uriel Delgado's good looks were reason enough to spend time and money on researching him, but if Gabi is transitioning, then it's proof that he's an immortal."

A growl rose in Kian's throat. "He must be a Doomer."

Onegus shook his head. "Doomers wouldn't have done such a great job of creating a fake identity, so he might not be a Doomer." He chuckled. "Perhaps Gabi has stumbled upon one more of Toven's children. The dark hair and handsome face match, only the eye color doesn't, but maybe Uriel is wearing contact lenses to fool the facial recognition at airports."

It was an interesting hypothesis. Orion had created a fake identity for himself and had managed to survive on his own, believing that he was the only immortal until his chance meeting with his father. Uriel might have done the same after realizing that he was immortal.

They even had similar occupations. Orion dealt with antiques, and Uriel dealt with flea market finds that were just a cheaper version of the same thing. Someone who had lived through history had a better chance of recognizing valuable old finds and profiting from them.

"If Uriel is Toven's son, his meeting Gabi on the plane must have been fated."

Onegus regarded him with amusement in his eyes. "The heretic turned a believer."

The door to the war room was slightly ajar, and as a knock sounded on its other side, Kian called out for Gilbert to come in.

"So, this is the famous war room." Gilbert looked around. "I'm impressed. What's on the screen?"

"Take a seat." Kian motioned for the chair next to him. "What did Gabi tell you when she called?"

"What I texted you. She's not happy with the care they are giving her at the medical center, and she wants me to take her out of there. I would love to bring her to the village and deliver her into Bridget's capable hands, but if that's not possible, I'll just transfer her to another hospital. Gabi might sound like a spoiled princess, but she isn't. If she says that the level of care is subpar, it is."

Kian glanced at Onegus. "Should we tell him our suspicion?"

The chief nodded. "She's his sister. He should know."

"I should know what?" Gilbert asked.

"Remember how I suspected that the guy she'd met on the plane was an immortal? We didn't have a good enough reason to dig deeper, especially since his identity and backstory were convincing. But he might be an immortal after all, and he could have induced her transition. That might be why she ended up in the hospital, and if that's indeed the case, we have to get her out of there."

The color drained from Gilbert's face. "A Doomer induced my sister?"

"Not necessarily." Onegus smiled. "Uriel Delgado might be Toven's son. There is some remote familial resemblance."

"I'll be damned." Gilbert ran a hand over his spare hair. "It's a small world after all."

"It's just speculation," Kian said. "First, we need to get you out of here. If it looks like Gabi is transitioning, we will send out a team to retrieve her. If not, and it's just a bug or some other medical problem, you should prepare to stay with her."

"When can I leave?"

"As soon as you are packed," Onegus said. "I'll get a Guardian to escort you out."

Aru

As Aru and Negal made their way down to the canyon floor, their four guests waited patiently.

Amidst the harshness and aridity, there was a certain raw beauty to the canyon. The rugged rock formations, shaped by centuries of wind and water erosion, displayed nature's grandeur, and the colors of the rock, now intensified by the unrelenting sun, seemed to glow with an inner fire. Blessedly, the wind picked up a little, rustling the leaves of the gnarled bushes and trees and reducing the temperature by a few miserly degrees.

As Aru wiped the sweat from his forehead, he was tempted to take off the hardhat and let the breeze cool the top of his head, but he wanted to preserve the illusion of being human for a few more minutes.

If the Kra-ell females recognized him and Negal for who they were, they might attack first and ask questions later. There was no love lost between the gods and the Kra-ell, and for good reason.

What Jade and Morgada didn't know, though, was that the gods had evened out the playing field and that some of the young gods born after the settler ship had left had been enhanced to be just as strong as the Kra-ell. The Eternal King was closing every possible gap in his consolidated power, making every effort to prevent the possibility of future rebellions.

If Jade and Morgada decided to attack, they would be in for a surprise.

"We come in peace." He lifted his hands to show that he wasn't armed.

Negal did the same.

Dagor was on the roof of another building, and he had his disruptor, but it was not a weapon to be used against biological beings. It could disable equipment that was powered by anything other than muscle, and it could become useful if these people decided to use the drone to attack them.

"So do we." Jade removed her sunglasses, and Morgada did the same.

"Hello, Jade." He smiled. "I'm so glad to see that both you and Morgada are alive. We were very worried about you."

If looks could kill, her glare would have done him in. "How do you know who we are?"

"We've been watching you for a while." He motioned toward the blanket. "Let's sit down."

"First, tell me who you are and how you know my name."

Behind him, Negal cast a shrouding bubble around their group. Regrettably, it was only good for keeping human prying eyes from seeing them and ears from eavesdropping, but not for keeping the sun from baking their heads.

As the male standing next to Jade moved closer to her, the small hairs on the back of Aru's neck prickled, and he rubbed his hand over them. Usually, the sensation only happened when he met new, unfamiliar male gods, but not with humans. They were of no consequence to him, no threat, and there was no reason for his built-in alarm to go off.

The guy wasn't a god, that was obvious by his less-than-perfect features, and neither was the other one who was regarding him with surprising calm given the loaded situation.

Perhaps they were descendants of the gods?

There was a strong prohibition on gods procreating with the various species they had created, but the gods who had been sent to Earth had been rebels, so they might not have followed the rules in that as well.

The two males might possess a trace of godly genes, and that was why the hairs on the back of his neck were tingling.

To make sure, he turned to Negal. "Do you feel it, too?"

The trooper nodded. "Not as strongly as with others like us, but these males are not fully human."

"Who are you?" Aru asked the male wearing a strange red vest that didn't match the rest of his elegant clothing. "Or rather, what are you?"

The male smiled. "I would like to know the same about you, but let's start with simple introductions and continue from there. You already know Jade and Morgada. My name is Magnus." He offered Aru his hand.

"Aru." He shook what was offered. "And this is Negal."

"I'm Phinas." The other male offered his hand.

Once all the handshakes were exchanged, Aru lowered himself to the blanket and sat down cross-legged Kra-ell style.

With a look of approval in her big eyes, Jade followed suit and sat across from him, and Morgada did the same.

When Phinas sat on Jade's right, Aru noticed the earpieces he was wearing. A quick glance at Magnus revealed that he was wearing them, too. Jade and Morgada had their hair down, so he couldn't tell whether they were wearing them as well.

He pointed at the earpiece in Magnus's ear. "I assume that our conversation is not private."

"It's not," the guy confirmed. "My boss is listening in. For full transparency, we are also flying a drone overhead that is filming us and, if need be, can provide an aerial defense. In addition, a force of Guardians is on standby not far from here. Both are defensive measures in case you turn hostile. If you don't strike, we won't. We just want to talk and find out who you are and what you want."

Aru was sure that it was far from full disclosure, but admitting it was a step in the right direction.

"I assume that you expect a similar disclosure from me, but all I can say is that we want the same thing you do, and whatever measures we have in place are defensive and not offensive."

Magnus didn't look happy with his answer. "Is anyone listening to our conversation on your side?"

Aru could have lied and answered in the affirmative, but he preferred the truth whenever possible. Lies by omission were necessary, and in most cases, he could get by without crossing that line.

"No one is listening to our conversation, but we are not without backup. We are expected to report periodically. If we don't, a large force will come looking for us, and believe me, none of us want that."

Dagor was watching, but his only recourse was to summon the patrol ship, and it would take years for it to come back.

The truth was that if they had nothing of interest to report, years could pass without anyone checking in on them. Their commander had a large sector to patrol, and

Earth was of little interest to anyone except for the two most powerful people on Anumati, each for their own reasons.

Magnus

Why me? Magnus thought while pinning the other group's leader with a hard look, which was hopefully not too threatening and not too soft either.

The only reason he'd been selected for this mission was his seniority. He was the highest-ranking non-head Guardian. That, however, didn't make him a good candidate for a diplomatic mission. In fact, he was probably one of the worst people Onegus and Kian could have chosen to represent the clan in a meeting with the gods.

Not that he was sure they were gods yet, but they weren't Kra-ell, and they weren't human, so the only option other than gods was that they were immortals like him.

"You're being vague," he told the leader. "Who are you, and who do you report to?"

"And how do you know our names?" Jade added.

The guy smiled. "Let's do things in their proper order and make it an equitable exchange of information. First, tell me who and what you are. You are definitely not human." He rubbed the back of his neck. "Do you also have this built-in alarm?" He glanced at Phinas, who neither confirmed nor denied.

Aru's admission, though, confirmed that he and his friend were either gods or immortals.

"You can tell him what we agreed on," Kian said in Magnus's earpiece.

"We are immortals," Magnus said. "We are the descendants of the gods. Your turn. Who are you?"

The guy arched a brow. "Fascinating. I assume that you are the product of dalliances between gods and humans?"

Magnus tilted his head. "I thought that was self-explanatory. How else could I be a descendant of the gods and not a god myself?"

"It is forbidden for gods to procreate with anyone other than their own, but your parents were known rule breakers."

Magnus's blood chilled in his veins. How did Aru know his mother? Had these beings been watching them as they had been obviously watching the Kra-ell?

No, that wasn't possible.

Aru didn't know who and what Magnus and Phinas were, and the only reason he'd figured they had godly genes in them was the built-in alarm system that male gods and immortals had—the prickling sensation when in the presence of possible male adversaries.

Perhaps Aru had misspoken.

"I assume that you meant our ancestors were known rule breakers. There is no way you know my mother, who is not a goddess but an immortal like me."

Aru's eyes widened. "I actually thought that one of your parents was a god. How many generations of immortals are there?"

The guy was either clueless or pretending to be.

"Many," Magnus said.

Negal leaned forward as if wanting a better look. "That's incredible. I had no idea that immortality could be hereditary. How does it work?"

Magnus shook his head. "Let's save the scientific explanations for later. I told you who we are, and it's your turn to tell us who you are."

"We are gods, of course. Who else could we be?" Aru removed his hardhat and his protective glasses, leaving behind only the dark sunglasses he'd worn under the shield. "It's way too hot out here."

Jade chuckled. "Your kind avoids the sun at all costs. You are not used to harsh sunlight."

"No, we are not, but we are better equipped to deal with it than Magnus's ancestors. The heat and the harsh light must have been torturous for the exiled gods, which was no doubt the Eternal King's intent. After all, he wanted to punish them."

"It's getting interesting," Kian said in Magnus's earpieces. "Keep him talking, but don't reveal what we have agreed upon no matter what he tells you."

Magnus had no intention of mentioning the surviving gods, but since Aru and Negal were gods themselves, they could just reach into his mind and take the information from there. Kian should have sent Turner, who was immune, and Magnus had even suggested him, but both Onegus and Kian had rejected the suggestion.

"What do you know about the exiled gods?" Magnus asked.

Perhaps if he kept Aru talking, the god wouldn't be able to peek into his mind at the same time. Thralling required concentration, and if Magnus couldn't thrall humans while talking, the god shouldn't be able to thrall immortals while talking either.

Aru grimaced. "I know what our history records tell us, and it's nothing good, but my teammates and I are well aware that it's all propaganda meant to besmirch the heir's name. Now, it is blasphemous to even say his name out loud."

Jade cast the god a hard look. "That wasn't what we were told back in my day, but I don't really care about the lies the Eternal King spreads about his own people."

Magnus narrowed his eyes at the god. "You said, 'teammates.' That implies more than one."

Aru nodded. "The third member of our team is not here for security reasons. We didn't know what we were walking into, and bringing our entire team would have been foolish."

It was a valid concern. "Makes sense. Where is he now?"

Aru smiled. "Do you really think I will tell you that?"

Magnus lifted his head and looked at the roof the gods had been working on. The third member of their party was no longer there, but Magnus was willing to bet that he was on one of the other roofs, watching his teammates.

"We saw you on that roof," Jade said. "You overlooked one item of your disguise, and it gave you away."

"What is it?" He'd thought that they had blended in seamlessly.

She looked at his boots. "Those are not made for construction work. I knew all along that you left one of your teammates behind, but what I don't get is how you know who I am. You even know my adopted name. Have you been tapping into the compound's communications?"

"Something like that."

To answer Jade's question truthfully, Aru would have to reveal much more than he was comfortable with at the moment, but since he'd already shown his hand by recognizing her and Morgada, he had no choice.

The cloud that had provided a little respite from the sun had moved over, and the limbs of the tree they had spread the blanket under were so gnarled and devoid of leaves that it was like sitting out in the open.

"I wish we could have this meeting in an air-conditioned place." Aru put the hardhat back on his head.

Sweating was better than having his brain fry in the sun.

Jade rolled her eyes. "Stop stalling already and answer me. 'Something like that' is not an answer."

He nodded. "It's a long story that I don't want to get into detail with, but the gist of it is that we were sent to find you, see what you are up to, and report back. We periodically surveyed the compound to see what Igor was up to and whether he had captured more Kra-ell, but we were not allowed to intervene or to let our presence be known."

She arched a brow. "Really? So why are you here now, talking to us?"

Aru shifted his gaze to the two immortal males. "When we realized that new players had showed up on the scene, we had to find out what they were about."

As the implications sank in, the alarm in Magnus's eyes betrayed his thoughts even before he voiced them. "Where did you come from and why? Was it a nearby outpost or straight from Anumati?"

The immortal feared discovery by the Eternal King, and rightfully so.

"We left Anumati a hundred and one Earth years ago, and we've been here five years. Our arrival wasn't in response to any particular event. We are on a standard tour of duty in the sector."

"Where is your ship?" the other immortal asked.

"The ship dropped us off and continued on its tour. It will collect us on its way back and continue to the next sector."

"When will it come back for you?" Magnus asked.

Aru hesitated and then decided to go with the truth. As long as Magnus and whoever was listening to their conversation were afraid of an imminent strike by a superior force of gods, they wouldn't reveal anything about themselves. To gain the trust of the immortals and their Kra-ell charges, he needed to give them something else to focus on and show them that they were on the same side of the divide.

"Our ship will return in one hundred and fifteen years, give or take a few. The round trip from Anumati and back takes over seven hundred years, and the last time anyone checked on humanity was about six hundred years ago. Your world was very different back then, and the Eternal King had no reason to get involved in what was happening here. But things have changed dramatically since then. The human population has exploded, and its technological progress has advanced exponentially. Our primary task was to find out whether the settler ship had arrived, and we reported that it had and that only some of the settlers had survived. I didn't report what else we found on Earth even though it was much more important than the Kra-ell." He smiled. "It's also much more important than discovering that the descendants of the rebel gods are hiding among the humans." He sighed. "What I'm trying to say is that you don't need to be alarmed on account of us discovering you. There are much bigger concerns to worry about."

Beside him, Negal groaned in frustration, probably appalled by how much he was revealing.

Their four guests stared at him with wide eyes.

Jade was the first one to speak. "Aren't you a soldier in the king's army? Isn't it your duty to report everything?"

Aru nodded. "Officially, yes. The three of us were conscripted into service but not at the same time. Negal has been serving longer than the other teammate and me. But that doesn't mean that we are fully aligned with the Eternal King and his agenda."

Just to be safe, he'd worded it in a way that didn't sound like treasonous intentions but rather a difference in opinions.

"A lot longer," Negal grumbled. "And yet you got the command."

"Conscripted?" Magnus asked. "Service is not voluntary for gods?"

"For most, it is not. There are always the privileged ones who get exempt from duty under various guises of alternative service. But in my case, and in the case of my teammates and everyone on the ship patrolling this sector, we are here because we wanted to be stationed together. We are a ship of kindred people."

The new rebellion was thousands of years in the making, and it would take many thousands more. Ahn's mistake had been rushing in without enough support. This time around, they were building a solid foundation and waiting patiently for it to reach critical mass. When the time came to end the Eternal King's rule, what they were building would be so vast and powerful that no bloodshed would accompany the transition of power.

Hopefully.

"Why are you telling them all that?" Negal took his hardhat off and wiped the sweat off his forehead before putting it back on. "We don't know who they are or who they work for. You are endangering thousands of lives by revealing our most guarded secret as casually as describing the weather."

Aru shifted his eyes to him. "These people are obviously not working for the Eternal King, and they are in much more danger from him than we are. If we want them to trust us, we have to show them trust first." He shifted his gaze to Magnus. "In the eyes of the Eternal King, you and everyone like you is an abomination. You are not supposed to exist. He will exterminate you like bugs before listening to anything you have to say, and he will do that from afar so none of your blood will stain his pristine robes. He will also not allow humanity to keep growing. The last time a team reported from Earth, there were less than four hundred million humans. Now, there are more than eight billion people on Earth, and their technological progress has grown at an astounding rate. When the Eternal King learns of that, he will send a plague the likes of which Earth has never seen before, decimating the population and bringing it back to what he considers manageable, both in numbers and in technology. He might not act right away in human terms, and a couple of hundred years might pass before he makes his move, but once humanity gains interstellar travel capability, he will act swiftly. The king will not tolerate competition from what he views as inferior creatures."

"How do we stop him?" Magnus asked.

Aru smiled sadly. "The resistance is steadily gaining ground, but it is still far from being ready. Gods think in terms of thousands of Earth years. It will be a long time before we can do anything and hope to succeed. The best we can do for now is not report humanity's state until we are picked up in a hundred and some years."

Unless Aru came up with a brilliant excuse for failing to report that, he would be punished for the omission by exile to a rock at the end of the galaxy, but he wouldn't be executed. After all, his team's job was to find out whether the settler ship had arrived and if the twins had been found. He'd reported that some of the Kra-ell had survived and that the twins probably hadn't, so technically, he had fulfilled his duty.

The weight of leadership had always rested heavily on Kian's shoulders, but he'd faced the many challenges with a resolve born of hope for a better future.

Aru's words had shattered that hope, bringing about a despondency that pressed down on Kian like a mountain of boulders. The walls of his war room, previously symbols of strength and resolve, felt like they were closing in on him.

All the work his mother and he and his sisters had put into helping humanity evolve could be undone in one swipe of the Eternal King's hand.

As the saying went, it wasn't the things he fretted over that would bring their downfall, but the unexpected that caught them off guard. His own great-grandfather would be the engineer of humanity's demise, and there was nothing Kian could do to stop him.

He let out a breath. "I really want someone else to take over my job." He leaned back in his chair and scanned the faces of his teammates. "Does anyone want it? Because I'm tired of the never-ending struggle."

He wasn't even joking. The only other time in his life he'd felt as helpless as this had been when he'd been forced to leave his first wife and their unborn child, but at least then, he could ensure that their future was as secure as he could make it.

That wasn't the case now.

What chance did he and his clan have against the might of the gods? How was he going to protect humanity from the Eternal King?

The immortals would not be affected by a plague, but they had spent their entire lives helping humanity, and none of them could even conceive of another global disaster wiping out most of the population.

It would be so devastating that it would break even his mother.

"I thought that the Doomers were our biggest problem," Onegus said. "I've been waiting for them to make their next big move, like start the third world war, but they are nothing compared to an army of gods and their biological weapons."

"Navuh would never be so reckless," Turner said. "He wants to control humanity, not destroy it, and the more humans there are, the bigger his empire would be."

The Eternal King had no such qualms, and the one thing he was determined to prevent was competition in any shape or form. If he suspected that humans presented a threat to his hegemony over the known universe, he would strike preemptively before they reached critical mass, and probably not for the first time. The flood described in Sumerian and other mythologies around the world might have been a natural disaster, but Kian believed that the gods would have intervened if the Eternal King had allowed it. The story of Noah's ark described one god's desperate attempt to save humanity from complete annihilation, but the other gods had obeyed the king's orders to do nothing and had watched with horror as their subjects drowned.

Birth rates were slowly declining all over the world, though, so the king might opt to just wait and see whether the trend continued. If it did, then no action was required. The human population would shrink in size, and its technological advancement would decline along with the shrinkage. There wouldn't be enough economic thrust to enable it, let alone propel it forward.

Trends were unpredictable, and intervention might reverse them, but it didn't always work. The Chinese were an excellent example of that. Even after the one-child policy had been lifted and having more children was encouraged, the populace refused to adopt the new policy. Socio-economic factors were such that people preferred to have only one child so they could adequately provide for it.

Except for a few pockets where birth rates were still high, the same was happening all over the world.

The more advanced the nation, the fewer children it produced.

Turner gave Kian a sympathetic look. "Don't despair. We have a hundred years to find a solution. In godly terms, it might not be a long time, but it is in human terms. If introducing biological agents is how the Eternal King controls populations across the galaxy, we need to focus on finding a way to make everyone immune to them like we are. If we work with these rebel gods, they could help us understand the information in Okidu's journals, which might contain the blueprint for turning humanity immortal or at least immune to diseases."

Turner was the last person Kian had expected to provide words of encouragement, and coming from him, they weren't just platitudes to make him feel better.

"I never expected a pep talk from you. Thank you for your attempt to cheer me up."

"It wasn't a pep talk. I just stated the facts as they are."

Kian stifled a chuckle. That was such a Turner response. "The other factor we must consider is the steady global decline in birth rates. The Eternal King has nothing to worry about right now because humanity does not possess interstellar travel capabilities, and the population might significantly shrink before it does, if it ever gets there."

Turner arched a brow. "I've seen estimates of Earth's population halving in five hundred years and others predicting that it will shrink to below five hundred million. But keep in mind that those are highly speculative estimates based on simplistic assumptions. In reality, population trends are influenced by numerous factors like technological advancements, socio-economic changes, and unforeseen events. It's difficult to accurately predict the direction of global birth rates over such a long timeframe."

"Indeed, but all the factors you've mentioned point toward further decline, not reversal. The global economy is in trouble, and people know how to prevent pregnancies. My gut tells me that the more extreme estimates are the correct ones, but that could be a blessing in disguise. I'd much rather the human population shrink because fewer babies are born than to have them suffer another plague. I can only hope that the Eternal King is not in a rush and will wait and see what the next five hundred years will bring before making his move."

Onegus rubbed his jaw. "Do we even believe these gods? Introducing a mutual external threat is a perfect way for Aru to create rapport with us and gain our trust. He might have made up the prediction about what the Eternal King would do if he discovered how far humanity had advanced."

"That's possible." Kian wanted to believe that, but regrettably, Aru had probably told them the truth. "What their leader said was in line with what Jade has told us about the Eternal King and his politics."

Onegus nodded. "He also sounded sincere. Unless Negal is a superb actor, which he very well might be, his response reinforces the veracity of what Aru was saying. Negal sounded genuinely alarmed when his commander spoke about what could be perceived as treasonous intent, and his shoulders slumped in resignation."

Kian had been watching the same feed, and he hadn't seen the change in the god's posture.

The drone was flying high above, the camera feed was grainy, and the dried-out tree they were sitting under partially blocked the view, making it impossible to see the gods' facial expressions or even posture.

Kian had been relying on what had been said, and for long moments now, no one had said a thing. Magnus and the rest of them were stunned, and Aru was giving them time to process what he'd revealed.

Kian tapped his earpiece. "Ask Aru how often the Eternal King checks up on Earth and how come he doesn't just pick up transmissions from Earth's satellites to learn all he needs from there."

Aru

Aru waited patiently as Magnus and his team absorbed what he had told them. They were probably also listening to their boss in their earpieces.

Regrettably, the devices were very well-fitted, and he couldn't hear what was being said on the other side. He could've reached into Magnus's mind and gotten a good impression of what the guy was hearing, but he didn't know whether the gods had imparted their immunity to thralling to their immortal offspring or if the immortals were as susceptible as humans. He was itching to test it, but if the immortals could feel his mental probing, it would be considered a hostile move.

Most of the Kra-ell were immune, which was probably one of the reasons the old gods had made every effort to keep them in a disadvantaged state.

If they couldn't control their minds, they could control them economically.

The rebels had sought to correct that wrong and had paid with their lives for their effort.

"How often does the king check up on Earth?" Magnus asked.

Aru arched a brow. "Is that the only question your boss has for me?"

The guy listened for a moment and then smiled. "For now, he only has a few more questions. He says that we should meet again somewhere more comfortable."

Aru wiped the sweat off his forehead with the sleeve of his shirt. "I agree wholeheartedly. This heat is unbearable."

Magnus nodded, but Aru had a feeling that it was in response to something his boss said. "We find it difficult to believe that a society as technologically advanced as the gods' needs boots on the ground to investigate. Aren't they monitoring Earth's broadcasts?"

"That's a good question, and it requires a long answer." Aru reached for the water jug, uncapped it, and took a long sip. "Anyone else thirsty?"

Magnus chuckled. "Now that you drank from it, I'm less apprehensive about it being drugged or poisoned." He took the jug from Aru, lifted it to his mouth, and poured the water into it without touching the rim.

"I could be immune to what's in it," Aru teased. "It could contain a drug that will loosen your tongue. Are you sure you want to risk it?"

Smiling, Magnus made a show of gulping down a substantial amount of water and then returned the jug to Aru. "If I start talking nonsense, my boss will have to send the backup force to extract me."

"Understood." Aru offered the jug to Jade. "It's not drugged."

Casting him a defiant look, she took it and drank.

"Signals from Earth can't be transmitted directly to Anumati, not with the technology available to humans. We used to have satellites that transmitted to a relay station, but they were destroyed. The official version was that the rebels blew them up to avoid answering questions from Anumati journalists about the so-called war crimes they were accused of, but a conspiracy theory claims that the Eternal King ordered the satellites destroyed."

"I've never heard that one," Negal said. "Where did you hear it?"

"From a reliable source." Aru would never reveal his source. Not even to his most trusted friends.

"Why would the king want to destroy communications with Earth?" Magnus asked.

Aru cast a quick look at his companion while formulating his answer. Some of what he was about to say was common knowledge, but some was not, and he needed to frame it accordingly. "Shortly after the settler ship went missing, the Eternal King had war-crime accusations trumped up against Ahn and the other rebels. Supposedly, new information had surfaced of crimes severe enough to warrant entombment. The Eternal King even brought up the flood that, in all likelihood, he had ordered himself. When reporters tried to get Ahn's response to the accusations, the communication satellites around Earth conveniently exploded. The king claimed that Ahn blew them up out of spite and to avoid being asked uncomfortable questions and being brought to justice."

Jade pursed her lips. "I assume you were not the only one who suspected the king was behind the destruction of the satellites. Anumati is ruled by a monarch, but it's supposed to be a semi-democratic monarchy, at least for the gods, if not for the Kra-ell. How come no one in the media investigated the allegations?"

The king's propaganda machine worked so well that even a Kra-ell like Jade, who was by no means a sympathizer of the gods and didn't support their king, believed in the lies as long as they had no bearing on her and her people. For some reason, people always found it easier to believe what they were told rather than use their critical thinking and analyze what information they were being fed and why.

Aru's rule of thumb had always been to look for who benefited from what. It wasn't always readily apparent, though, and in the past, he had often been left with no answers, but now that he was serving someone much smarter than himself, the web was much more transparent.

"The reporters knew what was good for them and their careers. They were afraid to push the envelope and lose their jobs or get sent to the farthest corner of the known universe to report on the seeding of a new planet." He leveled his gaze on Jade. "No one dares go directly against the king. Have you ever heard any reporter ask him an uncomfortable question that he didn't have a ready answer to? He always has the perfect answer to every question, and not because he's so brilliant, although he is. "

Jade shrugged. "He's the Eternal King for a reason."

"Yes. He's shrewd, and he knows how to manipulate public opinion. Every interview that you ever saw with him was scripted and rehearsed. He gets the questions before the interview and has time to prepare the answers. In fact, I'm sure that the answers are prepared by his army of assistants."

She let out a breath. "I always believed that the gods were deeply corrupt. I just didn't know the extent of it."

"The majority of people don't." Aru shifted a couple of inches to the right to move away from the rock that had been digging into his bottom ever since he sat down. "After the satellites were destroyed, the king made a mournful address to the nation, saying that he couldn't bring himself to entomb his children, but given the atrocious war crimes they had committed, he could not pardon them either. He would do the next best thing—they would be abandoned and forgotten on Earth forever. He ordered Earth's location expunged from all records and asked everyone to forget the rebels who were sent there as if they were never born. The Eternal King is a powerful compeller, but even he couldn't compel everyone through the televised event to forget the rebels and the location of the solar system they were exiled to, but many did nonetheless."

"Wait a moment." Jade lifted her hand. "The Kra-ell were supposed to arrive on Earth at some point. The Kra-ell queen would have never agreed to forget about her people."

"The queen who sent you here was dead by then. When the new Kra-ell queen protested, the king said that the prohibition to visit Earth was on gods, not the Kra-ell, and once they developed their own vessels, they could go visit their people on Earth whenever they pleased."

Jade

Jade grimaced. "Let me guess. The Kra-ell never got to develop their own interstellar ships."

Aru nodded. "They got to settle on many new planets, but they were brought there by the gods' ships. The gods never released their technology for building stasis pods, and without them, the Kra-ell couldn't travel to faraway places even if they managed to build the ships, which they didn't. The technology is closely guarded."

What else was new? The gods didn't part with any of their knowledge unless they were forced to.

"I've noticed you said it took you only a little over a hundred years to get to Earth. That's much faster than what was possible when we left."

"There are ships capable of even faster speeds than that, but they are much smaller. To this day, settlers' ships are slower than patrol ships."

"What happened to my queen? She was still a young female when we left."

The god cast her a sad smile. "She suffered an unfortunate accident forty-some years after your ship left. The official statement claimed that she fell off a cliff. Naturally, there were rumors about her daughter assassinating her to get the throne, but we both know that wasn't what happened."

"That's not the Kra-ell way." Despite the queen's duplicity, Jade felt a pang of sadness for her untimely death. "If the queen's daughter wanted to ascend to the throne before her mother was ready to step down, she would have challenged the queen to a duel, but that has only been done a couple of times throughout our history when the reigning queen was so terrible that she needed to be removed." Jade let out a breath. "The queen didn't have another daughter when I was still on Anumati. The new queen must have been born after our ship left."

Aru smiled apologetically. "I suppose so, but I'm not that well versed in Kra-ell history. For me, that happened a very long time ago."

Perhaps the queen had fallen to her death because the ship had been lost along with her children, and she'd been overcome with grief. It was a great sin to take one's own life, but maybe in her sorrow, the queen had not been as careful, and the fall was indeed accidental? Anumati's terrain was rugged, and losing footing on one of the narrow mountain passages was not uncommon.

"Do you know if our ship was already lost at the time of her death?"

"It was," Aru said. "After the Eternal King decreed that Earth was to be forgotten, the new queen pleaded with the Eternal King to turn the ship around. The answer from the command center was that they had lost contact with the computer running the ship."

"Hold on," Morgada said. "If Earth was to be forgotten, how did you learn about the queen's request? I assume that the king gave the order to forget Earth long before you were born."

"Only the location of Earth was expunged. The planet itself was not forgotten. It became a cautionary tale—the hell where sinners and evil doers dwell."

It was funny how that aligned with some of the human religious beliefs. Perhaps the Eternal King had found a way to drip-feed that into human mythology, or maybe it had arrived on the wings of some kind of cosmic awareness.

"What about the gold?" Magnus said. "The main reason the rebels were sent to Earth was to oversee the mining of it. Didn't they need it on Anumati?"

"We've been manufacturing a synthetic alternative that does everything gold was previously used for, for a very long time. No one uses gold for anything other than jewelry, which is quite expensive."

"Do they use money on Anumati?" Phinas asked.

Jade cut him a look. "Out of everything you've heard so far, that is what intrigues you?"

He shrugged. "That will be among the first things Kalugal will ask me."

"Who's Kalugal?" Aru asked.

"My boss."

The god frowned. "Isn't that the same person Magnus reports to?"

"No, but I also answer to that one. It's complicated."

Surprisingly, Aru smiled. "I get it. I know all about answering to several bosses. And to answer your question, we use credits, which is the equivalent of money. Generally, our society functions similarly to human societies, just on a much larger scale." He looked at Jade. "How are you enjoying living among humans?"

"I don't really live among them." She glared at him. "You said that you arrived only five years ago. How much did you learn about our history from observing us? You still didn't tell me how you were monitoring us. Was it through the compound's communication or by some other means?"

The god hesitated for a moment before answering. "We flew drones undetectable by human technology, so we had eyes and ears in the compound."

She cast him a glare. "So, you knew that we were subjugated, and yet you did nothing to help us."

"I'm sorry, but we couldn't. We were not allowed to intervene."

"Did you know what Igor's secret mission was?" Magnus asked.

The question seemed to take the god by surprise, but since his eyes were still hidden behind his sunglasses, the only indication was the tightening of his lips.

"How did you find out about his mission? I'm sure he didn't volunteer the information."

Neither Negal nor Dagor knew about Gor's primary directive. There had been no need for them to know, and Aru couldn't tell them without revealing his secret source of information.

The Eternal King believed in compartmentalization, and sending different teams to do the same thing without them knowing what the others were doing was a common tactic of his and others in his chain of command.

"We have our ways." Magnus looked at Jade. "She made a bargain with him. His life for information."

Aru shifted his gaze to Jade. "What did he tell you?"

When she hesitated and didn't respond right away, he wondered whether she was also listening to the immortals' boss. He still didn't know why and how they had liberated the Kra-ell and what their angle was, and so far, he had revealed much more than he had learned, and it was time to flip things around.

"He told us that he was sent to assassinate the royal twins. Was that your mission as well?"

"Our mission was to check whether the Kra-ell settler ship had arrived. When our patrol ship entered this sector, we started receiving signals from your trackers, but given that only a small number of them were broadcasting, we realized that not everyone had made it safely to Earth. Our job was to find out whether the twins were among the survivors. After locating your compound, we reported that the twins were not there. Our next task was investigating the crash site and searching for the other pods. That was what we were doing when the trackers suddenly stopped broadcasting, came online again, and started winking out one at a time. We were afraid for your lives, but we couldn't get to you because we were too far away. We were investigating a potential lead to a pod location in Tibet, and getting to Karelia took us a long time."

"Right." Jade crossed her arms over her chest. "You cared so much about us that you left us under Igor's rule. But I get it. You followed orders until they no longer suited you, and you disobeyed them because you had a mystery to solve."

She wasn't wrong, and perhaps he owed her an apology. "The truth is that we had nothing to gain by helping you, and we had a job to do. But once you were taken by a superior force, we were obligated to investigate it." He shifted his eyes to Magnus. "I've told you many things I probably shouldn't have to gain your trust, but you haven't returned the favor. Tell me how and why you aided the Kra-ell."

"Hold on," Jade said. "Before Magnus answers your question, I need to know whether you were sent to kill the twins."

"We were not. We were only supposed to report whether they were alive, and we were forbidden to engage them if we found them."

Jade nodded. "You aren't powerful enough to deal with them. I wonder, though. When was it revealed that they were on the ship? I only discovered by chance that they were there, and I wasn't sure until Igor confirmed it."

"I didn't know that," Aru admitted. "I thought that everyone knew they were aboard the ship. The official story was that they were sent with the settlers as their spiritual leaders, and when the ship was lost in space, the Kra-ell queen mourned their loss. She was despondent, and there were rumors that her death wasn't an accident but a suicide."

"That possibility has crossed my mind," Jade said. "She wouldn't have committed suicide because that would have barred her from ever entering the fields of the brave, but she might have been less careful and more reckless with her life. It's difficult for a mother to keep on living after her children die."

After eavesdropping on several of her conversations with Kagra when they were still Gor's captives, Aru knew that Jade spoke from personal experience.

Dipping his head, he put his hand over his chest. "I'm sorry for your loss. I don't know all the details, but I know that you lost two sons."

She nodded. "The need for revenge kept me alive, but in the end, I gave it up for the greater good. Getting information out of Igor was more important than the satisfaction I would have felt from taking off his head."

"What did you do with him?"

Jade looked at Magnus, and when he nodded, she said, "We put him in stasis."

"I'm surprised that you didn't kill him."

Jade uncrossed her arms. "I gave him my word that he would not die by my hand. Besides, the things stored in his brain would have died with him, which would have been a waste. This way, we can wake him anytime we need to retrieve that information." She looked him in the eyes. "You know what I'm talking about."

He shook his head. "I suspect that you know more than I do."

Jade

Did she believe him?

From what Aru had told them so far and from the little that his companion had said, Jade's impression was that he was a young god, not high on the totem pole of command and that he and his friends were part of some resistance. Except, he seemed to know a little more than Negal did, which made her suspicious.

Well, more suspicious. Gods were not trustworthy in the best of circumstances, especially not when they had something to gain by manipulating and lying.

"How did Igor know to decipher the signals?" she asked. "How did you know to do that?"

"We have a receiver."

As he reached into his pocket, Jade tensed, and so did Phinas, but what Aru pulled out was a phone.

"It's all in here." He tapped the device. "It can locate and identify the signals from the trackers."

Magnus leaned forward. "You can do that from your phone?"

Aru chuckled. "This is not an ordinary phone, but yes. It can do many more things, including communicate with our mother ship, but it's turned off right now."

She eyed the device with suspicion. "How do we know that? And besides, they could be listening to what you do without your knowledge, even when you think the thing is turned off. If human technology can do that, I'm sure the gods can do that as well."

"It can, but this one cannot. Everyone on Anumati, with even the most basic technical education, knows how to ensure privacy. Our society would have disintegrated without that ability. Even the Eternal King knows not to mess with that. He would lose support overnight."

Glancing at the other god, Jade noted that his expression and body language confirmed Aru's statement, but she would be a fool to forget even for a moment that gods were master manipulators.

Still, there was no harm in telling them about Igor's abilities. "Igor was not a regular Kra-ell. He was enhanced by the gods, and part of his enhancement was the ability to decipher where the signals were coming from. He needed a receiver to amplify the signals, but his mind supplied the location once he heard them. For some reason, he didn't have a receiver in his pod, and he had to wait for human technology to reach the stage where he could have one built to his specifications. Once he had it, he found every Kra-ell who woke up from stasis, and he came after us. He killed the males and took the females. He wanted to create a male-dominated Kra-ell community, and that was precisely what he did."

"We are aware of that part," Aru said. "I thought he told you more about the Kra-ell royal twins and how he planned to get rid of them."

As if she was going to tell him how Igor had planned to do that. She wouldn't risk Aru using the knowledge to take out the twins himself.

"He was an incredibly powerful compeller and had numerous enhancements. But what I can't understand is why the Eternal King thought that the queen's children were a threat to him. If they were as powerful as he believed, their mother wouldn't have felt the need to smuggle them off Anumati. They would have been safe where they were."

She didn't know whether Aru knew about the twins being the Eternal King's grandchildren, and her pretense of ignorance was a good way to find out.

"I don't know why he's so scared of them, but if they are so powerful, they are a threat to the king, and they might be helpful to our cause."

"Provided that they're still alive," Phinas said. "After so long, that's not very likely."

Aru nodded. "I share your opinion, but we will keep looking for the missing pods regardless, if only to put the occupants to rest and usher them on their journey to the other side of the veil." He looked at Jade. "It would be a good idea for you or another Kra-ell to accompany us to perform the ceremony. I know how to do it, but I doubt the souls of these Kra-ell would appreciate a god performing the ritual."

Surprised by the offer, Jade nodded. "There is much that still needs to be discussed, but once we all reach an agreement of cooperation of some sort, I will assign a couple of my people to assist you with the search and, if needed, the passing ritual. The custom calls for at least two adult Kra-ell to be present."

"Why not you?"

She lifted her chin. "I took it upon myself to lead our community, so I can't just leave them behind to go looking for what are most likely dead settlers."

"Understood." Aru shifted his eyes to Magnus. "I've waited patiently for you to explain why you aided Jade and her people and who you are aside from being the hybrid immortal descendants of the gods. You are obviously well organized and possess impressive military power, yet you let Jade govern her people independently. Not only that, she seems to trust you implicitly, which speaks volumes to the character of your organization." He turned to her. "Am I right?"

Jade nodded. "Despite being descendants of the gods, these immortals are honorable people, and they came to our aid without expecting anything in return. They did that because it was the right thing to do, and I owe them a debt of gratitude that I can never repay in my lifetime. My descendants will have to continue repaying the favor for many generations."

As she'd expected, Kian groaned in her ear. "I told you a hundred times. The only gratitude I expect is your people's loyalty and cooperation."

The young god smiled. "After such an enthusiastic endorsement of the immortals, I'm less apprehensive about trusting them with our secrets."

Jade had a feeling that he'd shared only a tiny portion of his secrets with them, but that was understandable. In time, he might feel more comfortable sharing more.

"Not too long ago, I was in your position," she said. "I'm not the trusting type, and I was very suspicious of my rescuers' motives, but after they proved time and again that they meant me and my people no harm and even welcomed us into their community, I laid my suspicions to rest and offered their leader my oath of loyalty. I wanted to give him a life vow, but he refused to accept it, which is another testament to his character."

"Indeed." Aru turned to Magnus. "The stage is yours, my friend. I want to hear your side of the story."

Magnus

"What do you want to know?"

Aru chuckled. "Everything. Who are you and what do you stand for, and how did you find Igor's compound? But I'll settle for whatever your boss is comfortable with you telling me."

"You can tell him about Emmett," Kian said in Magnus's ear. "They already know about Safe Haven because of Sofia's tracker. They might not make the connection right away, but I have no doubt that they will eventually get to investigate the place."

Magnus brushed his fingers over his short beard. "I'm not a good storyteller. Jade can tell you how we found her. She can also tell you about her capture by Igor."

She'd heard Kian's instructions and knew the backstory of what led them to her.

Aru arched a brow. "I'd rather hear that from you."

Magnus shook his head. "It's really not my story to tell. Once Jade is done, I'll answer your other questions."

Hopefully, Kian had gotten the hint and would instruct him on what he should and shouldn't say. They had covered the basics before the meeting and had agreed to keep things as vague as possible, but after Aru's revelations, they had to tell him more.

The god nodded. "Very well. While Jade tells me the story of her liberation, you can discuss with your boss what to tell me."

"You are a smart guy." Magnus chuckled. "No wonder you are in command even though you are less experienced than your teammates."

"One teammate. Dagor and I were drafted at the same time."

"Since you know what I'm about to do, there is no point in me whispering and talking in hints." Magnus pushed to his feet. "I'll walk over to that boulder over there to talk with my boss in private."

As Aru nodded again, Magnus turned and walked away. With how well these gods could hear, he would need to walk much farther than that, but he wasn't going to say anything that was of importance to them anyway.

"I'm about fifty feet away from the gods," he said quietly. "That's probably not far enough to keep them from hearing me, but it's enough not to interfere with Jade's story. What do you want me to tell them?"

"I want you to find out what they know about Ahn and what happened to the gods, and I have a feeling that he's not going to tell you anything unless you share some information with him. You can tell him about the Doomers, but keep the two people we discussed out of the story. Refrain from mentioning my ancestry, too. I'm just an immortal like you and Phinas."

"How am I going to explain the clan's origins?" Magnus lowered his voice to barely a whisper. "Or the animosity between us and the Doomers?"

"I'm sure you can think of something."

Magnus let out a breath. "I'm not good at things like that. I need guidance."

He heard Kian chuckle. "Talk slowly and pause frequently so we can feed the story to you."

"Thank you. That will be much appreciated. What else do you want me to ask?"

"I want to know whether he and his team were sent to discover if any of the gods survived and to finish the job, but there is no chance he will answer that truthfully. I also don't know how to ask it without revealing that we know Igor's mission was not only to eliminate the twins but also the gods."

"Neither do I," Magnus admitted. "Since we are going to schedule another meeting with them, you or Onegus should consider participating." He sighed. "After the initial exchange of information, the talk will move to diplomatic territory, and I'm really underqualified for such important negotiations. Also, where do you want to hold the meeting?"

"Agreed. They already know about the keep, so we can meet there. Not in the underground, I'd rather try to keep it a secret, but in my old penthouse. Let them think that's our alternative headquarters. Also, make sure that they know that most of the building is occupied by humans, just in case they get any ideas about blowing the place up."

"Why would they do that? They seem interested in cooperation. Besides, what makes you think that they care about humans getting hurt?"

"They seem to want to protect humanity at large, so I assume that they care. What I'm puzzled about is what they hope to gain by allying with us. They don't need us, and if they disclose our existence, we are toast."

Magnus swallowed. "I hate to suggest this, but maybe it's in our best interest to prevent that from happening?"

Hopefully, Kian would get the hint.

Eliminating the three gods was the safest way of preventing the information about humanity from getting to the Eternal King.

"Not really. The other god mentioned that thousands of lives were at stake, referring to the patrol ship. If something were to happen to Aru and his team, they would come to investigate, and I don't want to think what they might do to avenge their friends. Especially since they will most likely assume that humans were responsible."

Aru

"Exoskeletons?" Aru arched a brow. "Isn't that the external covering of animals without backbones? Like insects?"

Jade chuckled. "Where have you been during the five years you spent on Earth? Haven't you heard about power exoskeletons? They are in almost every science fiction movie."

"That would explain why I haven't heard of them. I don't watch science fiction movies." Aru preferred romantic comedies and historical dramas—the first because they were lighthearted and took his mind off depressing subjects, and the latter because they gave him an overview of human history without having to spend time reading about it. "But I can guess what exoskeletons are since you said the immortals wore them to enhance their strength. I'm just curious about the technology. As you know, we prefer to fix biological disadvantages biologically. We only have stasis pods because it took our scientists a long time to enhance our physiology so we could enter stasis without the aid of technology."

Jade's lips twisted in distaste. "I know all about your tampering with nature."

"Humans had to find other solutions," Phinas said. "But our exoskeletons are not the kind you can find in a store or order online. They were built for immortals and are too heavy and cumbersome for humans to wear."

That was a clue about the immortals he'd been curious about. Apparently, they had inherited the gods' strength. Not that it was a problem. Aru and his teammates were among the gods who had been enhanced to match the physical strength of the Kra-ell. After the revolution, it had taken their scientists several centuries to isolate the genetics and develop the enhancement without giving gods a Kra-ell appearance. Not all gods were given the trait because it came at the cost of others that parents might have valued more than physical strength.

"Interesting." He smiled. "I follow the news, and I haven't heard exoskeletons mentioned as being used in warfare. What do humans use them for?"

"You can look it up," Jade said. "Do you have a phone? I mean, something that connects to the internet?"

"Of course." He pulled the device from his pocket.

"Not now." She waved a dismissive hand. "You can do that after the meeting is over in the comfort of your hotel room." She looked at him from under lowered lashes. "You are staying in a hotel, right? You didn't thrall some poor human family into giving you their house?"

"What do you take us for? Amateurs? And even if that would not undermine our cover, we would never take what wasn't ours to take by force or mind manipulation."

Never was a strong word, and they had used their mind manipulation powers on multiple occasions, but never to cause harm to innocents.

Jade lifted her hands in the air. "Just checking. As you've learned from my story, I wasn't always very considerate of humans. Although, in my defense, their conditions outside my compound were even worse." She cast a quick look at Magnus. "The immortals were always much more mindful of human rights. Their mission is to elevate humanity, not enslave it or keep it from prospering, but that's Magnus's story to tell, and he's getting instructions from the boss. All I can do is continue the story of our rescue."

"Before you continue, will I ever learn the name of that mysterious boss you are referring to?"

She made a face. "Again, it's not my decision. My people and I are guests in their community, and we were given many more privileges than we've earned. The least I can do is honor their preferences regarding what I can tell you."

"I understand."

He was growing fond of Jade. She wasn't the same female he'd observed in Gor's compound, which could only be attributed to the immortals' influence. He also had a strong feeling that Phinas was her consort. She regarded him with a fondness that she did not accord to Magnus, and it wasn't because of deference to Magnus as their team leader.

"I have the definition for you." Phinas held his phone up. "Powered exoskeletons are used in healthcare, military, industrial, and entertainment applications. In the medical field, they can assist patients with mobility impairments or aid in physical therapy. In military applications, exoskeletons may be utilized to support soldiers in carrying heavy loads or enhance their capabilities on the battlefield. In industrial settings, they can improve worker safety and productivity in physically demanding jobs." He lifted his eyes from the screen. "Ours make us as strong as the Kra-ell and impervious to bullets, swords, daggers, and the like. They can even protect us from grenades."

"Impressive." Aru shifted his gaze to Magnus, who was heading back their way. "I think you will need to finish your story at a later time because your leader has received his orders and is ready to talk."

As Jade turned to look over her shoulder at Magnus, Aru peeked at his messages, but there were no new ones, and he didn't know whether it was a sign that Gabi was feeling better and not in a rush to leave the hospital, or that something was wrong and she couldn't communicate.

He hoped it was the former, and he wanted to wrap up the meeting so he could go to her.

Magnus

Magnus sat down on the blanket the gods had provided. "Before I tell you what my boss allowed me to share, he has one more question. If Earth's location has been expunged from the official records and visiting it was prohibited, how and why are you here?"

The god chuckled. "That's such a naive question. Your leader must be young."

"He's not." Magnus was offended on Kian's behalf.

"My apologies." The god dipped his head. "I've heard a clever human saying, but it was in Russian, and I can't do it justice by translating it because it wouldn't rhyme. The gist is that rules and laws do not apply equally to everyone. The king can prohibit citizens from visiting Earth and yet send patrols to monitor it, and no one will even question his right to do that. The public no longer has access to navigation charts that include the location of

Earth, but the same is not true of the royal archives and interstellar fleet's records."

"Makes sense. My boss also wonders about the trumped-up war crimes. What exactly was Ahn accused of?"

Aru frowned. "The gods are gone, and you said that you are many generations removed from them. How do you know the heir's name?"

"You just made one hell of a slip of the tongue," Kian said in Magnus's ear. "Tell him that the stories were passed down from one generation to the next, and remind him that he has referred to Ahn several times already, but as a leader of the rebels, not as the heir."

Magnus nodded even though Kian probably couldn't see him. He also had a question that Kian hadn't thought to ask.

"Legends about our godly ancestors were passed down through the generations. You yourself have mentioned Ahn several times as one of the rebel leaders. What I wonder, though, is how do you know with such certainty that the gods are gone?"

Aru smiled sadly. "The Kra-ell weren't the only ones who were implanted with trackers. All the rebels had them, too. When they died, the trackers stopped transmitting. We didn't know that until many years later when a patrol ship arrived at the sector and couldn't pick up their signals."

"Our bodies heal fast, which means they reject all foreign objects," Magnus said. "But I assume the gods found a way to overcome that problem."

"We did," Aru agreed. "Every god who leaves Anumati is implanted with a tracker. After all, the king wants to know where everyone is at all times. In the case of Earth, he lost that ability when he blew up the satellites, which is why the rebels' demise was only discovered many years later."

Luckily for them, the only surviving gods had been born on Earth and hadn't been implanted with trackers, so the Eternal King didn't know of them.

"So that means that you have trackers in you as well. How come we didn't pick up the signal?"

Aru shrugged. "Different technology. We figured out that you somehow knew how to decipher the signals from the old trackers, and in order to find you, we needed them. Luckily, we knew where the original Kra-ell scouting team had settled and where to find the resting place of its members—those who had died before the communication satellites were destroyed. We had to go to China to find them and return here, where the last of the still functioning Kra-ell trackers led us before winking out as well."

"Where in China?" Kian asked in Magnus's ear.

When Magnus repeated the question, Aru shook his head. "Enough. I've been very patient and accommodating, but this wasn't a fair exchange of information. I need some answers from you."

"Fair enough." Magnus took a deep breath and recited the speech Kian had given him. "There are two known groups of immortals, and by known, I mean to each other, not to humans. Our group calls itself Annani's clan, and we are named after one of our godly ancestors. The leader of our clan is named Kian, or the boss, as we've been referring to him so far. The other group calls itself the brotherhood of the Devout Order of Mortdh, with Mortdh being their godly ancestor, and their leader's name is Navuh. We are adversaries. Our clan works to elevate the human condition, perpetuating the work that our godly ancestors began when they got to Earth. The other group wants to rule humanity and enslave it, and they hate us for enabling human progress. The feud between us has been going on ever since the gods perished. Sometimes, we gain the upper hand, and sometimes they do. If one of your patrol ships visited during the Dark Ages or before that, during Sumer's decline, it would have witnessed the fruits of their success."

Aru smiled. "From what we have seen so far, you seem to be winning the war. Humanity is doing much better than it has ever done."

"Thank you, but it's a never-ending struggle, and we've learned not to celebrate our triumphs. Regrettably, more often than not, they are temporary."

Gabi

Gabi was having the most delicious dream. She and Uriel were on a beach, walking along the shore and eating ice cream, and he looked so dreamy that she wanted to throw the ice cream away and lick him all over instead.

Why was she so cold, though?

The sun was shining bright, and the sky was cloudless. Maybe it was the ice cream dripping over the back of her hand?

It was so cold.

"What's the matter?" Uriel asked. "You're shivering."

"My hand is cold." She lifted it and examined the back.

Nothing had dripped. Dreams were so strange. And how the hell did she know that she was dreaming? Maybe it wasn't a dream, because if it was, she wouldn't be so cold when the sun was shining so bright.

"I'll warm it up for you." Uriel took her hand between his. "Better?"

"Much." She smiled.

"Gabi."

"Yes?" She looked up at him.

"Gabi. Please wake up." Uriel's mouth was moving, but the voice coming out wasn't his.

"Uriel?"

"It's Gilbert, sweetheart."

Gilbert? What was he doing in her dream?

Gabi's eyes popped open. "Gilbert. How did you get here so quickly?"

"You were unconscious for hours. It's after five o'clock in the afternoon."

She tried to calculate the time in her head, but everything was fuzzy, and she just wanted to go back to sleep and dream about Uriel and a sunny beach.

"Why is it so cold in here?"

"I'll ask the nurse to bring you another blanket."

As he let go of her hand and pushed to his feet, she noticed the IV line and the needle in the back of her hand. That was why it felt so cold.

When Gilbert returned, he had the nurse with him and a warm blanket, which she tucked around her.

"Thank you." Gabi felt the ache in her muscles subside.

She must have been clenching all over from the cold. What kind of crappy operation was this hospital running? Were they trying to freeze their patients to death?

"What's wrong with my sister, doctor?"

So that wasn't the nurse. It was the doctor. Why the hell didn't she wear a white coat and eliminate the guesswork? How were the patients supposed to tell the difference?

"We didn't find any evidence of bacterial or viral infection, and her CAT scans are normal, so it's not a brain tumor or stroke, and we have no idea why she's been losing consciousness. At this point, all we can do is observe her for the next twenty-four hours and hope she pulls through."

Gabi reached for Gilbert's hand. "I don't want to stay here. Please don't leave me here overnight. I might never wake up."

"Don't worry." He gave her hand a light squeeze. "I'm not going to leave your side."

"Perhaps she needs something to calm her down," the doctor said. "I'll send the nurse with a sedative."

"That won't be necessary." Gilbert used his boss voice. "Gabi gets a little anxious sometimes, and the last thing she needs is a sedative."

The doctor looked at him as if he was a bug she'd squashed with her orthopedic shoe. "As you wish."

"I wish to transfer my sister to a different hospital. Are there forms that I need to sign?"

"Are you your sister's legal guardian?"

"She's an adult. She doesn't need a guardian."

The doctor's cold smile would have petrified anyone other than Gilbert. "Then you can't sign her out. Only she can do that, and if she's unconscious, her spouse."

"Gabi is not married."

"Oh, for Pete's sake. I'm right here, and I'm conscious. Bring me the paperwork, and I'll sign it."

"Very well." The doctor looked down her nose at her and then turned to Gilbert. "You need to arrange medical transport to the hospital to which you want to transfer your sister. I can't just discharge her when she's going in and out of a coma. Once you are done making the arrangements, you can tell the nurse that you are ready to leave, and she will double-check that there is indeed a hospital bed for Gabriella in another hospital and that you've secured an ambulance to transfer her. Once that is done, Gabi can sign herself out."

"I'll get right on it." Gilbert cast Gabi a reassuring look. "I'll just step outside and make the arrangements."

"Thank you." Gabi closed her eyes and let herself relax for the first time since waking up in a hospital bed.

Gilbert was with her, and she had nothing to worry about. He would take care of her as he had always done.

Kian silenced his earpiece and turned to Onegus. "Them having trackers is bad news. Should we try to grab them and remove the trackers? We know that the third one is on the construction site, and as soon as the meeting is over, the three of them will get into a car, which we can follow with the drone and send the backup forces after."

Onegus shook his head. "We have to consider that they might have superior weapons and also that they can communicate with the patrol ship that is supposedly staffed with thousands of gods. I think we should tread very carefully with them."

Kian shifted his eyes to Turner. "What do you think?"

Turner regarded him for a long moment before answering. "I agree with Onegus. Since the three were dropped off five years ago, it would take the patrol ship about the same time to get back here, so Aru was bluffing when he implied that they could get here immediately. Our best bet is befriending these gods and getting to the bottom of what they want from us while keeping them at arm's length. I can't see how we can be of any help in their rebellion."

"We are not on the map," Onegus muttered. "We are not important. The patrol ship cruises by Earth twice in the span of seven hundred years, and the size of the crew they send down to investigate indicates that Earth is not of much interest to the king. It's almost perfunctory. That means Aru and his friends can build a base here that can fly under the radar. Earth's status as a forbidden planet provides a unique opportunity. Perhaps that's also the reason humanity was allowed to spread to such an extent. Other planets that the gods have seeded apparently get visited frequently or are even governed by the gods, and the growth of their populations and what they are allowed to do is restricted."

That was a very insightful observation, and Kian was surprised that it hadn't occurred to him before. If what Aru had told them was true, Earth was the perfect place for the rebellion headquarters, but if that was the gods' angle, he would not agree to help them. Humanity was at risk from the Eternal King just for thriving. If they were to assist the rebels in any form, Earth's annihilation was guaranteed.

On the other hand, if the clan couldn't come up with a way to make all humans immune to diseases in the next century or so, the rebels might be the only thing standing between humanity and the Eternal King.

Turner nodded. "I hadn't thought of that angle. That's a very good point." He shifted his gaze to Kian. "Perhaps you and I should attend the next meeting with them. Magnus is obviously out of his element and can't continue representing us."

"I intended to do that even before you suggested it."

Onegus shook his head. "I don't like exposing you. I should go."

The chief was a great diplomat, but Kian wanted to meet those gods in person. He would be taking a risk, but in this case, it was worth taking. Too much was at stake for him to sit on the sidelines and act like a puppeteer, telling Onegus what to say.

"If they agree to meet in the keep, we can have sufficient backup in place. I'll even take a couple of Odus with me."

Onegus uncapped his bottle and took a sip. "That would be one hell of a surprise for them. They are going to freak out."

"I don't know why," Kian said. "The gods used the Odus to fight the Kra-ell, and if the Kra-ell didn't react strongly to them, the gods shouldn't either."

Turner chuckled. "The Kra-ell who joined our village weren't subjected to seven thousand years of propaganda. If the Eternal King decided to vilify the Odus, which he obviously did, since they were decommissioned and the technology to create them was destroyed, he has made sure to reinforce that message until it became indisputable in the mind of the populace."

When Kian's phone buzzed with an incoming message, he knew who it was from even before looking at it.

"Gilbert's sister seems to be transitioning." He lifted his gaze to Onegus. "She is slipping in and out of consciousness, and they can't find what is causing it. We need to get her to the village and erase all traces of her ever being admitted to the hospital, and the tests they ran on her."

Onegus's forehead furrowed. "I'll be damned. That guy she was with was a Doomer, after all. How did I miss it?"

Turner didn't look surprised. "Evidently, the Doomers have gotten much better at creating their fake identities. From now on, we will have to investigate any suspect much more thoroughly."

"I don't think the guy is a Doomer." Kian got to his feet and walked over to the big screen where the feed from the drone's camera was broadcasting. "Is there a way to zoom in further?" He turned to Onegus. "Do you still have the passport picture of Gabi's guy?"

Onegus had reported Roni's findings to him, and Syssi had told him about the lunch she'd had with Gilbert's sister and what she'd told them about her lover.

The guy didn't sound like a Doomer.

That being said, Phinas and Rufsur were former Doomers, and yet they were as attentive and devoted to their mates as any clan immortal, so it wasn't as if all Doomers were misogynistic bastards. But it was safe to assume that most of them were.

"It's no use zooming in," William said. "The gods are still wearing their hard hats; the leader has dark sunglasses on, and the other is still wearing the construction protective glasses. Unless they lift their heads and look in the drone's direction, we can't even see the structure of their faces or the shape of their lips."

"Here is Uriel Delgado's passport picture." Onegus swiveled his laptop for Kian to see. "He's a handsome dude, but he's not a god."

Kian had to agree, but the picture could have been Photoshopped to make the guy's face less attractive but still recognizable. Besides, most people's mugshots looked terrible.

"We can fly the drone lower," Onegus said. "That will force them to look up."

"It might scare them off," Turner said. "If one of them is indeed Gabi's guy, we don't want him rushing to the hospital and bumping into our people while they are getting her out and erasing all traces of her presence there. We need to keep the gods talking until our people are out of the hospital and Gabi is in a safe location."

"Good point." Kian shifted his eyes to Onegus. "Take care of Gabriella's extraction. We missed a whole chunk of conversation, and Magnus might need our help."

"He's doing fine," William said. "I've been listening the entire time."

"Good." Kian turned to the chief again. "When choosing the extraction crew, don't include head Guardians or council members. I don't want Arwel or Bridget in the hospital. Julian is in the downtown warehouse anyway, so he can go." The young doctor was waiting for the team to be done to check them for bugs before they could return to the village. "And choose Guardians who are good with thralling and shrouding."

"Naturally." Onegus pushed to his feet. "I'll make the calls from my office."

The silence in Magnus's earpieces was starting to worry him. He wasn't sure whether the answers he'd provided to Aru's questions were approved, because Kian wasn't guiding him. While he was telling Aru about Navuh and his band of hoodlums, the war room team was probably talking about strategy, and he should give them as much time as they needed, but Aru seemed to be overly interested in the Brotherhood, and Magnus couldn't blame him.

As a god, Aru might be able to take control of the Doomer army, and if he needed soldiers for his rebellion, the Brotherhood had many more than the clan.

"You say that your strategy is to hide," Aru said. "Is that because your enemies are stronger and more numerous or because your clan prefers to avoid armed conflict?"

Damn, Magnus really needed Kian to tell him how to answer that.

When the familiar hum sounded in the earpieces, signaling that the war room crew was back online, Magnus sighed in relief. "Could you please repeat the question?" he asked the god.

Aru tilted his head. "Is it for the benefit of your boss?"

"Yes," Magnus admitted. "He went offline for a few minutes, and I'm not sure how he wants me to answer this question."

The god's lips narrowed into a tight line. "Your boss should have met us, but I understand his caution. Perhaps we should meet again with him present this time?"

"I need you to keep the conversation going," Kian said in Magnus's ear. "Drag it out as much as you can. Gabi, Gilbert's sister, is transitioning, and I suspect the guy she's been seeing is one of these gods, and he induced her transition. We need to get her out of the human hospital and bring her here, and I don't want to chance the gods showing up at the hospital in the middle of the extraction."

"What did your boss say?" Aru asked.

Magnus let out a sigh. "I'll repeat your question."

"You can tell him the truth," Kian said. "Explain in detail why the Doomers are horrible, and why aligning with them would be a colossal mistake."

It was maddening to conduct two parallel conversations, especially out in the open, where the sun was still baking their heads and the hard ground was flattening his ass. So yeah, he'd become spoiled, but right now he would pay a king's ransom for an air-conditioned room and a cup of coffee.

"The Doomers are a far superior force, and they have no problem playing dirty. They thrall and shroud indiscriminately, and human lives mean nothing to them. They have instigated countless wars, causing the death of millions."

Aru's brow furrowed. "How did they become so powerful? Were there more of them to start with than you?"

"Yes, and they are also not choosy about who produces their next generation. Our clan members are much more discriminating, and we procreate at a much slower pace."

These gods seemed not to know about Dormants and their activation, and Magnus was not about to volunteer the information, especially not in light of what Kian had told him. Aru was an intelligent guy, and he would put the puzzle pieces together just as quickly as Kian had.

The less he knew, the better.

"I can see how that's a problem." Aru smiled. "Hiding is also the resistance's way, but we are building up our foundation so one day we will become so powerful that no one will dare oppose us. The idea is to win without a fight."

Was that even possible?

Magnus wasn't sure, but a philosophical discussion about the merits and pitfalls of revolutions would be just the thing for dragging out the time.

"What starts as a need for reform, a wish to correct a wrong, often results in a much greater harm. The rebellion led by Ahn and the young gods had all the best intentions. They saw the suffering of the Kra-ell and wanted to end it. The result was a bloody war with countless casualties on both sides. Do you think it was worth it?"

"No," Aru admitted. "But doing nothing would have been wrong. Your clan did the same thing, just on a much smaller scale. You found out about the Kra-ell, welcomed a few members into your clan, and when you learned about Jade's plight, you assembled your forces and flew across the globe to free her and her people."

Magnus smiled. "But we were smart about it. We suffered no casualties and managed not to kill any innocent Kra-ell either, so it was definitely worth it. We also seized the money Igor had stolen from the tribes he'd attacked and reimbursed ourselves for the expense. It was a definite win-win for all except Igor and his cronies."

"You made a good plan and didn't rush into it, which was why you succeeded." Aru reached for the jug, uncapped it, and took a long gulp of water. "We should continue our talk tomorrow. We've been here for hours, and Negal is tired of keeping the shroud up. I'm sure you are all as tired of sitting on the hard ground and baking in the sun as I am."

"Yes, we should definitely reconvene," Magnus agreed, "but I have a couple more questions." He smiled. "I answered many of yours, so now it's your turn again."

That was true. He hadn't expected Magnus's candid answers about the clan enemies. They didn't seem like the kind of people Aru wanted to associate with, but they were a formidable force that merited a closer look. The thing that bothered him was that in the five years since his arrival, he hadn't gotten even a whiff of a rumor about immortals still roaming the planet. Human mythology was rife with gods and their shenanigans, and it also talked about the many children born half-god and half-human. The thing was, even mythology didn't claim that the descendants of those hybrids were immortal. They were supposed to be humans with a godly pedigree.

"Fine, but try to keep it short."

"I'll do my best." Magnus smiled politely. "When you first noticed what was going on with the signals and then discovered that the compound had been invaded and vacated, who did you suspect had done it?"

That was a fair question. "We considered two options. The most likely one was that some of the pods had come online before Igor found a way to build a transmitter and that those Kra-ell discovered that they had trackers and removed them, which was why we didn't pick them up. The other option was that the compound was liberated by humans, which was the more troubling scenario. I'm glad that wasn't the case."

"So, you didn't expect immortals or other gods?" Phinas asked.

"Not at all. We knew that the rebel gods were dead, and we assumed that the myths about the gods taking human lovers and having hybrid children with them were not based on reality because it was such a strong taboo in our home world. We assumed that it was the humans' way to aggrandize themselves. Did any of these mythological children of the gods really exist? Were they based on people like you?"

Magnus shrugged. "Our own mythology confirms the existence of gods, and we are proof that the stories about them taking human lovers were true, so perhaps there was a Hercules. Immortals are much stronger than humans. I'm curious, though. What happened after the king was informed that his children and all the other gods were dead?"

"That's actually funny if it wasn't so tragic. After ordering everyone to forget about these gods, the king couldn't admit that he was still checking on them. What he did instead was to say that the oracles told him about the rebel gods' demise, and he declared a day of mourning. When reporters asked him how these gods perished, he said the oracle didn't specify. It could have been a natural disaster, or perhaps the savage humans turned on them and killed them."

Jade nodded. "Sometimes that happened on the gods' remote settlements. The people would rebel against the tyrants and kill them."

Aru chuckled. "That was what everyone was told. What was more likely was that the Eternal King got rid of meddlesome gods that didn't toe the official line or were born with undesirable traits."

That got Magnus's attention, or perhaps his boss's. "I thought that the gods determined all traits with genetic manipulation?"

"Not every trait can be pre-programmed." Aru looked at Jade. "Mother Nature does not reveal all of her secrets."

"What are the undesirable traits?" she asked.

"Immunity. The Eternal King does not want gods who are immune to his compulsion to remain on Anumati. They usually get shipped off to faraway places, and many fall victim to the so-called savages."

"My sister was an immune," Negal said. "She was sent to one of those hellholes and was murdered by the locals, or so her family was told."

"Was she a soldier like you?" Morgada asked with surprising kindness in her voice.

"Goddesses are not conscripted into military service. They are sent to outposts as doctors, nurses, and scientists. It's a civil duty."

"Interesting," Magnus said. "So, everyone gets drafted on Anumati, but for different tasks. Is it only the young gods or everyone?"

"It's mostly the young children of gods who are less influential. After the rebellion, the king realized the problem was the young gods who wanted to change how things were done. His power base is the old gods, so he keeps them close while sending the young on missions of seeding and developing other civilizations."

"That's a great tactic," Phinas said. "The young are by nature more adventurous, and they probably look forward to traveling to remote locations and living in the wild, so to speak."

Aru nodded. "Very few bother to look under the thin veneer of the Eternal King's fake benevolence."

"He's evil." Jade crossed her arms over her chest. "All he cares about is preserving his power. I bet he didn't feel an ounce of remorse or real grief when he learned that his own children died in exile. He was glad to be rid of the troublemakers."

"I wonder if he views himself as evil," Magnus said. "Or whether he makes excuses for himself for why he must do those things."

Aru had a feeling that Magnus and the others were dragging the meeting out for some reason.

Were they amassing forces?

What for?

The two immortal males and two Kra-ell females could overpower two unenhanced gods, and they had no way of knowing that Aru and Negal were as strong as the Kra-ell males.

"We really should be going." He pushed to his feet and offered Magnus his hand.

Reluctantly, Magnus got up and took the hand he offered. "It was a pleasure to meet you, and I'm not just being polite. I've learned a lot today." He looked at his companions. "We all did. Thank you for sharing your knowledge with us."

"It was our pleasure as well." He pulled Magnus closer and clapped him on the back, attaching a tiny drone to the back of his shirt.

The device was smaller than a mosquito and undetectable by human technology. Even the Kra-ell hadn't been aware of the tiny things attaching themselves to their clothing and hitching a ride into the compound to preserve their limited energy.

He'd told Jade about the drones, but he had intentionally omitted supplying any details. The tiny things had very limited independent flying capability. That's why they usually attached them to the people they wanted to spy on. To infiltrate the compound, they attached it to the guards at the first tunnel entrance. The things were so small and made so little sound that even the Kra-ell hadn't noticed them.

After repeating the embrace with Phinas and only shaking hands with the ladies, Aru turned to Magnus. "When are we meeting again to continue our talk? Preferably indoors, in an air-conditioned room."

"My boss suggests a building we own in downtown Los Angeles for our next meeting."

"Perfect. Will your boss be there?"

Magnus nodded. "My boss plans to attend, provided nothing else comes up."

"What time?"

"Same time as today," Magnus said. "One-thirty in the afternoon."

Aru chuckled. "Something bigger than three gods showing up on his doorstep?"

"About that." Magnus looked in the direction of the construction project. "Will the third member of your team attend the meeting? You really have nothing to worry about. We mean you no harm as long as you don't mean us harm. We are honorable and peaceful people."

Jade put her hand over her chest. "I vow that no harm will come to you from the clan immortals or me and my people. You know that I wouldn't have given you my vow if I believed differently."

He nodded. "I know how seriously the Kra-ell take their vows, but are you sure you know what your new friends plan?"

"I do, and I vouch for them."

"I will take your word and bring the third member of our team to the meeting, provided that nothing else comes up."

Shortly after Magnus and his team left, believing they were out of Aru's earshot and talking freely, he would find out exactly what they had in mind.

"Excellent," Magnus said. "Give me your phone number, and I'll send you a pin to the precise location along with a text with instructions."

If they thought they could track him by his phone, they were mistaken. It was a burner phone, but he'd had it modified by an expert who promised it would be untraceable.

Hopefully, the guy was worth the outrageous payment he had demanded in exchange for his services.

As Magnus pulled out his phone, it looked like the same model Gabi had. It resembled a popular brand but wasn't. Aru had thought it was a cheap knockoff, but the immortals didn't seem like the kind of people who needed to save money and purchase cheap equipment. Perhaps the knockoffs were easier to modify.

"Thank you." Magnus finished inputting the information. "How far is your hotel from downtown?"

"It's right there. The location is very convenient."

"Excellent. I'll send you the pin twenty minutes before the meeting."

So, they didn't want him to know where it was ahead of time. He could understand that. Jade's vow reassured him that these people were trustworthy, but they had nothing to reassure themselves about his intentions, and although those were good, he had just done something underhanded.

That being said, Aru would be very surprised if Magnus's boss didn't do the same. He was willing to bet the drone would follow them after they left, or at least try to.

Naturally, he had a plan to ditch it.

"Until tomorrow." He waved as their guests turned to leave.

"Let's clean up here," he told Negal.

They folded the blanket, and once their guests were no longer in view, they removed their hardhats and glasses.

The sunlight was no longer as harsh, and the sky transformed into a canvas of vibrant hues as the sun began its descent.

The colors differed from the reddish hues in Anumati's sky. The symphony of shades transitioned from a warm and fiery orange to a soft, delicate pink that gradually melded into serene blues. Wisps of clouds caught fire, their edges igniting with hues of magenta and lavender and then deepening into shades of indigo and violet.

"Are you looking for the drone?" Dagor asked.

Absorbed in the beauty above them, Aru hadn't even noticed his teammate joining them. "I can't see it."

"Neither can I, but I can hear it, and it's getting closer."

"We knew that they would try to follow us." Negal put the blanket over his shoulder and handed Aru the jug.

"Yeah." Dagor took up his monitor. "They drove away. Let's hear what they are saying."

"Don't activate the spy drone yet," Aru said.

"Why? It's soundless."

"Fine." For some reason, he felt uncomfortable activating it while the immortals and the Kra-ell were still in the car. It was safer to wait until they got out, but on the other hand, the drone was utterly soundless when stationary, and since it was on Magnus's back, which was pressed against the back of the seat, it was well hidden.

"Here we go," Dagor said.

Surprisingly, no one was talking, but given the sound of the car engine, Aru knew that the audio transmission was working just fine.

Negal chuckled. "We must have stunned them into silence."

"The drone is getting closer." Dagor pulled out his disruptor and aimed it at the bird as it came into view. "Why are they flying it so low? Do they want us to know that they are following us?"

"Their boss is curious about what we look like." Aru smiled at the drone and waved.

"Are you crazy?" Dagor removed the safety from the disrupter. "That thing is filming us."

"So what? We are meeting them tomorrow in their stronghold." He put his hand on Dagor's arm and lowered it. "I'm sure that they are going to record the meeting."

"Not if I fry their equipment. We shouldn't let them have proof against us."

"That's okay." Aru patted his back. "Jade gave me her vow that we have nothing to fear from these people. She seems to trust them implicitly, and she's not someone who trusts easily. These immortals have earned her trust. They are not going to betray us, and even if they wanted to, who are they going to tell?"

"I'll be damned." Kian got up and walked over to the large screen on the wall in the back of the war room. "I was right. That's the guy." He turned to Onegus, who was watching the screen with an annoyed expression on his face.

"The passport picture was doctored," the chief said. "He didn't look half as good in it. I thought that Gabi was exaggerating, but evidently she wasn't. What do we do now?"

"Good question." Kian glanced at Turner, who just shrugged.

The guy wasn't interested in the romance part of the story and wasn't concerned with the Fates and the intricate tapestry they were weaving. To him, it was probably mumbo-jumbo, as it had been for Kian until not too long ago.

Aru and Gabi's encounter wasn't accidental. It was a sign, just as Syssi's vision was, and they pointed toward a future collaboration between the clan and these gods, but Kian couldn't risk his people's safety based on superstition.

Pulling out his phone, he dialed Julian's number. "What's your status?"

"We are in the hospital. We are wheeling the gurney out."

"Good. Get her out of there as soon as you can. The guy who induced her transition was one of the two who met with our team, and I'm sure he will head that way as soon as he leaves the canyon. Luckily, it's an hour's drive, so you have plenty of time. Just don't delay unnecessarily."

"We won't. Can I tell Gilbert?" Julian asked.

"Of course. He's going to get a kick out of that."

Julian chuckled. "I'm not so sure. He's going insane with worry, and it won't matter to him who induced Gabi, only that she's transitioning and intermittently losing consciousness."

"Make sure you don't miss any of the staff that need to be thralled. Check if there were any shift changes."

"Theo and Jay will take care of the hospital staff. I'm here to take care of Gabi."

"Naturally. Let me know when you are out of there."

"I'll call you from the van." Julian terminated the call.

Roni had already erased Gabi's record from the firm employing the paramedics who had brought her to the hospital, and he was on standby, waiting for Onegus's signal to erase her from the hospital records as well.

Julian and the two Guardians were not great thrallers or shrouders, but between the three of them, they were good enough.

"Do we lift the lockdown and bring her in?" Onegus asked. "Or do we take her to the keep?"

"I'm not ready to lift the lockdown yet." Kian walked over to the fridge and pulled out a bottle of Snake Venom. "Anyone want a beer?"

When there were no takers, he returned to his seat, removed the cap, and took a long swig from the bottle. "Syssi's vision and the so-called chance meeting between Gabi and Aru indicate that the gods are here for a reason, and it is not to harm us, but I don't like to rely on signs and visions when the safety of my people is involved. I'm just wondering whether we should tell Aru about Gabi when we see him tomorrow."

Leaning back in his chair, Onegus crossed his arms over his chest. "The gods are not supposed to procreate with humans or other created species. Aru seemed very surprised by the existence of immortals, and yet he had sex with Gabi and probably many human females before her. How does he reconcile the two?"

Turner swiveled his chair to face the chief. "Maybe the rules are different for gods who are stationed on remote outposts without female companions? Surely, they don't expect them to remain celibate."

"Maybe they do," Kian said. "Aru and his teammates are part of the resistance, so maybe they enjoy breaking the rules. Or maybe the prohibition is only on actually procreating and not the sex part."

"I'm sure the prohibition includes sex," William said. "Do you remember what Jade said about the gods and the Kra-ell? Both societies deemed mixing the two species a taboo."

"Gabi was quite taken with the guy." Kian cradled the cold bottle between his hands. "I think we should tell him. Maybe he feels as strongly about her. After all, Toven mated a Dormant and is as happy as can be with her. Maybe Gabi and Aru can also have their happily ever after."

Onegus chuckled. "I never took you for a romantic. Aru can be with Gabi for the next one hundred or so years, but then he will be picked up by the patrol ship. It's not like he can decide to end his tour of duty without consequences. If he goes AWOL, his people will come looking for him."

Kian didn't think of himself as a romantic either, but Syssi said he was, and his wife was always right. "A hundred years is a long time." He took another swig from his beer. "A lot can happen between now and then."

Gabi

An abrupt jolt pulled Gabi out of a deep sleep. Disoriented, she felt as though her bed had suddenly gone airborne. "What's going on?" she murmured, blinking her eyes open.

The surroundings seemed to suggest the interior of a van, or more accurately, an ambulance, given the array of medical equipment. She clutched the guard rails and attempted to hoist herself up. Relief washed over her at the sight of her brother's face smiling at her from the ambulance's open doors.

"Gilbert?"

"It's okay." He climbed after her into the ambulance. "We are transferring you to another clinic."

"Hi." A striking man leaned over her. "I'm Doctor Julian, and I will be taking care of you from now on."

"I'm Theo," said one of the paramedics.

"I'm Jay," said the other.

Gabi's eyes danced between their too-handsome faces. "I must have died and gone to hunk heaven," she murmured. "But since you are here," she smiled at Gilbert, "I know that I'm not dead, or at least I hope that I'm not because I don't want you to be dead."

He leaned over and kissed her cheek. "You are not dying, Gabi. It's the exact opposite."

"What do you mean?"

He hesitated for a moment. "Let's get out of here first, and I'll explain on the way. I just hope you will stay awake long enough so I can do it all in one go."

That sounded very mysterious, but she was too spaced out to try to guess what he'd meant by the opposite of dying. Usually, it implied thriving, but she was definitely not doing that. In fact, she felt miserable and longed for the respite from the aches and pains that sleep provided.

Her body knew when to knock her out to minimize her discomfort, and there was nothing wrong with that.

Gabi just wanted to know what was causing the aches and pains and disorientation, but despite Gilbert's previous comment about the opposite of dying, he wasn't looking or acting like his usual jovial self, and that worried her.

Had he learned something new while she'd been out? Perhaps they had found something, and she was dying from some little-known disease? She'd read about deadly bacteria and viruses that weren't diagnosed in time. And given how incompetent everyone in that hospital had seemed, she wouldn't be surprised if they had overlooked something.

"Did any of my test results come back while I was asleep?"

"They all came back negative."

"That's good, I think." She lifted her head once more. "Did you get my things? My phone in particular?"

"I have everything right here." Her brother lifted a large plastic bag that hopefully contained her clothes, her purse, and all its contents.

"We need to get rid of the phone," the doctor said.

"Right." Gilbert reached into the plastic bag.

Gabi pulled herself up again and glared at the guy who claimed to be a doctor. "Why would you want to get rid of my phone?" If not for Gilbert being right there, she would have panicked that someone had kidnapped her from the hospital to cut her up and sell her organs on the black market, but Gilbert would never allow that. "I need to tell Uriel that I'm no longer in the hospital and the name of the new one you are taking me to."

The doctor and Gilbert exchanged loaded looks, and then the doctor leaned toward the driver. "I made a mistake. Her phone is still here, and it's active. We need to employ Turner's evasive techniques."

"What's going on, Gilbert? Who are these people, and where are they taking me?"

"Everything is okay." He took her hand and gave it a gentle squeeze. "You know I will never let anything bad happen to you if I can prevent it, right?"

Gabi nodded even though she didn't like the caveat he'd added.

"I will explain in a little bit." He looked at the doctor, who Gabi was pretty sure wasn't a doctor at all. "Do you think he put a bug in her phone?"

"Why would he? He thought that she was just a human."

Just a human? What else could she be?

"I don't want to risk it," Gilbert said. "Maybe he suspected something and bugged her phone."

Gabi's eyes were closing again, and she felt herself slipping away, but she had to know what was going on.

"Who is he?" she murmured. "Who are you talking about?"

"Get some rest, sweetheart." Gilbert lifted their conjoined hands and kissed her knuckles.

"Promise me that you won't get rid of my phone, or at least write down Uriel's phone number so I can call him from another phone."

"I promise."

It was so difficult to hang on, but she had to make sure her wishes were obeyed. "Swear it on our parents' souls."

"I swear," Gilbert said.

Letting out a breath, Gabi closed her eyes and let herself drift away.

"She is out again." Gilbert stroked his sister's hair like he had done so many times when she was a kid.

"Gabi is doing well," Julian reassured him. "The fact that she's waking up quite often is an excellent sign. All the Dormants who exhibited this pattern transitioned easily."

"That's reassuring," Gilbert said while continuing to stroke Gabi's soft hair. "What do we do about her phone?"

"Maybe we can use it to set up a trap?" Jay asked.

Gilbert arched a brow. "For the god? What for?"

"I don't know." The doctor shrugged. "Maybe Kian wants to catch them. I wasn't in the war room, so I don't know what the status is."

"Weren't you in the warehouse? Waiting for the team to put them through your detecting machines?"

"I was, but I wasn't getting live updates."

Julian pulled out his phone and placed a call. "We have her."

"Good," Kian's gruff voice sounded loud and clear as Julian activated the speaker. "Did you get everyone who had any contact with Gabi?"

"We did," Theo said from the front of the van. "One obstinate doctor took more work than the others, but I got her memories of Gabi shoved deep. For some reason, she really didn't like Gabriella."

Julian shook his head. "Doctors shouldn't let their personal preferences affect their attitudes towards patients."

Gilbert chuckled. "Gabi was very vocal about how she didn't like the way they were treating her in that hospital, and knowing my sister, she voiced that opinion to everyone who cared or didn't care to listen. I can't really blame that poor overworked doctor who had probably been on her feet for the past twelve hours."

"Is the meeting over?" Julian asked Kian.

"It is. Our team drove away first, and the gods followed several minutes later. We were lucky that they chose Simi Valley for the meeting. It will take them about an hour to get to the hospital, and by then, all traces of Gabi will be gone. Roni is hacking her hospitalization records as we speak."

"Did you decide where we should take her?" Julian asked. "I vote for the village, but then the team will have to wait for me to get back to take care of the scanning. If we take her to the old clinic at the keep, I can make it in time to the warehouse, but I will have to leave Gabi with no medical supervision. Gilbert and the Guardians can watch her while I'm gone, but it's not ideal."

"Nothing is ever ideal," Kian said. "Take her to the keep. We are meeting Aru and his friends at the penthouse tomorrow, and I thought that Gilbert might want to meet his future brother-in-law."

Gilbert nearly choked on his own tongue. "Are you serious? You will let me meet the new gods?"

"I'm only semi-serious. I wonder how he will react to the news that the human woman he's been seeing is a Dormant transitioning into immortality. We've learned today that the gods consider procreation with all other species a taboo—not just with the Kra-ell. It's beneath them. They also have no idea about Dormants or how immortals create other immortals."

Gilbert's baby fangs started itching despite his venom glands being inactive. "So, it's okay for them to have sex with what they consider lesser species, but just not to make children with them?"

"That's how it would appear," Kian said. "Throughout history humans weren't much better, and they were discriminating based on nonsensical differences like social status or skin color."

"Let us make men in our image, after our likeness, and let them have dominion over the fish of the sea, and over the fowl of the air, and over the cattle, and over all the earth, and over every creeping thing that creepeth upon the earth," Julian quoted. "I guess that likeness is in all things, for better and for worse."

Gilbert rolled his eyes. "Never mind that. I don't care about meeting the damn god. What I care about is getting my sister the best medical care, and that's not going to happen in the damn keep. I want her in the village, where Bridget and the nurses can watch her twenty-four-seven. If Fates forbid something happens to Gabi while Julian is gone, I wouldn't know what to do, and neither would the Guardians."

"We have basic emergency medical training," Jay said.

"And the warehouse is less than ten minutes away," Julian added. "I can be back right away."

Gilbert looked at the young doctor. "If we bring Gabi to the keep, all of us will have to stay in the keep until the village is no longer in lockdown. Are you okay with being away from your mate for several days or a week? Because I'm not."

Julian's mood soured. "Right. I didn't think of that. Can you let Ella out? And maybe one of the nurses?"

"Let's see how tomorrow goes," Kian said. "You can survive one night without your mates." He ended the call.

Gilbert sighed. "I'd better call Karen. She won't be happy about having no help with the kids."

"I can ask Ella to lend her a hand," Julian offered. "She studies and works online, but she can spare a couple of hours, and she loves kids." He grimaced. "Other people's kids. She's not ready to have some of her own yet."

"Are we going back to the hotel?" Gabi mumbled with her eyes closed.

"No, we are not." Gilbert cupped her cheek. "Do you need anything from there?"

"All my things are there. You need to get them."

"I can go later and collect them." He lifted his gaze to Julian. "But it will have to wait until the doctor returns, and I know you are in good hands. I won't leave you before then."

"Good." She gave him a faint smile. "I'm so glad that you came."

"Of course." He leaned over and kissed her forehead. "I would move mountains and fight dragons to get to my baby sister."

Her smile widened. "How big?"

It was a game he'd played with her when she was little. He would say he would fight dragons for her, but only if they were really small.

"This big." He spread his arms wide.

Gabi's eyes twinkled, a hint of the playfulness they used to share as children lighting up her pale face. "That's a pretty big dragon," she teased.

Julian watched their interaction with a fond smile. "It's nice to see a brother and sister as close as you are."

Gilbert's expression sobered. "For a long while, all we had was each other."

Gabi's hand found Gilbert's. "Tell me more stories," she whispered. "Like the ones you used to tell me when I couldn't sleep."

He chuckled, brushing a stray strand of hair behind her ear. "Alright, do you remember the one about the mischievous fairy who stole the moon's light?"

She nestled deeper into the pillow and closed her eyes. "I love that one."

"I still don't trust them," Jade said. "Gods are master manipulators."

Magnus cast her a warning look.

Kian had instructed them not to say anything they thought that the gods shouldn't know until Julian put them through the scanner and they changed clothing. The third god could have attached a tracking device to their car, and Aru and Negal could have attached miniature listening devices to their clothing or their hair when they all shook hands.

The instructions they had gotten were to discuss what they had learned from the gods and not say anything negative about them or anything that could betray things Kian didn't want the gods to know, Gabriella's transition being one of them. Kian suspected that one of the gods was responsible for inducing her, and he didn't want them to learn about it just yet.

Jade winked at him and continued. "Aru was full of smiles, and he said all the right things, but he kept the hardhat and dark sunglasses on. I don't like talking to people whose eyes I cannot see. Besides, I gave him my vow, and he didn't give me one in return."

"Gods don't take their vows as seriously," Phinas said. "Aru knew that it wouldn't affect your judgment of him."

"He was sincere," Morgada said. "But he was hiding things even from Negal."

Magnus put a finger on his lips, reminding her that she shouldn't be saying things like that.

"He's the team leader," he said out loud. "In most organizations, the leader knows more than the others."

Given Jade's frown, she wasn't happy with his explanation. She turned to Morgada. "What makes you say that? I've known you for a very long time, and you were never any more intuitive than others."

Morgada shrugged. "When you were engaged in the conversation, I was observing, and Negal wasn't very guarded with his expressions. He seemed like a simple guy, for a god, that is, and he often looked surprised when Aru spoke. So, it might have been because Aru wasn't supposed to reveal those things to us or that they were news to Negal as well. I might be wrong, though. It was just my impression."

"Hello, team." Kian's voice sounded in Magnus's ear, and given the startled expressions on the others' faces, he was speaking to them as well.

He must have heard the exchange and was about to reprimand them for not following his instructions to the letter.

"I don't want you to react verbally to what I'm about to tell you," Kian said. "We know now that Aru was the guy Gabi has been seeing. After you left, we flew the drone low enough for the gods to lift their heads and look at it, and the resemblance to the guy Gabi was seeing was unmistakable. He called himself Uriel Delgado and had an excellent fake identity that was based on a real person. Roni tells me that sometimes American citizens living abroad sell their identity to foreigners so they can enter the United States. He thinks that's what the real Uriel Delgado did, and Aru bought the identity through a broker dealing in those things."

"Okay," Jade said. "What does it have to do with us?"

"I'm just giving you an update. Julian has brought Gabi to the keep, and he's going to meet you in the warehouse as scheduled. As for the gods, they used the same technique as we usually employ to ditch the drone. They got into the parking lot of a mall, and they either switched cars or went shopping. My bet is on the first option."

"So is mine," Phinas said. "I have a question. Given the news, is it wise to have a meeting in the penthouse?"

The four of them were going to spend the night in the other penthouse, which used to belong to Amanda, and Magnus thought that it was very convenient. He would have preferred to spend the night at home with Vivian, but this wouldn't be the first time they had been separated, nor would it be the last. He was a Guardian, and although Onegus tried to make accommodations for the mated Guardians, it wasn't always possible.

"It's fine," Kian said. "The entrance to the underground facility is well hidden, and they won't have time to snoop around because we will give them the address only twenty minutes before the meeting. When they get to the building, someone will be waiting for them to escort them straight to the penthouse. "

Magnus wanted to ask whether Kian still planned to attend the meeting, but the question would have to wait for after they'd changed clothing and gone through the scanner.

"Thanks for the update, boss," he said.

As soon as Negal pulled up to the hospital, Aru threw the vehicle door open and rushed in through the sliding doors.

Where to go from here?

He stopped the first person he passed. "How can I find a patient who was admitted to the hospital today?"

The woman smiled. "Labor and delivery is on the third floor. Is this your first?"

He frowned. "Is it obvious that this is my first time in a hospital?"

"I meant, is this your first child?"

Finally, her previous words about labor and delivery registered. "Oh, no, I'm not having a baby. I mean, my girlfriend is not having a baby. She fainted earlier today and was brought here."

"Aha." The woman nodded. "Check the ER. You can't get in, but you can ask the nurse at the admissions window. It's down the hall where it says Emergency Room."

"Thank you." He dipped his head. "Have a wonderful day." He dashed in the direction she'd pointed.

"Such a charming and polite young man," he heard the woman murmur. "If only I was thirty years younger."

Aru couldn't help but smile. He was a young god, but he was at least that woman's age, if not older. She looked to be in her mid-fifties, and he was sixty-eight years old, not counting the years he'd spent in stasis en route to this sector.

There was a line in front of the window of the Emergency Room, which was strange since emergency implied urgency, and yet no one seemed in a rush to assist the people standing in line.

When he finally got to the window, he leaned to look at the nurse and used a slight thrall just to make her more cooperative. "I'm looking for Gabriella Emerson. She was admitted earlier today. She fainted on the street."

The nurse pursed her lips. "I don't remember anyone by that name." She typed on her keyboard and frowned at her screen. "How does she spell her name? Is it with one L or two? An E or an A at the end?"

"I'm not sure." He pulled out his phone and checked Gabi's contact. "It's with two Ls and an A at the end."

"We don't have anyone by that name. In fact, we don't have anyone with the last name Emerson. Are you sure she was brought into this hospital?"

"She texted me the name." He turned the phone so the woman could see Gabi's text. "City Medical Center."

"Maybe she meant City Clinic. People often confuse the two. City Clinic is only ten minutes away. You should check there."

"Can you call them and ask whether they have her?"

The nurse tilted her head and looked behind him. "I wish I could help, but there are people in line who need help."

Aru looked over his shoulder and winced. The guy behind him was cradling an arm that looked broken, and the woman in the wheelchair behind the guy looked like she was about to throw up.

"Yeah. You're right. I can call them myself."

When he got back to the car, Negal asked, "Well? Did you find her?"

"She's not here." Aru closed the passenger door and turned to Dagor. "I need to call other hospitals in the area. Can you find the numbers for me?"

The guy didn't look happy to do it, but he did it anyway, and then it was time to make the calls.

They divided the seven possible hospitals and clinics between them. Fifteen minutes later, they had exhausted the list without finding Gabi in any of them.

"I don't understand it." Aru raked the fingers of both hands through his hair. "Where can she be?"

"Maybe she used a different name," Negal said. "She might have given you a fake name like you gave her. Did you see her driver's license or her passport?"

"Why would she do that? She doesn't have to hide who she is."

"She could be married," Dagor said. "Humans are very possessive of their mates, and she didn't want her husband to find out."

Letting out a frustrated groan, Aru lifted a hand to stop them from suggesting any more absurd ideas. "You are not helping. What's going on with our new friends? Did they reach their destination?"

"They are still driving, but you'll be glad to know that they are close by. They also talked about us. Jade doesn't trust you, and Morgada thinks you are hiding things from us."

Morgada wasn't wrong. Aru was hiding things from his teammates, but he didn't have a choice, and it was better for them not to know. Humans called it plausible deniability, and it was a very apt term.

"They have no reason to trust us." He shifted in his seat. "What radius did you specify when searching for hospitals and clinics?"

"Five miles. Do you want me to expand the perimeter?"

"Yes, please. In the meantime, let's go to her hotel. Perhaps she was discharged and is back in her room."

"Did you try calling her?" Negal asked.

Aru nodded. "She's not answering. Calls go straight to voicemail, and texts don't get delivered. I suspect that her phone has run out of charge."

She'd texted him from the hospital, so he knew she had it with her, but he didn't know whether it had just run out of charge or something was very wrong with Gabi.

Magnus

When the team got to the warehouse, Julian wasn't there yet, but there was plenty to do before the doctor ran them through the more advanced scanners after they changed clothing to make sure that nothing was attached to their skin and hair.

Regrettably, there was no shower, so they would have to put clean clothes on their sweaty bodies.

The first step, though, was running the handheld bug detector over each of them, and Magnus performed the scan as soon as they entered.

"You are all clear." He handed the bug detector to Phinas. "Can you check me?"

"Sure." The guy did a thorough job of it, scanning every inch of Magnus's clothing, but the device hadn't beeped even once.

“You’re clear as well, but we won’t know for sure until Julian performs his body scans, and maybe not even then.”

"Morgada and I will change over there." Jade pointed to the large scanner. "So don't look that way."

Magnus lifted the duffle bag with his change of clothes and slung the strap over his shoulder. "Don't forget to brush your hair, rub disinfectant on your skin, and then moisturize everywhere your skin was exposed."

Later, when they got to the keep, Magnus planned on taking a long shower, scrubbing his skin, and changing his clothing again. He would advise the others to do the same.

"I remember Julian's instructions." Jade took her own duffle bag and followed Morgada behind the scanner.

The problem was that all of their precautions were based on known technology, but the gods possessed technology that was far superior to anything humans and immortals had. They could have bugs made from materials that were undetectable by the scanner and so small that Julian couldn't see them on the screen even if detected. Heck, they could have created biological bugs that were indistinguishable from real flies or even mosquitos.

After all, they were genetic experts.

William had said that they might have spy nanos that transferred through contact and advised them not to shake hands with the gods, but when Aru offered

Magnus his hand, he knew that refusing to shake it would undermine the negotiations.

Jade's vow had done a lot to make the gods trust them, but it wasn't enough.

The truth was that the meeting had left him unnerved despite Aru being perfectly polite and seemingly mellow. The gods' might was terrifying, and the prospect of the Eternal King turning his attention to Earth was enough to induce a panic attack even in a hardened Guardian like Magnus.

Perhaps having a family had softened him, but Magnus couldn't remember ever feeling as out of sorts as he felt now.

"Here." Phinas dropped an empty cardboard box at his feet. "You can put your old clothing in here." He had a similar box for his belongings.

"Thank you."

Removing his Kevlar vest, Magnus folded it in two and put it inside the box. Next went his shirt, then his pants, socks, and shoes. There was no need to change underwear since the gods couldn't have touched it.

He brushed his hair thoroughly, put an oily moisturizer over the parts of his skin that had been exposed, including his face, and then got dressed in fresh clothing.

"I feel like a new man." He looked at Phinas, who was pushing his feet into a new pair of short leather boots. "Nice soles. What brand are they?"

"Blundstone. They are from Australia." He glanced in the direction of the scanner. "Jade and I got matching pairs."

Magnus's lips twitched with a smile.

It was such a couples' thing to do, and to think that only a short time ago, Jade had not believed in monogamous relationships.

As the warehouse door opened and Julian walked in with Jay, Magnus asked, "How is Gilbert's sister doing?"

"Given the circumstances, she's doing very well. I've left her in the keep clinic with Theo and her brother. He is freaking out, but I told him that I can be back there in less than ten minutes and that nothing can happen to her in such a short time."

Magnus arched a brow. "Is that true? Or did you just say that to reassure him?"

"It's mostly true." Julian smiled at Jade and Morgada, as they emerged from behind the scanner. "Who would have thought that one of those naughty gods would induce Gilbert's sister? I still don't know whether it's a good thing or bad."

"Good for her," Jade said. "She saved herself a lot of trouble looking for an immortal to induce her, and her transition will probably go smoother. Other than that, I doubt it's a good thing. She might be enamored with him, but he will think of her as nothing more than a temporary plaything. By and large, his people do not mingle with what they consider lesser beings."

"I don't like that term," Julian said. "It's derogatory."

Jade shrugged. "It's true, though. They are superior, and they are the creators."

"But they are not more intelligent," Julian said. "That's why I don't feel superior to humans even though physically I am. There are so many people who are smarter than me and knowing that keeps me humble." He pushed his shoulder-length hair behind his ear. "Frankly, it surprises me that the gods didn't breed for intelligence. With their genetic manipulation ability, they could have easily done that."

"Maybe they didn't want to," Jade said. "And by 'they' I mean the Eternal King. He wouldn't have wanted young gods to be born who could be smarter than him." She braided the ends of her long hair. "That would also explain why compulsion ability is so rare among the gods. The king doesn't want competition."

Julian nodded. "That's a good observation and one more question to ask the gods tomorrow, but I shouldn't waste time talking and delay my return to the keep. Let's get the scanning over so we can get out of here. Who wants to go first?"

"I do." Jade toed off her boots, which were indeed identical to Phinas's. "I want to be done with it. I can't put my weapons back on before I go through the scanner, and I feel naked without them."

The good news was that Gabi's things were still in her hotel room, and she hadn't checked out, but that was the only good news.

Aru and his teammates had called every hospital and clinic in downtown Los Angeles and its periphery, and none had any record of her ever being there.

It just didn't make sense.

Had Gabi invented the whole hospital thing to get his attention?

She had some dramatic tendencies, but she was mostly reasonable, and she wouldn't have scared him like that for nothing. Besides, where could she be if she wasn't in her room?

The receptionist downstairs hadn't seen her coming in since she'd left earlier.

Could she have been kidnapped?

Perhaps her brothers had finally returned from their business meeting, and she was spending time with them?

But then she would have called him or sent him a message.

Unless her phone was out of charge, and she hadn't noticed.

With a sigh, Aru lifted one of the pillows and buried his nose in it. Gabi's scent still lingered on the fabric, providing a momentary relief from the aching void in his chest.

He was so worried about her.

Yeah, it was worry, nothing else.

He couldn't have feelings for the feisty human with intelligent eyes and pouty lips. The gods' taboo on relationships with created species was obviously bogus and needed to go, but a relationship between them was still impossible because of the long-term mission he had undertaken. He couldn't get attached to anyone.

Except, a small voice in the back of his head whispered that he was about to spend more than one hundred years on Earth, and Gabi wouldn't even live that long.

Damn, why did it hurt so badly to think of her inevitable mortality?

Shaking himself off, Aru dropped the pillow and left the room.

Down on the street, he opened the car's passenger door and got in. "She wasn't there, but her things were. I don't know what to think."

Dagor wasn't paying him any attention. Instead, he was looking at his laptop screen and smiling like he knew something that Aru didn't.

Nudging his arm, Aru got his attention. "What's going on?"

"They are onto us," Dagor said. "They didn't go back home as we thought they would. They stopped by a warehouse, changed clothing, and are about to enter a scanner. Jade is going first, and as soon as the machine starts making a noise, I'll fly our little spy out of the box."

So that's why there were no visuals, and since Dagor had his earbuds on, there was no sound either.

"What is the drone doing in the box?" Aru asked.

"I told you they are onto us. They took off the clothes they were wearing and put them in boxes. Thankfully, Magnus didn't close the box, or that would have been the end of our little spy."

"Take the earbuds off so I can hear what's going on."

"Yes, sir." Dagor plucked the devices from his ears and put them in their little container. "Here we go," he said as the scanner was turned on. "Fly little birdie, fly."

As the device flew out of the box, the warehouse came into view, and Dagor directed it toward a wall where it had a good view of the scanner and the people standing around it.

As Magnus lifted his head and looked in the direction of the drone, the three of them held their breath, but he must have assumed it was a mosquito and turned back to the scanner.

Aru let out a relieved breath. "This thing works better in open spaces."

Dagor nodded as he directed the drone to attach to the wall. "Landing was successful."

"Indeed." Aru clapped him on the back. "Good job."

On the screen, Phinas shook his head. "I still can't wrap my head around Gilbert's sister hooking up with Aru."

The words hit Aru in the chest like a ballistic rocket.

He had hooked up with only one female recently, and she had a brother named Gilbert. How the hell had these people found out about Gabi, and how were they connected to her brother?

"The Fates' fingerprints are all over this." Magnus crossed his arms over his chest. "What are the chances of a random encounter between Gilbert's sister, who doesn't even live here, and one of the gods? And what the hell was she thinking about, having unprotected sex with a stranger?"

Morgada frowned. "Why do you think she did that?"

"Maybe she wanted to get pregnant," Phinas said. "She's nearing forty, and childless human females start getting desperate at that age. Aru is an exceptionally good-looking, smart guy. If I were a human female looking for a daddy for my kid, I would have chosen him too."

Chuckling, Morgada slapped Phinas's arm. "I wasn't referring to why she didn't use protection. The question was how do you know that she didn't?"

"Condoms would have prevented her entering transition," Magnus said. "To induce an adult female Dormant, both a venom bite and insemination are required."

What were they talking about?

What did they mean by dormant and inducing an adult female?

Inducing to do what?

"Oh, I see." Morgada pursed her lips. "I didn't know that. I thought that an immortal male's venom bite was enough to induce a Dormant into immortality."

"What would be the fun in that?" Phinas nudged her with his elbow. "The Fates are interested in love matches, and according to the immortals' beliefs, they are three mischievous female spirits. They want to ensure that their pawns have fun while fulfilling their objectives."

"They belong in your tradition as well," Magnus said. "The fact that Doomers weren't taught anything about the Fates doesn't mean they don't govern your life. After all, do you really think you and Jade met by chance?"

"It was by chance," Phinas insisted. "Kalugal could have chosen Rufsur for the mission. I just happened to be in the right place at the right time, and Jade and I are kindred spirits."

Magnus regarded him with an amused expression. "If that's what you want to believe, it's your choice, but I don't think that you truly believe the Fates had nothing to do with it."

Phinas smiled slyly. "I didn't say that. Who am I to doubt the all-powerful Fates?"

"I don't understand," Aru murmured. "If Phinas is a Doomer, what is he doing with his enemies? And how did they find out about Gabi and me?"

Negal shook his head. "I told you that you shouldn't get involved with her. I had a feeling that nothing good would come out of it."

Nothing good?

How could what he and Gabi had together be described as nothing good?

It had been the best experience Aru ever had, and he couldn't tolerate the thought of anything bad happening to Gabi.

But what was happening to her was good.

She was turning immortal.

As Gabi's mind stirred into wakefulness, groggily pulling her out of a deep sleep, she blinked, struggling to focus in the unfamiliar room. The soft beeping of machines buzzed in her ears, indicating that she was in a medical facility, but none she recognized.

She took in her surroundings.

The room wasn't big, with walls that were painted off-white and dim lighting that was soft and calm. Machines with green and blue displays were scattered in the periphery of her gaze, with tubes and wires connecting her to them.

Her body felt heavy, and as she tried to lift her hand, she realized she was connected to an IV bag hanging above her. Confusion crept in, mixing with her grogginess.

Where was she?

Why was she there?

Turning her head slightly, she tried to see more of the room. Cabinets lined the walls, and there was a desk with a computer on it. The screen displayed data that didn't make much sense to her. Everything was so quiet, almost eerie, making the sound of her breathing seem loud in comparison.

Her fingers twitched as she attempted to reach for the call button on the side of the bed. It was harder than she expected, as if her body was moving through thick fog. She sighed in frustration. She knew she needed to figure out what was happening, but her memories were like puzzle pieces that just wouldn't fit together.

Closing her eyes briefly, she took a breath and tried to gather her thoughts. The beeping of the machines kept up a steady rhythm, distracting her and preventing her scattered thoughts from coalescing.

Had she been drugged?

She sure felt like it. Perhaps she should pull out the IV?

But what if she was sick and the bag contained necessary medication?

Taking a steadying breath, Gabi willed herself to grasp the fragments of her memory and recall how she had arrived here. But the events leading up to this moment remained elusive, a collage of pictures that didn't make sense. She remembered getting out of the hotel, then she remembered the face of a rude nurse, or was it a doctor?

Wait a moment. Gilbert was there. Had she dreamt him up?

As a door she hadn't noticed before opened, and her brother stepped in, the relief washing over her would have made her feel faint if she wasn't already feeling like passing out.

"Gilbert," she murmured.

He rushed to her side. "I'm here, sweetheart." He took her hand and clasped it between his large ones. "How are you feeling?"

"Terrible. I can't remember anything. How did I get here? What's wrong with me? Am I being drugged? What's in the IV bag?"

Chuckling, Gilbert bent over her and kissed her forehead. "You might be thirty-eight, but you haven't changed a bit. You still ask a million questions without waiting for an answer." Holding on to her hand with one of his, he climbed on the bed and sat next to her. "Do you remember fainting?"

"No. But I remember feeling sick and going to the drugstore. I don't remember getting there, though."

"That's because you never got there. You fainted on your way to the store. Someone called the paramedics, and they took you to a hospital. You called me, and I came as soon as I could. I got you out of there and brought you to the clan's clinic."

The clan.

Something about that sounded familiar, but her thoughts were still jumbled.

Lifting her hand, Gabi rubbed her temple. "Something is really wrong with me, Gilbert. My mind feels like it's stuffed with cotton candy. I feel like I should remember things, like they are on the edge of my conscious mind, but I can't bring them to the forefront. Tell me the truth. Do I have a brain tumor? Am I going to die?"

He frowned. "There is nothing physically wrong with you, Gabi. Orion's compulsion must have jumbled up your mind. Remembering things one moment and forgetting them the next, and then going through that cycle over and over again, while at the same time entering transition, must have been too much." He pulled out his phone. "I'm not a doctor, but that's just common sense. I'm calling Orion."

Who was Orion?

The name sounded familiar, but it was like everything else she was trying to remember. The end of the thread appeared to be within reach, but when she tried to grasp it, it slipped farther away, and she was getting a headache.

With a sigh, she closed her eyes and let her mind wander aimlessly. The headache subsided, and Uriel's handsome face appeared behind her closed lids. "Did anyone tell Uriel where I am?" she murmured. "He's going to be so worried about me."

Gilbert just patted her hand.

"Orion, this is Gilbert. I'm with Gabi, and she's transitioning."

That word again.

Transition.

It should mean something to her, but what?

Aru

Gabi was transitioning into immortality.

That was what had been wrong with her.

Was it dangerous?

"Your turn." Jade tapped Morgada on the shoulder. "We need to hurry up so Julian can return to Gilbert's sister. She needs to be supervised by a doctor."

Aru's blood chilled in his veins. If she needed medical supervision, the transition into immortality was dangerous.

"Getting induced by a god is a definite plus," Magnus said. "But I expect many immortal bachelors will be disappointed about not being given a chance with her."

"It's for the best." Jade waved a dismissive hand. "The competition would have been stiff, and the males would have gotten too aggressive."

"Immortals are not like the Kra-ell," Magnus said in an indignant tone. "We don't fight each other to impress females."

"Maybe not physically, but even humor can be a form of aggression." Jade cast Phinas a fond look. "Males compete by amusing females, and I, for one, am more impressed by that than physical prowess."

"Oh really?" Phinas pulled her into his arms. "So, me saving Kagra had nothing to do with it? I thought you were pretty impressed with my leap."

"I was." She pushed on his chest. "But your wit and your humor impressed me more."

As the group kept talking and the doctor ran everyone through the scanner, Aru tried to decipher what he'd heard so far.

Phinas was a former enemy of the clan, and as Aru had suspected, he and Jade were a couple. These immortals had formed the utopian community he and others like him were hoping to one day have on Anumati, and he couldn't wait to meet their leader, who had made this dream a reality, albeit on a small scale.

Right now, though, he needed to find a way to get to Gabi. They kept mentioning the keep as the place she'd been taken to, and the doctor was going to her.

They needed to attach the drone to Doctor Julian and have him lead them to Gabi.

Aru tapped Dagor's arm. "I need you to attach the drone to the doctor."

Dagor nodded. "I can do that, but what do you want to do? Force yourself into their stronghold? That wouldn't be helpful in finding out more about them and getting them to cooperate with us if we deem them worthy. I still don't think a bunch of immortals and Kra-ell would be helpful to us."

"I think they would. But I have to see her." He rubbed his hand over his chest. "It's like there is a void inside of me that only she can fill."

In the backseat, Negal sighed. "The young are so impetuous. Think about it, Aru. You don't know what transition into immortality entails, you don't know how to help her, and all you are going to achieve by barging in there is to reveal that we were spying on them."

"They were also trying to spy on us, but we outsmarted them. It's part of the game, and we won. They will understand that." He turned to face the front of the car. "If Gabi is transitioning into immortality, she will no longer be a human, and I can have a life with her."

"Really?" Negal scoffed. "You are a soldier. In a hundred years or so, you will have to return to the patrol ship and then back home. If you disappear, we will pay the price, and if we all disappear, our families will pay it."

For Aru, it was worse than that. He had an obligation to return that had nothing to do with his draft. "I don't intend to let you get punished because I want to stay behind. I have to return the same way you do. But in the meantime, I can enjoy Gabi's company. A hundred years is a blink of an eye for a god, and it won't be enough, but I can't turn my back on her." He shook his head. "I just can't."

Dagor sighed. "Maybe we can use it to our advantage. If these immortals know how strong the bond is between love mates, they will know that they can trust you will never do anything to endanger Gabi or those she cares for or her family."

Negal snorted. "He doesn't have a love bond with her. She was just a human while they were together, and gods cannot form bonds with lesser creations. I doubt a bond can form between a god and an immortal either, but at least there is a small chance of that."

Aru turned to look at his teammate. "You know that most of what we were taught about the horrible consequences of procreating with the created species was propaganda, right? These immortals are far from monstrosities. Jade bonded with an immortal and seems happier than I thought she was capable of. Also, a Kra-ell and god union did not create abominations. We know about the royal twins."

"We don't know that for sure," Negal said. "We suspect that."

"The twins are why we are here. Do you really think that the Eternal King would have bothered patrolling this planet to find out the fate of the Kra-ell queen's children?

His interest alone indicates that he knows that they are his grandchildren."

Negal swallowed. "It's blasphemy to suggest that, but by now, everyone knows that the king's heir and the Kra-ell heir had a dalliance. They just don't know that the twins were the result."

"It was more than a dalliance." Aru sighed. "They were in love, and they dreamt of a better future for both of their people, but their dream turned into a nightmare."

Gabi's consciousness fluttered drowsily, slowly emerging from the warm cocoon of pleasant dreams.

As her senses gradually came online, the soft, steady beeping of medical equipment reminded her that she was in a hospital room or a clinic, and she even remembered that Gilbert had brought her there for some reason.

Oh, yeah, she'd called him and asked him to get her out of that horrible hospital.

But where was she now?

Had he answered her questions, and she'd forgotten already?

Lifting her eyelids with effort, she was greeted with the view of Gilbert's broad back. He was holding a phone to his ear and speaking with someone.

"Gilbert?" she murmured.

He turned around. "Oh, good. You're awake. I thought I would have to call Orion again. Let me transfer the call to video."

Panicking, she lifted her hand. "Don't. I probably look like roadkill. I don't want anyone to see me like this."

Gilbert smiled. "You look lovely even when you are disheveled. Besides, you are transitioning, and no one expects you to look your best."

There it was again, that word.

"You keep saying that I'm transitioning. What does that mean?"

"Talk to Orion. Hopefully, things will make more sense after he does his thing." Gilbert unceremoniously turned the phone around.

The face on the small screen was strikingly handsome and familiar. "Hello, Gabi. I'm sorry about the mess my compulsion created in your head. In hindsight, it wasn't a good idea."

"I know you. You were at the dinner in the hotel."

"That's right. You were told things that needed to be kept a secret, but since you were seeing a guy who we suspected of possessing a certain ability, we couldn't let you remember what you were told when you had company. That was what created the confusion and eventually made you forget everything, even when there were no strangers around. I will remove the compulsion now, and hopefully, that will clear the confusion."

At the edges of her consciousness, Gabi knew what he was talking about, but the information was like a slippery noodle that refused to stay on her mental fork.

"How are you going to do that?"

"Simple. Look into my eyes and focus on the sound of my voice. You will remember everything you've learned about immortals, and you can speak freely about them with anyone. You are not restricted in any way."

For a brief moment, her head felt like it was going to explode. But then the sensation subsided, and she could feel things organizing themselves in her mind, until the pressure lifted, and she felt a refreshing lightness combined with clarity.

"Immortality. That's what I'm transitioning into. But how? I didn't have sex with an immortal, did I? Or did you make me forget that as well, and the memory just didn't come back yet?"

Orion chuckled. "I'll let Gilbert explain. This is one hell of an incredible story. I wish you the best of luck with your transition."

"Thank you." She rubbed her aching temples.

"I'll see you in the village soon," Orion said. "Or so I hope. Goodbye, Gabi."

"Goodbye, and thank you again."

Gilbert ended the call, put the phone on the table beside her hospital bed, and took a deep breath. "There is no easy way to do this. Your lover boy is not a human, after all. He's a god, and he induced your transition. What I want to know is, what the hell were you thinking having unprotected sex with a guy you'd only just met?"

She arched a brow. "Are you serious? That's what bothers you about this situation? And what do you mean by a god? Do you mean immortal, a descendant of the gods?"

"You were induced by a god. Not an immortal, not a demigod, but a pureblooded god." He surprised her with a grin. "And so was I. You don't have exclusive bragging rights."

"Wait a moment." She lifted a hand. "You said that all the gods were dead, and only their immortal descendants remained."

He arched both brows in mock innocence. "I didn't say that all the gods were dead."

Gabi tried to remember what exactly she'd been told, but evidently her memory was still a little fuzzy. Not that it was surprising, given what she was going through.

"I don't remember what you and the others said, but it was implied that there were no gods left on Earth and that only their immortal descendants remained."

He sighed. "The gods living in the village are our most guarded secret, even more so than the existence of immortals. It's like the Holy of Holies of secrets. They were supposed to be the only ones, but then Aru and his friends showed up, getting our attention by activating trackers that we knew were of godly origins."

"How did you know that they were of godly origins?"

"The history of those trackers is a long story for another day. When we identified the signals, we panicked, and the village went into lockdown. Do you remember that?"

She nodded. "It got so confusing. When I was alone, I remembered what you told me about a clan's location that got compromised and that the lockdown was a security measure. Was all of that because of Uriel?"

Gilbert nodded. "His real name is Aru, and he's not from Portugal. It's just a fake identity he bought. Anyway, a team of our people met with him today, and it seems like his intentions are not hostile, but further talks are needed to ascertain that. He and his friends are very dangerous."

"Why?"

"Because gods to immortals are like immortals to humans. We are powerless against them. They can get into our minds and thrall us, and some of them can even compel us. Also, they come from a planet of gods who don't hold humans in the highest regard. I don't know all the details of what Aru told the team, but it seems like he is on our side."

"Good." Gabi rubbed her temple. "I think. Will I be able to see him again?"

"It depends on how the talks are going. If Kian is convinced that Aru's intentions are good, he will not stand in fate's way."

"Fate?"

"The Fates, fate, it's all the same thing." He smiled. "Do you really think that your flight getting canceled and you getting a first-class ticket and sitting next to a god was coincidental?"

"No, I guess it wasn't."

Gabi's heart did a happy little flip.

Uriel was a god, and his secret mission had been to meet with the clan and negotiate something with them. Whatever it was, it had nothing to do with flea-market flipping or illegal activities, and since he had no reason to return to Portugal, they could be together.

On top of that, he had induced her immortality, meaning they could be together forever.

The question was whether he wanted to have forever with her.

After all, he was a god, and she wasn't.

"When can I see Uriel?" She murmured. "I mean, Aru."

"I don't know." Gilbert took her hand and gave it a gentle squeeze. "I guess it's up to Kian. It depends on how the negotiations go."

Fear accumulated in the pit of her stomach. "When will I know?"

He gave her an apologetic smile. "Your guess is as good as mine."

GABI & URIEL''S STORY CULMINATES

The Children of the Gods Book 76

DARK ENCOUNTERS OF THE FATED KIND

TURN THE PAGE TO READ THE PREVIEW—>

JOIN THE *VIP CLUB*

To find out what's included in your free membership, click HERE or flip to the last page.

As Aru and his team embark on a perilous mission, their past and present converge in a meeting that holds the key to their fate.

ARU

Aru stood motionless and silent behind Dagor's chair, watching the laptop screen. The video quality of the bug perched on Doctor Julian's shoulder was remarkably clear, and what Aru saw twisted his gut with worry.

Gabi looked drained, so pale and gaunt that she seemed almost ethereal. Her once vibrant and animated face was drawn, and her small frame barely made a rise under the blanket.

The contrast between the woman he'd known intimately over the last few days and the vulnerable figure in the hospital bed was jarring. In his memories she'd seemed like a force, a spirit that filled his heart and any space she occupied with her quirky personality and vivacious energy.

He was a damn god, and yet he was completely helpless to do anything about it. What were all his godly powers good for if he couldn't help her? Make her better?

Worse, Aru couldn't even hold the hand of the woman he cared for in her time of need, and putting his faith in the doctor was not something he was even remotely comfortable with.

Julian was the immortal descendant of the rebel gods, and Aru didn't know where he had gotten his education. Did he even know how to take care of Gabi?

As the urge to go to her became overwhelming, his grip on the back of Dagor's chair tightened to the point of the wood groaning in protest.

"Cut it out." Dagor looked at him over his shoulder. "You're going to break the chair."

"She doesn't look good," Aru murmured.

"On the contrary." Dagor turned back to the laptop screen. "She's a looker. I can understand now why you are so obsessed with her."

Over on the couch, Negal chuckled. "A human female's beauty can't compare to that of a goddess. It shouldn't affect you."

That was true. Gabi lacked the perfection of the goddesses back home, but her imperfections, her uniqueness, only made her more beautiful to Aru.

"Beauty is in the eye of the beholder," Aru said without sparing Negal a glance. "And there is much more to it than physicality. It's the bright soul animating Gabi's body that makes her beautiful."

"If you say so," was the trooper's sarcastic response.

"Your sister is doing very well." On the screen, the doctor turned to look at Gabi's brother, who appeared to be standing, given the angle of the bug's camera. "Her vitals are strong, and her bouts of unconsciousness don't last more than a few hours at a time. You should get some rest, Gilbert."

As relief flooded Aru, he let out a breath. That was good news.

That was excellent news.

"I told you so," Negal murmured from the couch. "She's in good hands."

"I'm not leaving her side." Gabi's brother looked around the room. "Is there a cot I can put in here? I plan on sleeping next to Gabi tonight."

"There should be one somewhere in the clinic. I'll get it for you."

"Thank you," Gilbert said.

As the doctor turned toward the door, Aru leaned over Dagor's shoulder. "Move the bug from the doctor to the brother."

"Are you sure? It's a small room. They might notice it flying over."

The outdated medical equipment in the room was making enough noise to mask the barely perceptible buzz the tiny drone would make as it crossed the short distance between the doctor's shoulder and Gilbert's. The device was smaller than a mosquito, made less noise than one, and was undetectable by human technology because it was mostly biological rather than mechanical.

"Do it," Aru commanded in a tone that brooked no argument.

"Yes, sir." Dagor moved his finger on the laptop pad, and the spy's viewpoint moved accordingly.

The doctor paused at the door. "Did you eat?"

"I didn't." Gilbert put his hand on his stomach. "But that's okay. I could lose an inch or two around the middle."

The doctor cast him an amused look. "I'll tell the guys in security to order us something. Anything in particular you're in the mood for?"

"Whatever you get is fine." The vantage point changed as Gilbert sat back down. "I want to call Orion and ask him to remove the compulsion from Gabi. It wasn't a smart idea to have her remember and forget things depending on where she was. Now, her mind is all scrambled, and she's confused. I hope that no damage was done, and she will go back to normal as soon as Orion removes his compulsion."

That explained so much—the memory lapses and the headaches. But why had they compelled her to forget things?

What were the secrets she held in her mind that she was allowed to remember in some circumstances and not others?

And who was Orion?

Was he a god?

Compulsion was a rare ability, and Aru doubted the immortal descendants of the rebel gods could have inherited that trait. Then again, the Eternal King's children could have gotten it from him and transferred it to their offspring, making these immortal descendants both dangerous and useful. There weren't many compellers left on Anumati, and those who had been sent to remote corners of the galaxy had usually met with one calamity or another.

The doctor frowned. "That worries me. The compulsion should be removed as soon as possible. Call Orion, explain the situation, and have him on standby for when Gabi wakes up again."

"That's precisely what I intend to do."

ARU

"I'm taking the laptop to my bedroom." Aru closed the device and lifted it over Dagor's head. "You two can take a rest."

Dagor cast him an amused look. "Are you planning on watching your human in the privacy of your bedroom?"

"You bet." Ignoring the innuendo, Aru tucked the laptop under his arm and headed to his room.

He didn't want his teammates watching Gabi in her vulnerable state, especially when the doctor was doing things that required exposing her.

Besides, he wanted to hear Gilbert's conversation with the mysterious Orion without them present. If Gabi knew important secrets pertaining to the gods and immortals, he wanted to hear them first and then decide whether to share them with Negal and Dagor.

"How is it going, Orion?" Gilbert asked when his call was answered.

Regrettably, Aru couldn't hear what Orion's reply was. The spy bug's receiver was not sensitive enough for that.

"Yeah, I know. The lockdown is maddening. But I'm not in the village. Kian let me out because Gabi is transitioning, and I begged him to let me be with her."

There was a short pause. "She wasn't feeling well and decided to walk over to the pharmacy around the corner from her hotel, but she never made it. She fainted on the way and was taken to a human hospital. Kian sent an extraction team to get her out of there, and we brought her to the keep."

After another short pause, Gilbert continued, "Yeah, we know who induced her, but I don't know if I can tell you. Since you're mated to Alena, and you are also Toven's son, you probably know what's going on, and I don't need to spell it out for you." Gilbert turned around to look at Gabi, giving Aru another glimpse of her before turning his back to her again. "Yeah, that's right. It was one of the gods. Anyway, the reason I'm calling you is your compulsion. It's messing with Gabi's head, and since she's no longer exposed to him and isn't going to be anytime soon or at all, you can release her, at least until she's out of the critical stage of her transition."

Critical stage sounded ominous, and Aru's gut clenched with worry. The doctor had said that she was doing fine, though, and he'd sounded sincere. So perhaps the critical stage didn't refer to how dangerous it was but to how important it was?

"Gilbert?" The sweet sound of Gabi's voice had Aru's heart flutter.

Her brother turned around, giving Aru the gift of seeing her with her eyes open. "Oh, good. You're awake. I thought I would have to call Orion again. Let me transfer the call to video."

Her beautiful eyes widening, Gabi feebly lifted a hand to shield her face. "Don't! I probably look like roadkill. I don't want anyone to see me like this."

Aru laughed. This was so like Gabi. Everyone was worried about her transition while she was fussing about looking presentable on the screen for Orion. Thankfully, Gilbert had said that the guy was mated, or Aru would have gotten jealous, thinking that Gabi wanted to look pretty for the guy.

But wait, did she know that Orion was taken? Perhaps she thought he was single?

"You look lovely even when you're disheveled." Gilbert echoed Aru's thoughts. "Besides, you are transitioning, and no one expects you to look your best."

Gabi frowned. "You keep saying that I'm transitioning. What does that mean?"

She didn't know?

So, Aru wasn't the only one who hadn't heard about Dormants and their ability to transition into immortality with the help of an immortal or a god's essence.

"Talk to Orion. Hopefully, things will make more sense after he does his thing." Gilbert turned his phone screen toward Gabi and activated the speaker.

Regrettably, Aru couldn't see Orion.

"Hello, Gabi," he heard the guy's voice. "I'm sorry about the mess my compulsion created in your head. In hindsight, it wasn't a good idea."

"I know you." She frowned at him. "You were at the dinner in the hotel."

Feeling like an idiot, Aru let out a relieved breath. Gabi could barely remember the guy, and she didn't sound interested in him.

"That's right. You were told things that needed to be kept a secret, but since you were seeing a guy who we suspected of possessing a certain ability, we couldn't let you remember what you'd been told when you had company. That was what created the confusion and eventually made you forget everything, even when there were no strangers around. I'm going to remove the compulsion now, and hopefully, that will clear up the confusion."

If they had suspected that the man Gabi was seeing was not human and could enter her mind, why hadn't they set a trap for him and caught him?

It would have been so easy.

He'd had no idea that she wasn't fully human or that she was related to the people he was searching for.

As it dawned on him that their encounter must have been destined, Aru lifted a hand to his chest. No wonder he felt so strongly about Gabi.

They were fated to be together.

"How are you going to fix that?" Gabi asked Orion.

"Simple. Look into my eyes and focus on the sound of my voice. You can remember everything you've learned about immortals, and you can speak freely about them with anyone. You are not restricted in any way."

Scrunching her nose, Gabi squinted as if she was in pain, but then her eyes grew large, and she lifted a hand to her temple. "Immortality. That's what I'm transitioning into. But how? I didn't have sex with an immortal, did I? Or did you make me forget that as well, and the memory just hasn't come back yet?"

Orion chuckled. "I'll let Gilbert explain. It's one hell of an incredible story, and he has more details than I do. I wish you the best of luck on your transition."

"Thank you." Gabi kept rubbing her temples.

"I'll see you in the village soon," Orion said. "Or so I hope. Goodbye, Gabi."

"Goodbye, and thank you again." She lifted a pair of questioning eyes to her brother.

He put the phone aside. "There is no easy way to do this. Your lover boy is not a human after all. He's a god, and he induced your transition. What I want to know is, what the hell were you thinking having unprotected sex with a guy you'd only just met?"

She arched an indignant brow. "Are you serious? That's what bothers you about this situation? And what do you mean by a god? Do you mean immortal, a descendant of the gods?"

"You were induced by a god. Not an immortal, not a demigod, but a pureblooded god. So was I, though, so you don't have exclusive bragging rights."

What in purgatory's name?

Who had induced Gabi's brother? Other than Aru and his teammates, there were no other gods on Earth.

"Wait a minute." Gabi lifted her hand. "You said that all the gods were dead, and only their immortal descendants remained."

That was precisely what Aru had believed up until a moment ago.

"I didn't say that all the gods were dead." Gilbert waved a hand.

Gabi cast him an accusing look. "I don't remember what you and the others said, but it was implied that there were no gods left on Earth and that only their immortal descendants remained."

Gilbert sighed. "The gods living in the village are our most guarded secret, even more so than the existence of immortals. It's like the Holiest of Holies of secrets. They were supposed to be the only ones, but then Aru and his friends showed up, getting our attention by activating trackers that we knew were of godly origins."

So, there were still gods left on Earth.

But how?

Had they removed their trackers?

Could the heir still be alive?

Hope surged in Aru's chest and then quickly winked out. Perhaps some gods had managed to survive, but it wasn't likely that the heir was one of them.

"How did you know that they were of godly origins?" Gabi asked.

"The history of those trackers is a long story for another day. When we identified the signals, we panicked, and the village went into lockdown. Do you remember that?"

She nodded. "It got so confusing. When I was alone, I remembered what you told me about a clan location that got compromised and that the lockdown was a security measure. Was all of that because of Uriel?" She asked in a whisper that carried a betrayed tone.

"His real name is Aru, and he's not from Portugal. It's just a fake identity he bought. Anyway, a team of our people met with him today, and it seems like his intentions are not hostile, but further talks are needed to ascertain that. He and his friends are very dangerous."

"Why?"

"Because gods are to immortals like immortals are to humans. We are powerless against them. They can get into our minds and thrall us or compel us. Also, they come from a planet of gods who don't hold humans in the highest regard."

"He wasn't condescending with me."

Gabi defending him to her brother brought Aru hope. Perhaps she wasn't angry about the deception and understood why it had been necessary.

"I don't know all the details of what the gods told the team that was sent to meet them, but from what I've heard so far, it seems like they are on our side."

"Good." Gabi rubbed her temple. "I think. Will I be able to see him again?"

She sounded hopeful, which reinforced Aru's belief that she didn't hate him for lying to her. There was still a chance he could salvage what they had.

To what end, though?

He couldn't stay. In a hundred and fifteen years, give or take a few, the patrol ship would return for him, and he would have to leave. But even before that, he couldn't be with her and endanger her and her community by his mere presence.

The tracker in his body made him into a beacon, a pointer, and Gabi's people had to hide not only from their terrestrial enemies but also from the Eternal King.

"It depends on how the talks go," Gilbert said. "If Kian is convinced that Aru's intentions are good, he will not stand in the way of fate."

Gabi arched a brow. "Fate?"

"The Fates, fate, it's all the same thing." Gilbert waved a dismissive hand again. "Do you really think that your flight getting canceled and you getting a first-class ticket and sitting next to a god was all a coincidence?"

She frowned. "No, I guess it wasn't. When do you think I will be allowed to see Uriel? I mean, Aru."

"I don't know." Gilbert took Gabi's hand. "As I said, it's up to Kian and how well the negotiations go."

GABI

The cycle of slipping away into unconsciousness, waking up, and then slipping away again wasn't so much scary as it was annoying.

Mostly, it was the unpredictability of it that got to her. She could be in the middle of a sentence and then find herself in the dream world or just drifting away into nothing.

Still, Gabi was grateful to be waking up at all.

According to the doctor, she was luckier than most, and other transitioning Dormants hadn't been as fortunate, spending the entire process unconscious.

Come to think of it, it shouldn't have been too difficult for them because they had been unaware of what was going on, but it must have been hard for those who cared for them and were helpless to do anything other than wait for the process to run its course.

Usually, though, the transitioning Dormants were accompanied by a mate, who worried about them and stayed by their side, sleeping on a cot in their hospital room.

Gabi had Gilbert.

Her eldest brother was the rock in her life, and he would probably remain the only male she could rely on, with her other brother being the runner-up. As far as a romantic partner, though, Gabi had never had one she could rely on.

Dylan was a self-absorbed cheater, others she'd dated hadn't clicked, and Uriel was a damned god who lied to her and whom she would most likely never see again.

"I miss you too," Gilbert whispered into his phone. "Where are you now?"

Gabi tuned him out, giving him privacy to talk to Karen the only way she could, which was by turning inward to the place where her heart ached from Uriel's betrayal.

He'd told her so very little about himself, claiming that he couldn't reveal more because he didn't want to lie to her, but even the little he'd told her had been a lie, including his name.

Why had he lied about that?

He could have told her that his name was Aru. What would it have mattered to her whether he was named Uriel or Aru?

It's not like everyone on the planet knew that there was a god named Aru roaming around, and she would have immediately recognized him by his name.

He wasn't a flea-market flipper either.

What did gods do for a living? Could they conjure gold from thin air?

The gods she'd read about had been worshiped and attended by the humans who revered them, so they didn't need to do anything other than look godly.

The same went for contemporary monarchs. They were figureheads, symbols, and, in a way, modern myths. The British didn't need their monarchs for anything, but the royal family was worshiped almost like deities.

Ugh, her mind was drifting again, and she couldn't even blame the transition for that. Or maybe she could?

Gabi lifted her eyes to the IV bag hanging over her bed. Perhaps they were feeding her relaxants in the IV, and that was why she was feeling so unfocused and scatter-brained.

Bringing her focus back to Uriel, she remembered fondly his offer to avenge her honor. He sounded so sincere when he'd offered to beat up Dylan. In retrospect, though, he'd probably had a different retribution in mind.

What did gods do to humans they didn't like?

Could Uriel summon lightning from the sky like Thor and smite those who incurred his wrath?

Nah, probably not.

Obviously, Uriel and his friends were just aliens who called themselves gods, the same as her ancestors, but she didn't know what powers they had other than mind manipulation.

Perhaps she could ask Gilbert to tell her what he knew about gods after he was done talking to Karen. He'd said that a god had induced his transition, so he must know a thing or two about these aliens.

Oh, crap. Why had he told her that?

That was so bad. If he felt free to tell her about the gods, he didn't expect her to ever see Uriel again.

Now that she was free of Orion's compulsion to forget what she'd been told about immortals, her mind was open to infiltration by immortals and gods, and she would never be allowed to see Aru again.

Hell, she would probably never be allowed to return to Cleveland.

The knowledge she'd gained was too valuable to risk infiltration by aliens or humans who could read minds.

Suddenly, the world seemed like an even scarier place than before. She had to worry not only about bodily harm but also about thought thieves.

Would they at least let her talk to Aru on the phone?

From what she understood about thralling, he couldn't peek into her mind unless he was physically next to her. But would they trust her to keep her mouth shut about what she knew?

Probably not.

So that was it. Instead of a child, Uriel's parting gift to her had been immortality. Not bad as a consolation prize, except Gabi didn't feel like a winner.

Too weak to fight the tears, she let them stream down her cheeks.

Gabi wasn't a pretty crier, but down in the clan's underground clinic, there was no one to see her and pass judgment.

Gilbert was there, but it wouldn't be the first time he'd seen her falling apart. In fact, he'd seen her in a much worse condition after she'd gotten proof of Dylan's infidelity.

Somehow sensing that she was distressed, Gilbert turned around and looked at her. "I gotta go," he told Karen. "I'll call you later." He ended the call and got up. "What's wrong? Why are you crying?"

"It's nothing. I hate being weak and sick, and that's how I feel now."

He arched a brow. "You know that I can always tell when you're lying. Out with it, Gabi."

There was no point in resisting because he would just keep on pushing.

"Now that you've told me about the gods, I can never see Uriel again. I can't even say goodbye to him over the phone because I might inadvertently blurt something out."

"Oh, sweetheart." He sat on the bed beside her and took her hand. "Orion is available whenever you need him, at least as long as the lockdown is in effect, and if you ask him, he can compel you again to forget what you've learned."

She lifted her hand to her temple. "But his compulsion is messing with my head. I don't want my brain to turn to mush."

Gilbert smiled. "And yet I can see that your mood has improved, which means that you like having the option, and you're considering it."

"Well, yes, of course. It's a door that was closed before and is now open if I wish to step through it. But I hope it can be done better so it's less bothersome to my mind. Maybe Orion can just make me forget about the gods. Uriel already knows about immortals, right? So that's no longer a secret, and I don't mind not knowing about the gods at all."

"I guess so." Gilbert shifted his position to get more comfortable on the sliver of space he'd claimed on her bed. "I'm not privy to the details of their talks. You and I will have to wait until we are told, and I don't know when that will be."

"Can't you ask? Perhaps Julian knows more?"

Gilbert leaned closer and kissed Gabi's forehead. "You can ask him yourself the next time he checks on you."

She shifted sideways to make more room for her brother. "Can you do me a favor and call Orion now? I want to forget about the gods."

Gilbert patted her hand. "There is no rush. We will worry about it when meeting Orion in person becomes an option."

ANNANI

Annani surveyed the somber faces of her family and let out a sigh. "We are gathered around the dining table, surrounded by our loved ones, and being served a delicious dinner by our dear Odus. We should treasure these precious moments with family and friends and not let outside worries ruin them, or we will never get to enjoy ourselves." She smiled. "Life is full of challenges, and that is never going to change."

The news Kian had delivered about the Eternal King and the future of Earth was far from encouraging, but nothing was imminent, and they had plenty of time to prepare. The grace period of one hundred and fifteen years might be a blink of an eye for the gods, but it was an eternity for humans. The technological advancements of the last century were staggering, and with the help of artificial intelligence, progress would be exponential. By the time the team of newly arrived gods had to report their findings, a solution might present itself.

Her grandfather might send a new plague to cull the number of humans and halt their technological progress, but Annani believed that Kian was right about their ability to make humans immune to disease and maybe even make them immortal. Doing so might introduce new problems that would have to be solved, but that was a worry for another day.

Amanda's lips twisted in a grimace. "It's hard to be joyful after hearing that Earth's population is in danger from none other than my great-grandfather." She shivered. "I always believed myself to be good, but with his genes inside of me, I'm no longer sure that I am." She turned to Dalhu. "I felt the call of darkness once, the need to rage and destroy. Fortunately, I didn't have the means to do damage, but what if I had? Would I have destroyed the world in my grief and anger? What if that darkness is still hiding inside of me, waiting to emerge in response to a strong enough trigger?"

When Amanda had lost her young son to a tragic horse-back-riding accident, Annani had sensed that darkness threatening to consume her daughter—its toxic allure sadly all too familiar. But she knew that she had raised Amanda and her other children to resist the lure of darkness and cling to the light with all their might, and she had trusted that her teachings would hold even in the face of such incredible tragedy and pain.

As sweet as the call of the dark side was, it was a trap, and one step too many into its hot embrace could be the point of no return.

Dalhu put his hand on Amanda's shoulder. "Your great-grandfather is not necessarily evil. He's brilliant and pragmatic and does what he thinks is best for his people. I wouldn't have minded having his blood running in my veins instead of the blood of the hoodlum my mother was forced to breed with."

Amanda's eyes softened. "Oh, darling. Thank you for reminding me that we are more than our genetics and that we always have a choice."

Toven, however, did not look encouraged by Dalhu's words, and his somber expression had not abated. "Even if we manage to make all humans immune to disease or immortal, we won't be able to save humankind. Once the Eternal King realizes that a pathogen his scientists have introduced hasn't worked, and humans haven't been infected by his plague, he will order a different way of culling the population, which will be no less devastating. Probably more so."

As silence stretched across the table, Annani searched for a rebuttal to Toven's grim prediction, but nothing came to mind. Humans, along with the immortals living alongside them, were no match for the might of the gods.

"Our only hope is the rebellion," Syssi said. "The king needs to be replaced with someone who sympathizes with the created species." She turned her gaze to Annani. "I happen to know his legitimate heir, and she is a big-time sympathizer."

Annani laughed. "Are you suggesting that I take the throne and become the queen of the gods?"

"Why not? The original rebels wanted to make your father the king. If they knew of your existence, the new rebels would choose you. You'll make a wonderful queen."

Annani had been groomed to take the throne, and as a young goddess, she had been ready to ascend if and when her father chose to step down, but she was not the same goddess she had been then, and she had no wish to rule anyone—not even her clan. She would not mind being a figurehead and being worshiped and admired, but she would leave the day-to-day affairs of the throne to others who were better suited for the job.

"I do not wish to rule the planet of the gods, but even if I did, it is not feasible. Not now, not in the near future, and probably not ever." She turned to Kian. "Aru said that the rebellion is thousands of years in the making and has many more thousands to go before it is ready. We do not have that long. We need to come up with a solution and implement it within the next century."

Kian shrugged. "Maybe we don't. As long as humans do not possess interstellar travel capability, the Eternal King will not deem them a threat. Perhaps all we need to do is ensure that they never get to that point. Besides, the Eternal King is not in a rush to do anything. He moves in godly time, and until he turns his sights on Earth, the natural shrinkage in human population due to declining birthrates might be enough for him to leave humans alone."

Toven reached for Mia's hand. "If the Perfect Match adventure the AI designed for us was a hint from the

Fates, then in five hundred years, the human population will have shrunk in size to what it was when the original rebels were exiled to Earth, and a new crop of gods will arrive to once again rule over humans."

ARU

"Have you learned anything new?" Dagor asked as Aru handed him the laptop.

He'd spent the evening of the day before, most of the prior night, and into the early morning watching Gabi through the little spy's eyes. She'd been unconscious for many hours, but when she'd woken up, she'd talked with her brother and the doctor, and Aru had gotten to eavesdrop on their conversations.

He'd learned quite a lot, but he wasn't about to share it with his teammates.

"I've learned a few things, but none of them are of much use to us. There were several mentions of a village, which is what they call the place they live in, and along with it, talk about a lockdown, which was done in response to our arrival. As soon as they identified the signals, they panicked."

As Negal unlocked their car, the three of them got in, with Negal behind the wheel, Aru on the passenger side, and Dagor in the back.

Magnus hadn't sent them the location pin yet, but thanks to the spy drone and what they had learned from listening to the feed, they knew where Gabi had been taken and that the meeting with the immortals' leader would take place in the same downtown location.

Scoping the area and the building itself was standard protocol.

They couldn't get inside, though, because thralling and shrouding were not going to work on the security cameras or the people watching the feed, but their little drone spies could be their eyes and ears and get into places they probably couldn't.

Most standard doors were not precisely fitted, and the bugs could pass under or above them. Anywhere a mosquito or an ant could go, their spy drones could go as well.

"I wonder if Jade and the other Kra-ell reside in the same village," Negal said.

"It would seem so." Aru turned around to look at Dagor. "Do you need the laptop, or can I use it until we get to the building?"

Rolling his eyes, Dagor closed the device. "You checked on her less than five minutes ago. Nothing has changed since then."

"You never know." Aru flipped the laptop open and brought up the feed from the clinic.

True to his promise, Gilbert hadn't left Gabi's side except to use the bathroom. During those brief breaks, Aru had muted the feed and busied himself with watching television to respect the brother's privacy until the guy was done with his business.

Thankfully, Gilbert hadn't showered or changed his clothing, so there had been no need to maneuver the bug. By now, the drone was running low on energy, and having it fly would drain what was left.

Aru would be lucky if the thing kept transmitting for a couple more hours.

They could attach new drones to their hosts, but Aru didn't want to push his luck. Security around the leader would be much tighter than it had been during the meeting in the canyon, and he wouldn't be surprised if they got strip-searched.

It hadn't been an easy decision to forgo bringing more bugs to the meeting with the leader, and as Aru had debated the pros and cons, he was well aware of what would happen if he lost contact with Gabi.

It was much worse than attaching spy drones to these immortals.

He was a god, and if pushed, he would use his mind powers over them.

No, diplomacy was always a better solution, and he would have to negotiate something with the clan's leader. The problem with that was having to admit that he knew they had Gabi. It would force him to also reveal the truth about the spy drone he'd attached to Magnus.

As hard as Aru tried to come up with a convincing lie about how he'd learned about Gabi's transition, he couldn't come up with one.

It had occurred to him that he could claim to have attached the drone to Gabi to make sure that she was unharmed when he wasn't with her, but in a way, it was worse than admitting he had attached the spy bug to Magnus.

The leader would be more understanding about the bug than she would, and rightfully so. Attaching the drone to Magnus wasn't personal. It was a strategically smart move. Attaching it to Gabi would have been an invasion of her privacy.

Come to think of it, Aru was crossing the line by monitoring her as it was.

"You still didn't tell us what you hope to get from them," Negal said. "We know now that the Kra-ell are not dead, and we know who took them. The question is what we tell the commander. We can't tell him about the immortals because our communications with the ship are recorded, and he will have no choice but to report our findings to headquarters."

"I'm glad that you arrived at the same conclusion I did." Just then, Gilbert turned to look at Gabi, and Aru got a glimpse of her sleeping face. "We will report that there was an uprising and that Gor and some of his males were taken out by the others."

Negal nodded. "You know what the problem with that is. We will need to report their new location, and that's where the immortals live. The Kra-ell will have to find a different place to settle."

"I know." Aru sighed. "Which is a shame. I love the idea of the Kra-ell and the immortal descendants of the gods living together in harmony and mutual respect. Also, Jade has an immortal mate, and she might not be the only one. Separating the two groups is going to be tough even though they haven't been integrated for long."

Aru hadn't told Dagor and Negal about the gods who also resided in the same location, and he didn't intend to, not because he didn't trust them, but because the less they knew, the safer the secret was.

Note

Dear reader,

I hope my stories have added a little joy to your day. If you have a moment to add some to mine, you can help spread the word about the Children Of The Gods series by telling your friends and penning a review. Your recommendations are the most powerful way to inspire new readers to explore the series.

Thank you,

Isabell

FOR EXCLUSIVE PEEKS AT UPCOMING RELEASES & A FREE COMPANION BOOK

Join my *VIP Club* and gain access to the VIP portal at itlucas.com
To Join, go to:
http://eepurl.com/blMTpD

INCLUDED IN YOUR FREE MEMBERSHIP:

YOUR VIP PORTAL

- **Read preview chapters of upcoming releases.**
- **Listen to Goddess's Choice narration by Charles Lawrence**
- **Exclusive content offered only to my VIPs.**

FREE I.T. LUCAS COMPANION INCLUDES:

- **Goddess's Choice Part 1**
- **Perfect Match: Vampire's Consort** (A standalone Novella)
- **Interview Q & A**
- **Character Charts**

If you're already a subscriber, and you are not getting my emails, your provider is

SENDING THEM TO YOUR JUNK FOLDER, AND YOU ARE MISSING OUT ON **IMPORTANT UPDATES, SIDE CHARACTERS' PORTRAITS, ADDITIONAL CONTENT, AND OTHER GOODIES.** TO FIX THAT, ADD isabell@itlucas.com TO YOUR EMAIL CONTACTS OR YOUR EMAIL VIP LIST.

Check out the specials at
https://www.itlucas.com/specials

Made in the USA
Las Vegas, NV
08 November 2023

80471298R00216